Return to Caer Lon

By

Claude Dancourt

RETURN TO CAER LON

Copyright © Claude Dancourt 2011
http://www.claudedancourt.webs.com

ISBN: 978-0-9880313-1-9

Cover Artist: Claude Dancourt
Editor: Cathy Moeschet

Acknowledgments

I have hyperactive muses, and sometimes I have to rely on trusted friends to help me keep them in line. I am very thankful to Ana Elias and Ethan Jones for their support during this journey, and their honesty when they reviewed my work. I'd like to thank Cathy Moeschet for her careful editing.

And finally, Zoe, who is my very first fan: this may not be the tale of your childhood, but it's close enough.

Nous ne savons pas encore ressusciter les corps, mais nous commençons à savoir ressusciter les rêves.

André Malraux

Return to Caer Lon

Camelot, fifteen years ago...

A loud bang erupted from the courtyard, instantly followed by furious yells of the aggressors and cries of pain from their victims. The stone walls seemed far from solid or protective as the world shattered in fireballs. The king's table was pushed to the side in case they needed to block the door. Chests were piled near the tapestry, hiding the domestic entrance with the same purpose.

Seated on the large four-poster bed, Queen Ylianor closed her arms tighter around her son. Her beautiful face was shadowed by terror, but she refused to let one sound come out of her throat, and her eyes were dry.

The young boy could not be more than five years old. He, too, was tearless, though he jolted as explosions shook the windows. He nestled in his mother's embrace, hiding his face each time a new clamor resounded outside.

Suddenly, the door of the royal chambers burst open. Two men entered the room, their swords in hand, both fully armored. When the taller man moved toward her, the crown dragon on his breastplate glinted in the dim light.

King William Pendragon ungloved his hand to brush his wife's cheek lightly. His face was pale with worry. He paused, letting the gentle caress speak for him. Then his hand fell down to his side as resolve shadowed his agreeable features.

"Ylianor, please, you cannot stay here. Hector will lead you to the border."

The woman lifted her head to face her husband. Her chin trembled despite her resolve to stay strong.

"I will not leave without you."

"Camelot is doomed, my love. I will fall with it. But you must live, for Derek."

Hearing his name, the boy glanced at his father with a proud expression on his face.

"I vant to fight viv you."

The child's pronunciation brought a smile to the tired man's features. He walked to the little boy, who had wriggled out of his mother's embrace, and scooped him up under his tiny arms so their faces were only inches apart.

"I am confiding your mother to your care, Derek. You must protect her. And you will come back one day to take what is yours by birthright."

"Yes faver."

The child's fierce nod got the better of the queen. She ran to her husband and son to embrace them both, her cheeks finally wet with tears.

The second man, who waited in a corner, casting frequent glances to the corridor, took a step forward. "We must go, my lord. I do not know how long my men can keep our path safe."

William put the child down gently and took his wife in his arms, holding her close for another instant, before he pressed one last kiss on her lips.

"I love you, Ylianor."

"And I, you."

The queen put her hood over her head and took little Derek by the hand, before she signalled to her escort she was ready. The king watched his family disappear in the dark before he took the opposite direction and joined his final battle.

Chapter 1

The door slammed so hard that its frame trembled. Ylianor grabbed her phials just in time before they fell on the floor.

"This is intolerable!"

Wiping her hands on her apron, she turned to face her irascible son. Derek had inherited her blondness and deep-blue eyes; from his father, he had taken his height and broad shoulders, and unfortunately a good part of his character. The young man paced the room furiously.

"Sebastian and Elwyn are going with a battalion near the border and I am stuck here! Sebastian is younger than I am and Elwyn is not nearly as skilled with a sword. Hell, he would hurt himself before hitting anyone! Geraint refused to consider my request to join them; he didn't even hear me out and…"

"Derek…"

The patient tone smoothed his temper, but barely for a second.

"It is Camelot over there, my kingdom, my people! I can't stay here and watch others fight! This is MY war!"

At twenty, childish roundness was all but completely gone from his face and had given way to well-defined male features. His firm mouth was pursed into a thin line at the moment, and his square chin aggressively moved forward as he straightened up to his full height. Even standing immobile on the other side of the room, Derek towered a full head and shoulders above his mother. She had to admit, his stature was impressive. Ylianor tried to repress a smile. Druidic quoits looked moveable compared to him when he squared his shoulders like this. Ylianor allowed herself a small smile. Her son was stubborn with an explosive temper, though his outbursts rarely lasted, as his heart was generous and kind.

Derek's eyes flashed when he sensed her amusement. She recognized the silver blue instantly. His furor was about to explode into a nasty outbreak he would regret later. She took off her apron and approached her son.

"Derek, I know this is hard." She silently thanked Geraint for keeping him away from this scouting and soothed her tone. "But what good will it do to Camelot if you die?"

"People will not accept a coward as their king!"

"Sometimes, it takes more courage to step aside than to fight. Waiting is harder you know that."

She guided him gently to a bench and bade him to sit. The young man obeyed reluctantly.

"I could have gone and just stayed out of trouble… It's just an intelligence gathering mission anyway…"

They both knew he would never have stopped at that. He was too much like his father. Ylianor brushed a strand of hair off his forehead.

"You will have your chance to prove yourself, Derek. Please, just be patient…"

"Right. I win tournaments and melées, while a murderer…"

Temper menaced to flare again and he trailed off. He got up and started walking back and forth once more, clenching and unclenching his fists by his side. The adamant refusal of Geraint to send him along with Sebastian and Elwyn *was* intolerable. He was second in command of the duke's troops, an honor he had *earned* with his warrior skills and not his birthrights. Erik, the duke's Captain of the Guards, was not a man to grant favors. He should be with the scouting, at least to take a glimpse of what he would take back one day; soon. His homeland…

Derek caught the flash of grief in his mother's blue eyes and stopped his rumbling instantly. Ylianor smiled and changed the subject, teasing, "Well, look at the bright side. Winning tournaments allows you to escort the Lady Sacha to the feasts."

Derek groaned. His mother and some of his closest friends - namely Elwyn and Sebastian - had the strange idea he fancied the beautiful daughter of Geraint. The thought was unnerving. They could barely stay within earshot without bickering. As far as he was concerned, her sharp tongue, fueled by stubbornness and pride, generally killed any idea of romance beforehand. Not that he had any, despite her breathtaking beauty and her admirable unbending spirit…

In addition, she had magic and so did her twin brother, Elwyn. Elwyn was fine, really; even if his habit of stirring the water and talking to animals was disturbing at times. Derek had learned not to take him to hunt, so that he actually managed to bring a prize or two back… Elwyn's magic was fine, really. Derek would trust Elwyn with his life. But Sacha's powers called to another kind of magic, one linked to Elemental Air, Spirits and Fire, just like Wolfryth. And Wolfryth had killed his father to usurp the crown.

Queen Ylianor had barely escaped with the five-year-old little boy he was at the time, a little boy too innocent to understand that he had hugged his father for the last time. They had been helped in her flight by William's faithful first in command. Hector had led them to the border of Pemfro, where Geraint' men were waiting, and he gone back to fight. They had never seen him again. Derek had no doubt Hector was dead, like his father and countless other good people who had stood against the sorcerer. And he was stuck in Haven, forbidden to do anything but parade around like a peacock, taking the Lady of the Castle to feasts, with nothing to do but wait.

Derek clenched his fists. Ylianor squeezed his forearm and stood.

"So when are they leaving?"

"Tomorrow."

The answer came out in a low growl typical of her son when he tried to control his temper. Ylianor tied her pinafore around her waist again.

"I have to finish this today then."

Derek conceded a glance around the room. Unable to accept charity from her former vassal, Ylianor had requested to assist the Court Physician in his duties. Her upbringing among the People - the followers of the Old Religion - had taught her about plants, so she prepared the potions and cataplasms that Jeffrey might need.

A puff of smoke was dancing over one of the bowls, and glittered in the light. Derek inhaled carefully. It smelled like butterscotch.

"What is it?"

His tone lacked the previous tantrum and had turned into childish curiosity.

"This potion is a pain killer," Ylianor answered, her attention focused on her mixture.

"It smells good."

"It probably tastes good too, though I have no wishes for anyone to confirm that any time soon."

Derek grinned. His mother's potions were generally as bitter as lemons. He pecked her cheek. "I will see you later. Elwyn is most likely to forget half his gear if I do not help him pack."

oOo

Derek found both of his friends in Elwyn's quarters. Sebastian was studying some maps while Elwyn tried to fit shirts and a pair of breeches into a too-small backpack. And his twin sister was, of course, haranguing them both. The twins shared the same dark hair, which Elwyn wore in a cut so short it spiked in every possible direction, while Sacha's long curls shone low on her back.

"Elwyn you must not go! Listen to me!"

"Sacha... Hello, Derek!"

The happy welcome would have made him smile if a pair of piercing green eyes had not attacked him at the same time.

"You are in this too, I presume."

"No. I am not allowed to join them."

The regretful answer would have gained him some sympathy from any woman at court, but the one in front of him simply glared and spun on her heels to face her brother again. He was glad to have her barbs directed at someone else for once.

"Please Elwyn... I have a bad feeling about this."

Sacha's tone blurred with worry. Derek took one step forward, amazed by the excessive pallor of her skin. Sensing his presence behind her, Sacha shot him another warning glance, before she decided that if she could not convince her brother to stay, at least she could make sure his packing was neat, and started arranging the folded clothes.

Derek ignored them both to join Sebastian near the table,

where several charts were unrolled for his perusal. The last one of their quartet was younger by two years and compensated for Elwyn's boyish enthusiasm and Derek's quick temper with intelligence and poise. Derek respected his opinion as a strategist as much as he appreciated his calm and dry sense of humor.

The young man nodded toward the twins on the other side of the room, ruffling his shoulder-length black hair with a half-smile.

"You are lucky to be off the hook like this. She has been on his case for nearly an hour. She did not even start on me yet."

Derek kept a straight face.

"Maybe she knows you are a lost case."

Sebastian pulled a face at him. Derek smirked, and pointed at the maps, dismissing the Lady of Haven's concern for their safety in one careless gesture.

"Those are good. Where will you be stationed?"

"Nowhere in particular, I think. Erik wants to know if Wolfryth is watching the border and how."

"The reports about the Dark Woods, hum?"

Derek referred to several accounts about mercenaries haunting the woods located near the eastern border of Pemfro. Sebastian nodded.

"We will probably not find anything. They cannot be stupid enough to confront a full battalion on Pemfro's territory anyway."

"At least you will be out of here for a couple of days…"

Sebastian noticed the frustration growing in his friend's voice and rolled his charts into a thick scroll.

"Your turn will come soon enough. And then-" he pointed at Sacha who was hitting her brother on the head with a pair of socks, "-she will make you regret it."

Chapter 2

The chattering of the women buzzed irritatingly in her ears. Usually, Sacha enjoyed seating in the small courtyard after spending so long closed inside the castle by bad weather. Haven's fortress overlooked the sea, and winter tempests were as hard as beautiful. Clear days were a deliverance everybody appreciated. Life bloomed again when the sun started to warm up the air. Vivid and light fabrics replaced the sober colors of winter clothes. Women assaulted the merchants for the latest fashion advice or gossip, while men flexed their muscles in riding or training in the field, happy to move after being inactive for so long.

Today, however, the soft warm spring air caressing her face and the early bird sing-songs were not enough to allow her ignore the acid barbs covered by hushed tones and knowing smiles from the gossips seated with her. Their high-pitched voices screeched on her nerves so hard she felt like screaming one moment, crying the next.

Sacha tried to concentrate on her embroidery and gave up within the minute. It had been four days since the battalion had left and each passing hour added to her anxiety. She hid it so as not to alarm her father, but every night she woke up more terrified, her heart pounding so hard she was sure it was going to explode.

Ylianor's most powerful draughts were ineffective to silence her dreams. Her visions were always the same: a pack of wolves, the flap of bat wings and feathers falling down on the ground. The ground was dampened with blood; so much blood that it suffocated her and she woke up screaming every time.

Even thinking about it in daylight sickened her. The young woman peeked around her; her companions had not noticed her sudden vertigo and kept gossiping about tokens, the past Easter celebrations and the upcoming May Day joust. Four days…

Sacha spotted Ylianor entering the courtyard from the corner of her eyes and put down her half-finished craft, standing gracefully.

"Please excuse me."

She was pretty sure the joyous gossips started on her case as soon as she was out of earshot. The beautiful (and still unsuitored) daughter of Geraint was among their favourite topics, especially when tournaments were around the corner.

Sonia's crystalline voice tickled the air. The brown-haired lady was probably purveying the others with some absurd tales about Derek's exploits. Sacha barely retained a snort. Sonia was obviously interested in him. Good for her.

She joined Ylianor near the colonnades on the other side of the terrace. The older woman smiled at her gently, and part of the weight in her chest lifted. They locked arms, and exited the gardens to enter the train-yard.

"You look tired, Sacha. How are you sleeping?"

Sacha sighed lightly. She could always confide in the former queen; Ylianor never made her feel foolish or spooky.

"The nightmares are so vivid, I fear they are real. Something terrible is going to happen, I know it."

The blond woman squeezed her hand, but did not try to deny her visions or comfort her with vain words of faith. Sacha appreciated her discretion.

"I wish I could see more clearly, but those images..." She trailed off.

Ylianor nodded.

"One day you certainly will, my dear. Ah, here comes Derek."

Sacha stiffened instantly. While Ylianor put her at ease, her son tensed her nerves to a breaking point. She suspected a good part of that came from Derek's infuriating habit of challenging her every word. He treated her either like some tapestry on the wall, useless, if pretty to look at, or like the brainless girls he pursued once in a while. Well, she was neither! She had a good head on her shoulders and knew how to use it, thank you very much, and if he had stopped his brattling for a minute to take a proper look, he would have noticed she was much more... More of *anything* than Sonia.

Sacha retained another undignified snort and looked for her best contemptuous smile with which to greet him. Ylianor handed her free hand to her son.

"Sacha and I came to interest you in a ride; it is such a beautiful day. It would be a shame to stay inside."

Sacha tried not to wince. Horse riding always ended with both of them competing, as Ylianor knew full well. Competition led to bickering, and bickering… She felt too tired to quarrel with Derek. She unhooked her arm from her elder's.

"Oh, Ylianor, I am not-"

Derek interrupted her excuse, like he always did, which annoyed her beyond reason.

"I am in charge of the training while Erik is away. But I will be happy to escort you after lunch, Mother."

Sacha frowned at the ceremonious tone, and the fact that his invitation was directed only to the queen. She needed no further incitement to change her mind.

"I will see to my duties, then, so they do not disturb your busy schedule, Sire."

Derek caught his mother's warning glance just in time to bite back his retort and settled for a smirk and a quick bow. Sacha made a point to look elsewhere while he jogged back to his training. Well, maybe she took a glimpse at his retreating figure when he stopped to pick up his sword, but only because Ylianor was talking to her again and she had turned to face the training yard to look at her.

The amused smile of the former queen made Sacha feel like a little girl caught with her hand in the jar of sweets.

"Sacha, you have to learn that one catches more flies with honey than with vinegar."

She blushed. She had no intention of catching Derek, with vinegar or otherwise.

oOo

The slap of air on her face lifted her spirits and Sacha urged her mount forward, exhilarated. She felt free, far from the burden of being the first Lady of Haven and far from her dreams. Nothing could imprison her or make her tremble while she rode like the wind. She was powerful and free…

A peal of thunder echoed behind her and she guessed Derek was trying to catch up. They both were excellent riders, but she had an early start and if she didn't want him to join her, he would never succeed. The young woman bent on her horse and whispered softly. The white mare whinnied and accelerated. The sound in her back decreased in the hurling of the wind in her ears and she focused on her race again, savoring the movement of the animal's hot muscles under her knees. The landscape moved so fast that she had to blink to accommodate the sight.

She had nearly reached the small bridge near the river when she allowed her mount to slow down to a more reasonable trot, then a peaceful walk.

Derek jumped down from his mount even before his horse had completely stopped and grabbed her reins, forcing her to halt abruptly. Her mare protested, but Sacha felt so happy she faced his ire with a brilliant smile, extending her hand so he could help her down.

Unsettled by her reaction, Derek caressed the hot neck of the horse for a second before he turned a furious glare to her.

"God almighty, woman, are you trying to kill yourself!"

Sacha frowned, her joy fading quickly, and withdrew her hand.

"You are ridiculous. I am an excellent rider; you barely kept up with me."

The blue eyes shone like steel.

"I *did* keep up with you, but you exhausted your mount and my mother had to ride by herself while I raced after you."

Sacha blushed at the reproach. Her mare's hair gleamed from perspiration, and Ylianor was a small shadow at a distance… She looked away, unwilling to concede that he was right and she had acted foolishly.

"I am fine, as you can see for yourself. Why on earth you feel you had to follow me is beyond my understanding."

Derek scowled, undoubtedly preparing an irritate lecture on responsibilities.

The argument had already chased the well-being the ride had provided, and she felt edgy again. A bird took off nearby and Sacha turned on her saddle nervously. Her heartbeat refused to slow down, pounding harder by the minute.

"Did you hear that?

"That was just a bird. What is wrong with you today?"

He really felt like twisting her neck. The idea of his mother riding alone was unnerving, but he could not leave Sacha now; she looked troubled enough to jump into the river. Damned woman... The growing tap of horseshoes on the ground pulled his attention back to the road and he glimpsed at the figure of Ylianor approaching them.

His distraction loosened the hold he had on her bridle and Sacha's horse danced away, probably because the incomprehensible nerves of its mistress were starting to reverberate on the usually docile animal. Derek tightened his grasp on the escaping reins, growling at the burning in his hand despite the gloves.

"You stay here, I am done racing after you."

Sacha squealed.

"Let me go!"

Abashed by her sudden panic, Derek glanced up. Sacha was shaking her head and pulling on the reins, suddenly eager to escape his grip.

The images in her mind were terribly clear; a black bird was being beat up, his soft feathers bloodied and flying everywhere. The animal's cry of agony pierced through her like a white-hot arrow. The swan was down, the swan was dying, the swan... She screamed.

"Sebastian!"

Her cry sounded barely human. Startled, Derek released her mount, but Sacha jumped down from her mare to run into the woods on foot. Ylianor stopped with a horrified expression on her face. Derek looked at her before he started after the young woman, who was running as if the devil were after her.

"Sacha!"

He was certain she was going to break a bone in her wild race; he half-hoped she would.

"Sacha!"

Her own calls echoed his.

"Sebastian!"

He accelerated his pace.

"Sacha for Heavens' sake! Sacha wait! Sebastian is not..."

And then he saw her fall.

"Sacha!"

Derek reached her side in a few seconds, and felt as if his heart had stopped.

The immobile form of her cousin was resting on the ground. He quickly knelt beside them. The pulse was there, weakening by the minute. Sacha had taken his head on her lap and she was rocking back and forth. For the first time since they were kids, he saw tears wet her cheeks. Her mumbling was foreign to him.

"I'm sorry... I'm so sorry... I didn't know, I didn't understand... Please don't leave me... I should have known... Please, I'm sorry..."

She sounded so desperate... Derek was at a loss of what to do, for her and for his friend, dying on the leafy ground.

"Derek, pull her back."

The poised voice of Ylianor sobered him up, and he reacted quickly. Taking Sacha by the shoulders, he gently forced her to move away from her cousin so his mother could tend to him. Sacha refused to let the inanimate body of Sebastian go at first, then she stood slowly, nearly falling when her knees buckled under her; Derek steadied her swiftly.

Then she realized he was leading her back to their mounts and he had to restrain her.

"Get your hands off me!"

She jolted violently to free herself. Her pale green eyes shining like jade, filled with rage or madness. One particular jerk hit his plexus at a vicious angle, and Derek grunted in pain.

"Do not make me calm you, Sacha."

The low-toned threat stopped her jittering at once. Unsure if she was going to lash him again, Derek did not release her immediately, but lightened his grasp slowly until he noticed her shivers.

Ill at ease, he rubbed his hands awkwardly on her shoulders. The fabric was soft under his palms, and warm… Then the urgency of the situation kicked back in, and Derek hardened his grip again.

"Damn it Sacha, now is not the time to act like a fainting maiden! You never played the act before, don't start now. I want you to go back to Haven. Alert the knights first, then Jeffrey and your father."

She didn't say a word, but her jaw clenched and she nodded firmly. Instead of freeing her, he hugged her tightly then sized her up and put her on her horse without ceremony. Before she could react, Derek handed her the reins.

"You'll dash me later. Just go!"

Sacha kicked her horse into a fast gallop before he could slap it to move. Derek watched her for a few second, then hurried back to his mother. Endless questions spun in his head. How did she know her cousin was here? What had happened to him? And where the hell was Elwyn?

Chapter 3

The knights patrolled the woods searching for Sebastian's attackers but came back empty-handed. No traces of a fight were visible, nor did they find a horse. As far as they knew, the unfortunate man could have appeared out of nowhere.

Derek concluded his report to the duke with an intense sense of failure and he hated it. Geraint shook his head gloomily.

"Thank you, Derek. Jeffrey and your mother are tending to my nephew. His wounds are bad."

The young prince read between the heavy words; Sebastian might die. Clenching his jaw in a vain attempt to mask his emotions, Derek bowed slightly and was taking his leave when the doors of the hall opened to give way to Sacha.

She hadn't taken the time to change. Her dress was stained with dust and her cousin's blood. With her hair dishevelled from the rides and her eyes still too bright, she looked like a mad fury. The beautiful lady ran to her father and grabbed his hands, visibly uncaring about Derek. Her disarray left him speechless. She always made a point to prove him she was so infernally perfect...

"Father, please... We have to go now! Elwyn-"

Geraint squeezed both her hands gently and led her to a chair. She refused to sit.

"Sacha, the knights did not find anything and we need to talk to your cousin before taking a course of action. Any harsh action may be quite disastrous; if an entire battalion was attacked within our borders-"

"But Father!"

Derek stepped forward.

"If you give me a couple of men, I-"

"This is out of question. You stay here, Prince Derek."

Geraint added the title only to remind the young man he had a duty that lay beyond running the woods and endangering himself. As long as he was safe and sound, people in Camelot could hope that one day their rightful king would overthrow the tyrant and claim back his throne. Derek growled but kept his mouth shut. Sacha was looking at him with blazing eyes. Whether she admired him for his offer or was furious at his yielding, he could not tell.

He bowed stiffly, and left the room without waiting. The last thing he heard was the striking lady, now fully enraged, shouting accusations at her father about careless handling and cowardice. He felt a pang of pity for the man. His passionate daughter had little idea how difficult it was to wait and do nothing.

He could not silence that part of himself that agreed with her. The quicker they went, the more chances they had to find survivors or avenge the dead.

oOo

Ylianor knocked and entered Sacha's chambers. The young woman was seated at her dresser, her maid braiding her hair for the night. The girl curtsied and exited quickly after the quick nod of her mistress.

The older woman picked up the job the maid had abandoned, twisting the dark locks together. Sacha said nothing, her eyes seeing beyond the reflection of their figures in the mirror. The former queen caressed her head gently.

"Your father has to see to everyone's well-being, Sacha, not just his son."

"And what will be our well-being, if his heir dies?"

Ylianor closed her eyes briefly. Behind grief and anger, Sacha's reasoning had its logic. She had said more or less the same thing to Derek in the morning. She tried another approach.

"Sebastian escaped, so maybe Elwyn-"

"Sebastian did not escape. He was sent back; as a warning."

Ylianor stiffened. The young woman met her eyes in the mirror.

"I saw it, Ylianor. Wolves attacked and our men lost the battle. All were killed but the Swan and the Cub. Sebastian's heraldry is a swan, with wings spread.. Elwyn…"

Sacha continued telling her dreams, so low her companion could barely hear the words.

"The wolf leader tortured and sent the black swan back to deliver a message."

"What is that message, Sacha?"

"Hand over the son of the Dragon, before I slaughter you all."

The blond woman swallowed, failing to suppress the fear rising inside her. She knew those names; dread them. The wolf was Wolfryth. And he was coming after Derek.

oOo

Unable to sleep, turning and tossing in his bed, the prince conceded and got up. He dressed quickly and stepped out his room into a dimly lit corridor. It was past midnight, and the castle was silent. Derek breathed deeply. So early in spring, the thick stones failed to retain warmth at night. The air stung with cold, even inside the castle.

Sebastian's quarters were a short walk from his. Derek decided to pay a late visit to his wounded friend. His mother had said he was 'sleeping', a gentle word to say he had yet to regain consciousness. That didn't mean he could not speak to him; only that Sebastian would not answer him. If he talked to his friend, maybe Sebastian would listen, and come back. He wanted his friend back.

A swift sound, like paper folding, caught his ear and he froze. The brush automatically resounded like danger. Derek unsheathed his dagger and listened. A squeal echoed behind him and he turned abruptly to peek at some dark grey fabric disappearing behind a door. *His* door.

The young man tightened his grip on his weapon and backtracked carefully to his chambers. He heard no noise coming from it, so his late visitor was either very quiet or had already found the room empty and was preparing to exit...

Derek moved away from the door just in time to avoid being seen when it opened, and grabbed the burglar by the throat, pressing his blade against its side.

Sacha yelped. Her jolt of surprise had her flank pressed harder on the dagger and she gave a little cry of pain. Derek discarded the blade quickly before he shoved her into his chambers and closed the door behind them. Footsteps echoed in the corridor a few seconds later and the lady's eyes widened in apprehension. Derek motioned her to silence. He did not mind having company at night, but if someone caught this particular lady in his quarters...

He was still holding her and the situation made him suddenly very aware of the softness of her skin under his hand. He could feel her pulse, just a little harried, and her body heat increasing... The person outside his room walked away and he released her.

Sacha took her hand to her throat where her skin tingled from his touch. Her eyes shone in surprise, along with some emotion he did not try to define. Derek stepped away and growled, "What the hell are you doing here?"

"Please mind your language."

The haughty tone annoyed him immediately and Derek smirked, bowing his head mockingly.

"I never suspected you liked me so much that you'd decide to sneak into my chambers; at night; my lady."

She glared, probably more irked by her sudden blush than his sneer. Her fingers were still smoothing the skin of her throat and he preferred to look elsewhere.

"Derek, help me."

He was waiting for some poisonous retort to match their growing argument. She knew she had his attention when his blue eyes flicked back to her, first to her face first and then to her attire.

Sacha briefly wondered if she should be insulted by the relief in his eyes when he noticed she was fully clothed under her wool cloak. Derek scowled.

"Are those Elwyn's old breeches?"

She chinned up, mute, and realization hit him.

"Oh no, absolutely not."

"He is my brother..."

And you are the only one who can free him... She didn't add the last part. Sacha deciphered hesitation in his eyes, the need to obey and stay put battling the urge to *do* something. She remembered the anger he had tried so hard to conceal from her father that very same afternoon in the hall. But he kept silent.

Sacha broke the eye contact, disappointed. She would find another way to save them all. There had to be another one…

She turned to leave and he grabbed her arm.

"I cannot let you go."

Sacha glanced at him defiantly and freed herself from his grasp. Derek placed himself between her and the door, folding his arms over his chest. She raised an eyebrow, temper starting to fire again.

"I only have to alert the guard, Sacha."

"Oh really? My father will be so delighted to learn how you lured me into your chambers at night and..." she put one hand on her throat again. "...assaulted me."

She was bluffing. She was surely bluffing and he should not buy her threat. He did anyway. Derek blamed it on the growing desire to go to Elwyn's rescue; and on the certainty Geraint would claim for reparation; most probably a marital one. The idea of spending the rest of his days and nights with her was enough to push anyone to act harshly.

Anyway, he refused to move away from the door, but he relaxed his stance a little.

"What do you have in mind?"

Sacha stamped her foot impatiently.

"My maid prepared our horses and some hoards. All you have to do is pack a few things and…"

"Did you say *our* horses?"

God, this man was impossible. She frowned and decided to change her tactic.

Sacha approached the stubborn prince slowly and placed one hand on his crossed forearms, her fingertips brushing his chest, and she plunged her clear stare into his.

"I took a chance on your heart, Derek, please…"

Derek swallowed hard. Suddenly, he was glad the proud Lady of Haven preferred threats and commands to more feminine ways to submit a man to her will. No man in his right mind would deny her anything when she fixed her impossibly green eyes on him, all innocence and sweet admiration. He certainly could not.

Derek untied the slender fingers from his shirt, and hid his surrender behind a severe "Give me five minutes."

The glint of triumph she quickly masked behind a thankful smile was enough to confirm he had been framed. But he knew that beforehand, and he had dived anyway. Derek shrugged his shoulders, and started packing.

oOo

They followed the servant's staircase to access the kitchens, which allowed them to go without encountering any guard. Derek took a mental note to add some patrols to those passages when they returned. Not only would it strengthen an obviously weak spot, but hopefully it would also prevent some reckless lady's nocturnal escapades in the future.

Sacha tiptoed across the vast room, careful to avoid the helpers who slept on the bare floor near the hearth. She had tugged her long cloak around her so it didn't swipe the floor tiles, and Derek quickly imitated her.

The kitchens' backdoor opened on a rear courtyard and the stables. They walked swiftly through the yard and found their mounts ready, held by Sacha's maid. The girl bowed to her mistress and confirmed that the northern door was free. Derek frowned; he really needed to talk to Geraint about security.

Already on her mount, Sacha spoke softly, "Remember, Agnes, you have to buy us as much time as possible. If someone asks about me in the morning, inform them that I had a bad night and I am resting. As for Prince Derek, should anyone wonder, simply say you don't know, or suggest he might have gone hunting."

"I will, my lady. Be careful!..."

Sacha nodded and kicked her horse, immediately followed by Derek.

The moon had finally set, which would cover their departure. The path to the northern door was unpaved and the bare ground muffled the noises from their horses' shoes. Once outside the castle Sacha immediately turned toward the woods, hoping the canopy would cover them. They progressed slowly until they reached a good distance from the walls. Then she urged her mount forward.

To ask where they were going was irrelevant. Derek knew where *he* wanted to go and apparently, Sacha had the same idea. They headed toward the Dark Woods.

Chapter 4

Elwyn returned to consciousness and instantly wished he had not. His entire body ached, from his wrists clasped in iron to his ankles, which felt like they were forming some unnatural angle with the soiled ground. He was pretty sure his chest was a rainbow of bruises; even breathing was painful.

Blinking several times, he was surprised to find out he could actually distinguish forms through one of his eyes. The other was too swollen and throbbed alarmingly when he tried to open it.

His prison was exactly what he could have guessed. It had bare stones walls, including the one he was chained to, absolutely no windows, and a massive iron fence forbade him to go visit the dungeons if he ever felt desire to do so. Only a rat would pass through that fence. A slim rat that was.

Without windows, he had no means to tell if it was day or night. The dim light seemed to come from torches outside his cell. He had no idea how long he had been here. All he could tell was that he was hungry; and maybe thirsty too. His tongue felt like parchment paper in his mouth. Sacha's trademark smirk crossed his blurred mind while her laugh echoed in his head.

'You are always hungry and thirsty.'

"Well, this time, Sacha, I really am."

Probably speaking aloud to his absent sister meant he had started to lose his mind, too. Words croaked out in an excruciating cough and he did not recognize his own voice. When he found his breath again, Elwyn was quite sure he might have sustained a broken rib or two, in addition to the rest.

The past events were a fuzzy blur. He recalled discussing with Sebastian the plunder they had come across, while the cook complained the wood was too damp for a good fire. And then darkness had fallen upon them. Afterward, he remembered only pain.

oOo

"We never saw them coming. I am not even sure how many they were... Men dressed in animal furs and armed with short axes... They killed half of us before we even realized we were under attack... I recall the horses were terrified and they broke free, at some point... Elwyn... Elwyn and I tried to reach Erik, but we were cut off from the group, and... I don't know what happened afterward... I remember being dragged on the ground. But..."

Ylianor helped Sebastian up and brought a cup to his lips. He gulped some of the liquid with difficulty. The tentative grin on his battered face looked like a grimace.

"I am sorry to say, it smells better than it tastes, Lady Ylianor..."

She smiled at the poor banter, trying not to wince as her heart squeezed for the young man.

"You will tell that to Derek when he-"

Geraint snorted loudly and Ylianor lost her smile.

"We let you rest now, Sebastian. You did well."

"I wish I had done better, Uncle, I-"

"Shush... Rest..."

The smooth caress on his forehead lulled him to close his eyes, and the young man lay back on his pillows without a protest, helped by Ylianor. Soon, the painkiller acted, and he dozed off.

Geraint glanced at his nephew from the door, before he escorted Ylianor out of the room. They walked in silence to the Great Hall, where a few knights were waiting. The duke quickly gave his orders and then turned to Ylianor, visibly fighting to keep his calm.

"I cannot believe Derek threw precautions to the wind like this! Does your son have any idea how much it has cost us to keep both of you safe all these years?"

Igraine faced him calmly.

"I am sorry, Geraint... I fear that when his friends are concerned, Derek tends to listen to his heart rather than his head."

Geraint breathed heavily.

"Please do not hear me wrong, my lady. William and I were as close as brothers in arms could be, and I will never regret giving you sanctuary, never. Derek is brave and honourable, just like his father was, and a great warrior. But my priority must be the security of this land and its people."

Ylianor considered his declaration for a moment before she put a friendly hand on the man's arm. His posture was still the one of a soldier, strong and rigid. His thick hair had greyed over the years, but the blue eyes were still alert and piercing. He had said nothing of Sacha, but she knew the father worried for his daughter, for both his children, just like her heart trembled for her only son.

Foolish, foolish Sacha who always did what she thought was right, and damned the consequences. She had little doubt that the impetuous lady was the mastermind behind their disappearance. Derek was quick-tempered, but he valued obedience and generally followed orders. Geraint had clearly commanded him to stay put.

The former queen gave a tight smile. That Sacha had managed to convince Derek to come with her was of little surprise. He never resisted a challenge from the fierce Lady of Haven, and if she had chosen to ply his resolve with coy eyes and trembling lips, there were even less chances he denied her anything. Especially if it meant going to his best friend's rescue. Ylianor wished she had not advised her to charm instead of demanding to obtain what she wanted. At any rate, whatever the weapon Sacha used, now both were gone.

The duke silently covered her hand with his before he glanced up to the blonde woman by his side with a humourless grin.

"I fear our children chose the worst moment to finally give into each other."

Finding nothing to answer, Ylianor nodded courteously before she took her leave. The memory of Sacha's dream worried her.

oOo

They stopped by midday to eat some bread and dried meat, and water their horses. Derek took a few minutes to check on their supplies. Sooner or later, he would have to ask Sacha about her plans, but he was not in a hurry to discover she had none. She always rushed head first toward whatever waited ahead, and thought later - generally too late - about trouble. The only difference was that generally, he let Sebastian deal with her.

In some ways, Elwyn was the same troublemaker. Except that Elwyn used to drag him along - mostly - against his will, and this time he had *agreed* to come. Correction: she had tricked him into agreeing. He dismissed the thought with a frown and focused on their packing.

Her maid had bundled about three days' worth of food; they'd have more if he was lucky on the hunt or they bought more supplies in the way. Examining the second bag, Derek found a map, visibly older than the ones Sebastian had shown him the week before, and several phials he recognized.

"Did you go through my mother's stock?"

Sacha put away her gourd.

"I did not know what we… What Elwyn would need."

He uncorked one and smelt it, suspicious.

"Well I hope you know how to distinguish cure draught from poison."

Her eyes gleamed dangerously, but Sacha kept her mouth shut. They were only a few hours from Haven and she could not afford to alienate him just yet. Or ever. If Derek did not accompany her, her chances of success were null. The young woman pursed her lips, irritated, and stood to stretch her legs before she walked to her horse to caress its soft nose before she mounted it.

Surprised by her silence, Derek put his discoveries back in the bags, save for the chart, which he unrolled.

"We should reach Worth Hall in about two hours; I prefer we avoid villages afterward. We will stop by a farm for the night."

"We could go farther. It is barely noon and-"

Derek let the chart roll up again, and cut in.

"We are tired and I have to draw our courses of action. You have a lot to explain, too. We will stop in three hours."

Sacha felt annoyance prickle the hair on the nape of her neck. Of course, he assumed the lead was his. It did not matter to him that *she* had organized their getaway by a safe road, nor did he prize her thinking about the food, the chart or the medicines. He simply implied she had *stolen* from his mother - borrowed without permission, if you please - and considered that being the male, *he* was in charge.

"Fine."

One word was all she could give him without shouting her frustration. *She* was not - that - tired. *She* had nothing to explain. They had to go to the Dark Woods and then… Of course, because he was talking about resting, she needed to yawn.

Derek shot her a quick glance, maybe astonished by her docility then he climbed on his horse.

oOo

It took them nearly the rest of the afternoon to reach the small town, and another hour to find a farm that Derek deigned to consider.

The first two were dismissed because of their proximity to the small city, while the third looked more like a ruin than a farm; "The perfect trap for unwise travellers," he declared, when they trotted away. The woman weeding the land near that one had a rooted smile that disclosed that more than half of her teeth were missing.

The fourth building they saw more than half an hour later was small, but apparently in good shape. The farmer nodded briefly at them before resuming his work, and his sober attitude suited Derek, who finally stopped. A man more interesting in farming his lands than in travellers felt safe.

After a short exchange, the man agreed to let them use the barn for the night. Sacha refused Derek's help to unsaddle her horse and did her best not to grimace under the load. By the time they had tended to their horses she was yawning so hard she could not mask it. Derek announced he was going to speak with their host to get some fresh food, and Sacha vaguely nodded, already eyeing the hayloft. She nestled against a big bail of straw and sleep took her quickly after she arranged her cloak around her.

The light was dim around him, but he was getting use to the semi-darkness by now. It was not as if his cell offered the nicest view anyway.

The headache was still there, pounding in his head and making it heavy. Elwyn fidgeted to activate blood circulation and the movement nearly sent him overboard. Only his instinctive grip on the frame saved him from falling. He was not chained anymore and the hard floor had transformed into a bed, as comfortable as his own. Maybe he was back in Haven. Or maybe he had developed a strong fever and he was still in his cell, and delirious.

The vertigo from his sharp jolt dissipated and he risked opening one eye again. He was not in his personal chambers. But this didn't look like the dungeon he had awakened in the last time. The room was small, yet agreeably furnished. In addition to the bed he was currently lying in, he spotted a chest and a large chair by a fireplace.

Elwyn blinked. The chair was occupied by a young woman with straight blond hair, and she was looking at him with interest. When their eyes locked, she grinned happily. She was pretty. He scolded. This had to be the fever. No one woke up with a cute girl as a nurse after being beaten up into a pulp then chained with rats; not even Derek. Well, maybe Derek…

"You are awake! I am Fillin. How are you feeling?"

She had a nice voice. If this was a hallucination, why not make the best of it?

"I am not sure. Where am I?"

His voice was coarse from being unused and he coughed. The blonde helped him with a drink, unfortunately not wine. For a dream, it needed improvement. The beverage was vaguely acid, and sweetened, like lemonade; refreshing. Maybe it was better than wine.

"You are in Caer Lon of course."

Her small laugh cascaded joyfully in the air. Elwyn closed his eyes. The name rang a bell, but he could not place it. He had probably read it somewhere on Sebastian's charts and his overworked imagination plotted a fictitious world around it.

"Why am I here? What about my cousin?"

His companion sighed. The sad little sound forced him to open his eyes again.

"I could not do anything for him. He was sent back. But I saved you…"

And just like that, the young woman bent over him and kissed his lips. All in all, it was a pleasant fantasy…

Chapter 5

Sacha straightened up, startled. She moved a little and realized her face and her hands were cold, whereas she felt hot with the nurse of a headache. Her eyes adjusted to the feeble light, and she finally noticed Derek. He was seated by the opening in the gable that served as an upper door, looking outside. He stayed immobile with his sleeves rolled up despite the cold air coming in, apparently deep in thought.

She moved to get up and join him but his voice stopped her. "There is some stew and bread if you are hungry. The stew is probably just warm by now."

The bowl was some feet away from her, close enough for her to smell the food. Her stomach growled in approval. The bread was a little crunchy from poor grinding but she devoured it to the last crumbs. The food helped to clear her head and she felt better, though still a little dazed from her nap.

Derek had put a clay jug beside the now empty bowl. It contained some home-made ale and she sampled it carefully, nearly choking when the bitter taste grazed her tongue. The ale was strong and savoury, so she drank more. The alcoholic beverage succeeded in warming her.

Sacha did not remember covering herself with her blanket, but it was spread over her legs. She curled under the thick cloth, propped up on one elbow, and squinted at Derek.

"How long did I sleep?"

He did not turn his head to answer her question, still watching the darkening fields.

"You took in only a few hours. The farmer confirmed he saw our troops passing by a few days ago, then no one else save an isolated rider or two. Sebastian was not taken back this way. We will head northeast tomorrow. I want to arrive from the back at…"

"Elwyn is in Caer Lon."

Derek stared at her in befuddlement and she calmly held his doubtful gaze.

"We have to go there."

Irritation perked through his answer.

"That is impossible. How would you know where Elwyn is anyway? We will ride northeast at dawn."

He did not believe her. How could she explain? He would simply laugh and dismiss her vision. Sacha took another swig of ale and immediately regretted it. The beverage was far stronger than what she was used to. She inhaled deeply to chase away the dizzying sensation. Derek chuckled and walked to her shelter to take the jug from her hands.

"You want to be careful with that."

She glared but her displeased glance was lost to him as he sat away from her, his attention entirely devoted to the recipient he started playing with, making it turn between his knees on the dusty floor.

Sacha took his pensive attitude for an opening and tried again.

"Derek, I know I am right. Elwyn *is* in Caer Lon. We need to go there…"

He continued his little game in silence, though she was sure he had heard her. Why could not he rely on her? Frustrating, stubborn, idiotic specimen of a…

"Sacha, Caer Lon is a myth. It was where the High Kings of Camelot held their court. The place was lost three hundred years ago. Elwyn cannot be there or it means he is dea-"

"He is not dead!"

She nearly screamed in anguish. He was her twin, her other half. If he had died, a part of her would have died too. He was alive. He was. She knew he was.

Surprisingly, her outburst brought Derek closer and he put one hand on her arm to comfort her, though he took it off almost immediately. When he spoke, she recognized Ylianor's reassuring intonations in his voice, soothing and warm.

"Where did you hear of that name? No one talks about the High places anymore."

His voice lacked the characteristic sarcasm that annoyed her so much. Maybe he would listen if she tried…

"Fillin told him. She is taking care of him; she had him removed from his cell and tended… She… She kissed him."

Disclosing the last part was a mistake, as she realized too late.

"Kiss?"

The prince roared in laugher. Sacha instantly jerked away from him to retreat into her lair of straw; bringing her cover up to her jaw, she turned her back on him. Derek was obtuse and closed minded. She should not even have bothered to try and tell him about her vision. She was going to Caer Lon, wherever it was. He could ride north or east or back to Haven for all she cared!

oOo

Something was wrong. There were the itch of straw on his cheek and the hard wood biting into his back, but something else felt absolutely out of place. Derek pushed up to sit and looked around. Turning his head, he waned. Sacha was missing.

He jumped on his feet instantly awake, looking for the traces of a fight. There was nothing. She was simply gone. He cursed loudly. The little she-devil had finally decided to leave him behind! Another bunch of colourful epithets escaped him.

Derek buckled his scabbard and slid rather than climbed down the ladder. How did she manage to go without waking him? He rushed outside and the rising sun blinded him.

The young man shadowed his eyes with one hand, the other automatically setting on the hilt of his sword. The crude light failed to show settling dust or some clue of her direction. She was long gone… He swore again. Why could not she be reasonable? How could he protect her if she took off like this? Was she so foolish she would follow some random dream, vision, or whatever it was? The idea left a mark in his mind.

Her brother being tended by some maiden in the mythic Caer Lon was as real as unicorns and fairies. Once he found her, he was going to seize her up and galloped back to Haven with her. He would knock her out if he had to. He would convince her father to jail her. He would put her in the stocks dressed only with a potato sack. He would…

"Derek!"

He whirled on his heels so fast he nearly lost his footing. Her brilliant smile half eclipsed the rising sun, infuriating him even more. Blind with a ferocious need to kill her, Derek charged toward the young woman. He grabbed her arms in an iron clasp. Her grin disappeared while shock bolted in her luminous eyes.

"You're hurting me…"

His grip tightened for a second before he mastered his fury and let go. She immediately took one step back. Derek barked:

"Where the hell were you?!"

Sacha massaged her painful upper arms and walked away swiftly, without answering. Four steps and the prince blocked her way, towering over her with his entire frame. Her forehead barely reached his chin. Unimpressed, Sacha stood her ground. He nearly lost his temper and seized her again. Sensing his storming mood, she scowled defiantly, doing her best to compensate for the difference of height with a haughty glacial gaze.

His wrath evaporated slowly. She looked like a pouting child. She was safe…

Derek held one hand up to brush her offended limb and she tensed. His arm fell back to his side.

"I did not mean to hurt you. I woke up and you were nowhere to be seen…"

This was the closest to an apology he was willing to give. Sacha shoved the plate of bread and cheese she was still holding into his stomach.

"I suggest that next time you check the horses before you fret."

The tip of his ears grew embarrassingly hot. He had not thought of the horses. Derek turned toward the opened door. Sure enough, their mounts were peacefully chewing hay, and he could spot their saddles in the corner where he had stored them the previous evening.

She had vanished and he had imagined the worst because… Because she was Sacha and her sole purpose in this life was to annoy him to no end; driving him crazy was just a side benefit. Derek groaned.

"Well *I* suggest that next time, you wake me up instead of disappearing like that. Where were you anyway?"

The young woman snorted and started toward the barn. Derek followed, putting the plate aside.

"I wanted to thank the farmer and his wife for their hospitality and I asked where we can find a proper library."

"A library?"

She was demented. Too little sleep and too much ale had finally pushed her over the edge. He was taking her back to her father. Now. Period.

Sacha was looking at him as if he were slow, her impatience barely contained.

"Yes, Derek, a library: you must have heard about it. It is a place stocked with books and charts. Scholars use them for knowledge."

She ignored his growl and went on:

"*You* may not know where Caer Lon is, but I will find out."

The way she hammered the first word, she could have poked at him in the chest with her finger. It felt like it.

"Sacha…"

He barely recognized his voice in the low defeated tone. She picked up her saddle but waddled under the load. It was too heavy for her to even think about reaching the back of her horse but she clenched her teeth and tried anyway. She never gave up and that he admired, even if her stubbornness irritated him senseless. Derek took the saddle off her hands to put it into place effortlessly before he tended to his own stallion. Sacha continued her explanation with only a short nod to acknowledge his gallantry.

"We have to go to Lann Stefan. The farmer told me the monks at Saint Stephen monastery are known for their scholars."

She kept including him in her nonsense. *Where we can find… We have to go…* She was assuming they were together in this, but she refused to listen to him if his words were not to her liking; as always…

Derek took a deep breath and reviewed his options quickly. One: he could go with her and try to convince her it was a wild goose chase. Two: he could go the right direction and worry about her safety all the way. Three: he could go back to Haven and explain to her father he had let her on her own. Four: he could grab her, tie her up across his saddle, and take her home.

Sacha had climbed on her horse and was looking at him, visibly waiting. He sighed.

"Fine. But next time, you *will* wake me up." He too could use words to make someone feel small. "I am serious Sacha; other places will not be as safe as this one."

She smiled beautifully. Derek couldn't help but return it. Lann Stefan was east, after all. Sacha pursed her lips, satisfied she had won this battle.

"You snore…"

"I do not!"

The little witch had already kicked her mount into a trot. Derek gritted his teeth and followed, forgetting about breakfast. Option four had its appeal; definitely.

Chapter 6

The servant put the tray on the table, eyes glued to the floor, before he retreated as quickly as he could into a corner.

This one would be gone in a week, he thought; ten days at most. Twice as clumsy as the slaves he bought in Londinium, and just as worthless. Those puppets were pitiful. His cup was only half full, and yet it was a miracle the wine had not spilled on the food. The man snapped his fingers and the boy yelped in terror, jumping forward to fill his goblet before he fled back to his corner. Their submission was disgusting.

He glanced at the boy's reflection in the cup and played with it, back and forth, making the image move sideways. A hiccup echoed behind him, nearly a sob, as the meagre body followed the impossible movements the sorcerer gave to its image on the cup, twisting at impossible angles. Finally tired of his game, the man crushed the goblet in his massive hand. A gasp of pain, followed by the muffled sound of boneless members hitting the ground answered the man's impatient grimace. Pitiful puppets. This one had lasted less than a week, after all.

Wolfryth negligently threw his now useless cup toward the crushed body. He stood up and the room suddenly felt smaller. Standing near the fireplace, the man's large shoulders almost hid half of the mantel. His grey hairs were pulled back with a leather bind. His yellow eyes gleamed dangerously under the light from the flames, adding to the impression of savagery. The sorcerer touched the fine line that ran from his left temple to his chin, a present from William Pendragon, so many years ago. Yesterday.

The man had been skilled with a sword, and sustained by survival instincts. He had broken him like dried wood nonetheless. No man-made blade could be a match for his magic.

He laughed and the sound rolled unpleasantly in the empty room. He had killed one Pendragon and now he needed one. How ironic.

Another twist of his hand, and the corpse disappeared, leaving only empty clothes on the floor. He hated to wait. Two days ago, he had used a simple spell of transportation to hurl her cousin back to the Seer, and she was yet to show up. He watched her dreams long enough to know her heart's desires. And what women wanted... She would come, along with Pendragon's offspring sniffing after her skirts like a well-trained dog.

The fire roared to mirror his growing irritation. He was the greatest wizard alive. He had mastered Air and Fire. Water obeyed when he commanded. No one for generations had controlled three of the Powers, and he needed a child, barely old to shave, to reach the ultimate one!

The man clenched his fist and the flames reduced to the size of a candle flick. Patience... The Seer would bring him the blood of the Dragon soon. Patience...

"Father?"

Wolfryth released his grasp on the fire and it burned normally again.

The young woman stepped swiftly into the room, her blond hair flying around her. Reproach shadowed her angelic face briefly when she noticed the piled clothes in the corner. Her voice transpired nothing but boredom when she approached him.

"You did it again... How can I hope to bring up satisfying staff if you dismiss them so often?"

"This one was beyond your teaching."

She sulked.

"I suppose."

Then her smile reappeared. Her golden eyes shone in childish pleasure.

"I have good news, however. Elwyn is awake and he will be up very soon. I like him. He is so cute!"

"I am delighted to hear you like your present. But you have to be careful, my child. He is very powerful."

"Oh, he can do me no harm... I gave him citraurantia."

Wolfryth laughed again. The plant would block the young man's powers. His magic would still be here, sleeping within him, but out of his reach.

"Very well, my crafty little fox. Enjoy his company, but do not hold him too dear; his utility will eventually come to an end."

The fire blazed again, and its light accentuated the resemblance between the sorcerer and a wild animal.

oOo

Jeffrey, the Court physician, patted Sebastian on the shoulder, probably the only place of his body that was not covered with bandages. It hurt nonetheless. This time, the examination had been less painful, thanks to Ylianor's decoctions, but he was glad it was over.

He felt like he had been trampled by a hoard of furious boars, then thrown into a ravine. Even wincing was painful, let alone breathing. His head felt so heavy on his neck he was sure it would have fallen sideways if the pillows had not maintained it in place.

The young man clenched his jaw to retain a moan and settled for a quick nod to the old man who bowed and exited the room, probably to give his report back to his uncle.

Geraint had not come back to ask if he remembered something else about the attack or the place he had been taken. Sebastian wished he had more to tell him. Truth was, he was not sure he had left the battlefield at all before waking up in his bed. Everything was so confused…

A light knock on the door pulled him out of his thoughts.

"Come in."

A young girl he thought he had seen sometimes around Sacha came in, holding a tray.

"Lady Ylianor said you would be hungry, Sir."

"Yes, I am."

He could do with some food, even if the idea of opening his mouth to chew and swallowing was not that appealing, especially after the cold sweat the simple fact of straightening up had brought. Not to mention the ache.

"Thank you... Pardon me I do not remember your name."

"I am Agnes, my Lord. I serve the Lady Sacha."

"Well Agnes you will thank my cousin for sparing your services so you could bring me some food."

Her sudden blush surprised him. Generally, servants were at ease with him, because he was easy going and polite; and to his limited experience, maid girls did not blush that easily. Sebastian pushed up a little more on his cushions. The effort tore a groan from his throat. The maid instantly put her tray down on the table and rushed to help him up.

"Thank you."

She smiled and Sebastian appreciated her gentleness as she helped him up on the pillows. He equally noticed something more disturbing. He had been in the castle for nearly two days, and no one had visited him except Geraint, Ylianor, and the physician.

"Agnes, where are my cousin and Prince Derek?"

"They are about their business, my lord."

Jeffrey could be pretty insistent when he wanted his patients to rest, but Derek and Sacha had never obeyed before. Sebastian narrowed his dark eyes on her, and the girl's already flushed skin turned a deeper shade of pink.

"They… They are on a trip."

A trip? Right after this attack? Not likely.

"Where did they go? I am surprised my uncle authorized them to go anywhere, even with a full cohort of knights to escort them."

Agnes was fidgeting with the lace of her apron, visibly ill at ease. Sebastian tried to keep his tone calm in order not to scare the girl away. Despite his efforts, worry started to tighten his throat.

"Agnes? I asked you a question. Where did the Lady Sacha and Prince Derek go?"

"I… I do not know, my lord. My lady did not say. She asked me to prepare their horses and some goods for three days and she went with the prince before dawn right after they found you… Please, My lord, I just followed her orders…"

She was on the verge of crying. No doubt his uncle had questioned her already, and probably less gently.

Sebastian closed his eyes. Sacha and Derek had gone to Elwyn's rescue. It could be only that. No wonder Ylianor seemed so worried and his uncle looked like he was ready to murder someone.

Oh, Sacha, what did you do...?

It was her plan, of course it was. Derek could be stubborn but he was not reckless. Or rather, he would have gone alone, especially if to leave in the middle of the night. It had to be Sacha, who cornered Derek into following her. He wondered if his friend had caught her while she was tiptoeing out, or if she had walked straight into his chambers to harangue him.

Sebastian could just picture the scene in his mind: Sacha stamping her foot and pouting while Derek looked at her with that stern expression he saved just for her. As if the prince were going to let her go alone... Maybe she had called him 'a good little soldier', 'a docile sheep' or another one of her favourite epithets, so he could not ignore the bait. He never resisted when she provoked him.

The young man wondered if instead of insulting him, Sacha had tried to charm him. Derek would dive after her without a second thought if she did. Or he would have run the other way as fast as possible. Whatever the case, Sebastian would have paid a fortune to see the scene.

The girl was still fixing him nervously, her velvet eyes widened in fear. Sebastian offered the best smile he could muster. With a split lip and bruises all over his face, it probably looked like the worst grimace she had ever seen. Indeed he had paid dearly to have them paired up. He sighed.

"What is done is done, isn't it? Didn't you say something about food?"

She jumped at the reminder, and quickly put the tray on his lap. Sebastian peered at the soup with a groan. Knowing both his cousin's and his friend's usual behaviour around each other, he doubted the greater risk for them came from their enemy, whoever that was.

Chapter 7

Lann Stefan was barely more than a village. But compared to Haven's castle and its dozen houses, it felt like a small city to Sacha.

With spring, merchants had started to travel again, and the coming May Day festivities were bringing a colourful crowd out to venture happily around the shops and bargain the prices with the tenants.

Derek had decided they were to stop at an inn to bathe and rest before they looked for the monastery. He doubted a day was going to be enough to find anything, even with the help of the monk-librarian. For once, Sacha had agreed with him.

Her clothes were stiff and itched from an entire day on horseback and a night in the hayloft. In addition, Sacha was in no hurry to repeat their performance of the morning. Her horse made a step aside and she had to pull on her reins to restrain it. The movement enhanced the sting in her sore arms. She was pretty sure she would sustain a bruise in the morning. She had not expected him to react so violently. Derek was certainly prompt to react and tempest, but with her he had always kept a strict rein on physical expressions of his temper, settling for arrogant retorts or mocking remarks.

It amazed her to know she could shatter his control like that. It made her feel... powerful. The idea of possessing that kind of influence over a man like Derek intrigued her, though she wasn't sure she liked it. Much.

Sacha glanced at her companion. Derek was riding beside her, his posture almost casual. She noticed he had only one hand on his reins; the other rested on his thigh, inches away from his blade. His blue eyes were scanning the crowd while his face was blank. Nothing in his attitude indicated he too was fazed with the stony road or the numbers of two story buildings. He looked like the known sleepy cat, which waited for some heedless mouse to come a little too close. The young woman shivered involuntary. Those were the moments that truly reminded her that Derek was lethal, more than his random outbursts of rage.

A bell rang to announce Terce. She pushed up on her stirrups looking both ways for the church. Derek's stern voice reminded her about discretion and she sighed before settling back on her saddle.

Some minutes later, Derek stopped his mount in front of a building larger than the rest.

"We will stay here."

A sign hung above the door. A big animal with twisted tusks was painted on the wood panel to announce the establishment's name: 'The Wild Boar'. Derek jumped down. Sacha didn't wait to dismount, ignoring his offered hand. The prince said nothing and gestured a servant to pick up their bags.

When he stepped forward to push the door and enter in front of her, Sacha had more than enough with his patronizing.

"You have more experience of taverns than I do. Please lead the way."

Derek frowned, visibly displeased by her comment. Shrugging his shoulders, he preceded her inside.

The room was brighter than she expected, almost welcoming. A few costumers were seated in front of a carafe in spite of the early hour. Others were eating. More than half of them snatched a glimpse at the newcomers and Sacha felt like a rabbit surrounded by foxes. Maybe having him entering first had not been such a bad idea...

Derek pushed his hood back and she could only imitate him, but she kept her face down, glad her long braid was caught beneath her cloak. At least the thick cloth protected her from more probing. With her delicate face and slender frame, she could hardly be mistaken for a boy.

The prince chose a table near the wall and she nearly sighed in relief at the idea of having the thick barrier in her back. Murmurs of thanks evanesced from her lips when she saw Derek take the bench near the wall while he invited her to take the open one.

"I prefer having my eyes on the room instead of it watching my back."

So do I. Sacha thought bitterly. She preferred swallowing her comment. No need to let her discomfort show. He would be too happy. Instead she sat down, trying her best to look poised and at ease with her neck exposed to curiosity.

A waitress with an outrageous neckline showed up within minutes with two cups and a jug. Derek did not let her enough time to take a proper look at them before he declared, "We need a room for the night and baths. Our horses are in the back."

"Yes; my lord."

Her low bow exposed more cleavage when Derek placed a silver coin in her hand to punctuate his list of requirements. Sacha quirked an eyebrow; the smirk on her companion was insufferable. As for the absurd behaviour of that woman... The waitress left, and Derek looked back to her, apparently sure she was shocked by the amount of money he offered, and obviously amused by her silent blame.

"There has to be some interest in winning tournaments."

Escorting her was the only valuable reward to the jousts. Knights told her so every single time, before Derek beat them methodically to win the day.

She fought not to slap his grin off his face. His smirk grew some more, as if he could see the wheels turning in her head. Sacha bit back a comment about greed, her cheeks burning. Couldn't her mind shut up about the way he glimpsed at that woman? He'd never looked at her that way. Not that she wanted him to. Did she? No. Of course not. She wasn't interested in the slightest in Derek or his frolics...

"My lady, my lord, your room is ready. If you please follow me..."

The young woman jumped to her feet to follow their guide upstairs. Derek imitated her with a glance toward the bar. Sacha did her best to ignore his hesitation. Her hands trembled with outrage.

Fortunately, Derek stayed in the room just long enough to peek at the two small beds and make sure their bags were intact.

Satisfied, he ordered the tub hidden behind an overused screen to be filled for bathing immediately and left her blissfully alone.

oOo

The tavern's main room was filling up quickly as the morning bloomed. Locals and merchants alike poured through the door for a drink or to exchange the current gossip, which was fine with him. Rumours travelled faster than light. By experience, Derek knew one could learn far more by listening rather than asking questions. Unfortunately, that took time, and time was a luxury he had not.

A bunch of old men now occupied the table by the wall. Derek overlooked his previous observatory to walk to the back of the room. The barman nodded at him, never stopping mopping the wooden surface.

"What's for you, lad?"

Derek fished a silver coin from his purse, and put it on the counter.

"Information."

The barman shrugged. Derek pushed the coin forward. The man stayed still, looking straight at the young man. After a few seconds, he grunted, "I have ale or cider. Which one do you want?"

Derek frowned. The barman held his stare steadily. Derek tried to think fast. Why offer a choice of drink when he had made it clear he didn't want to drink? He took a wild guess.

"Give me a pint of cider."

Apparently satisfied, the barman put a chop in front of him. When he glanced down, Derek noticed the money had disappeared. One coin of silver was way too high a price for cider, but at least he…

"You're lucky. Last bottle from a bunch I bought last winter. Was pretty surprised to have goods from the *other side* again at the time."

Derek sipped the beverage tentatively. His mind worked in a frenzy to process the two words the barman had put emphasis on. His mother often prized Camelot's apple trees and the talent of the peasants to exploit them. Tiny bubbles fizzled on his tongue, sweet and dry at the same time, an invitation to drain his cup. He resisted the temptation in extremis and bowed his head in appreciation. The barman bent forward.

"When the wolf is out of the woods, the forest breathes again."

The man talked in enigmas, but this one rang a bell.

"What else crossed the border?"

The barman stepped back. For a second, he feared he had been too direct. His source groaned, "Told you. Goods." The man lowered his tone, "and bad things."

The young man opened his mouth to push on the matter.

"That's a very nice squire you've got, Sire. Very nice…"

The sneer sent Derek's heart up his throat. He forced himself to take a long gulp of cider before he turned. The ruffian elbowed a poor costumer nearby.

"If pretty boy here is fed up of his *page*, I'll supply."

The salacious laugh shrieked on Derek's nerves, hard. His left hand looked for his sword. He gripped the hilt, and stepped forward.

"It won't be necessary."

Though hissed through clenched teeth, the new comer recognized the threat. He fisted hands large as ham. Derek prepared for the first swing.

Feminine curves appeared out of nowhere between them, and the blond who had first welcomed Sacha and him locked arms with the brute.

"Let me show you to a nice table…"

The intruder glanced down on the generous corsage, growled at Derek and deserted the scene. Breathing more easily, the young man noticed his informer had disappeared in the back room. Whatever *bad things* had crossed Camelot's borders would have to wait. His *squire* had soaked by herself long enough anyway.

oOo

Sacha relaxed, vaguely wondering how long she could indulge in the water before Derek claimed his turn. The man came haunting her thoughts all too often. He was probably flirting with that cheeky waitress and not at all in a hurry to use the cleaning facilities.

She closed her eyes, sinking deeper in the tub. The hot water started to wash annoyance and soreness away. Her unplaited hair sprang to life in the water, dressing her shoulders with a black web. Sacha pinched her nose to immerse fully in the water and rinse her mane. Underwater, she could not hear anything, but the low beating of her heart and she savoured the peaceful rhythm as long as she could. Finally she broke the surface for air, wiping water off her eyes.

"You have been in there for an eternity."

Sacha screamed and lost her balance, slipping to the bottom of the tub, spraying water everywhere. The shadow behind the screen jumped backward instantly. Her sore biceps hit the rim and she moaned in pain. The brutal invasion of water into her nose and down her throat brought up tears, as she choked and coughed.

"Get out Derek!"

Crouched in the tub with water up to her chin, she didn't dare moving one lash.

"I need to tell-"

His sentence floated toward her, muffled by the sound of her heart racing and thudding blood in her ears.

"How dared you!"

She shut up immediately, fighting to retrieve her composure. She refused to sound like a terrified little girl. There was nothing to be afraid of… It was nothing but Derek acting like an oaf! Taking a deep breath she spat, words angrily banging out of her mouth.

"Close your eyes while I dress."

"Don't worry. Your virtue has nothing to fear with me."

Oh, really. If she had not been so mad at him, she would have loved proving him wrong and adored every single minute of it. Arrogant, vulgar, ignominious...

Sacha risked a glimpse out of her hiding. Her change of clothes was on her bed. Derek was facing the door, hands crossed in his back. If he had heard the boil of water when she climbed out of the tub, it did not show in his nonchalant posture. She tiptoed to the bed and snatched her clothes before she retreated behind the screen in a flash. It took her less than a minute to vest despite the resistance of the fabric on her humid skin.

"You can turn around now."

Her voice was regal, and perfectly icy. Derek stayed immobile for a few more seconds. When he finally decided to grant her one look, she was seated on the bed, working her brush through her mane. The surprise on his face annoyed her even more.

"You are wearing a dress."

The brush stopped midway in her damp locks.

"Yes, I am. Is that a problem?"

"No, of course not."

She was not sure she liked the glint that sparkled in his eyes. The taunting smile was even more hassling. Sacha continued arranging her hair, falsely unconcerned.

"The water is still hot, if by any chance you feel like cleaning up."

His smirk disappeared at the insult. Excellent.

Derek put off his jacket and started unlacing his shirt. Sacha narrowed her eyes on him, unable to chase away the warmth spreading up her throat.

"The screen is over there, Derek."

His boots landed on the floor. Sacha turned to face the opposite side of the room but she refused to close her eyes. Her locks were already tangling, she had no reason to wait for him to discover the sense of the word 'modesty'.

"You really splashed water everywhere…"

God, was he insufferable! What need had he to always try and make her feel addled or futile!

"I am not used to have someone entering my chambers while I am bathing."

"This is reassuring… Hum, this is good."

The appreciative murmur when he entered the tub tore away a smile. Sacha focused on one particularly difficult knot; like certain prince. The sound of water caught her attention again. The knot gave in with a vigorous pull that echoed down to her arm and she could not stop a whimper to escape her lips.

"I asked a couple of questions of the barman. He was able to buy some cider from Camelot last winter."

She chocked. He hadn't intruded her privacy to talk about alcohol, had he? If this was an excuse for ill behaviour, this was the lousiest she had ever been served. And Elwyn had a bottomless stock of them. She put her brush away without a reply and started arranging her hair, wincing every time she pulled too hard at the wavy mass.

"I suspect beverages are not the only thing that came across. Apparently, *bad things* did too. Whatever they are. So, are you ready?"

Sacha looked up to find him dressed fresh, his hair shining a dark gold from the bath. Irritated at liking the image, she took her time to clip her braid up with a beautifully carved hazel comb Agnes had thoughtfully added to her packing. Then she stood gracefully, a perfectly composed smile on her lips. Derek's expression flinched, yet it was still too bold for her taste.

"Good. Let's go explain to the innkeeper why a lady dresses as a page and why said lady and her knight need to find the church…"

Chapter 8

Derek decided the furious embarrassment in Sacha's eyes when he served his story to their hostess was worth every second. She had no idea what her shriek had done to his heart rate. Especially given that he was still recovering from his encounter with one of her two admirers in the main room. What the hell was she thinking, screaming like that? He thought... No, he had just stopped thinking for a split second.

Afterward, the effort of calming the beast raging inside his chest had nearly made it easy to ignore her shadow playing on the wall as she dressed; well, quite easy. She had taken her sweet time vesting. Did she think he was made of stone? Good God, he was only human and she *was* beautiful...

"I cannot believe you told her we eloped!"

Her outrage cut through his distracting thoughts. Caught off guard, Derek managed a sneer.

"I did not recall using that particular word. I told only the truth. We did leave without your father's approval."

Derek paused to observe their surroundings and find the general direction the innkeeper had indicated for the church.

"But you *implied* we eloped. And you asked for the church! Now she is convinced we need a priest to... To... To marry us!"

Finding the church would automatically lead them to the monastery, as he was about to explain to the enraged lady before she started fustigating him. Then Sacha was so far gone he didn't bother. Derek continued to walk, his progression slowed down by the various spreads of market.

"We will not stay long enough for her to offer you a wedding crown, if that is your concern."

He avoided one cart offering flowers, before he half-turned to make sure she followed him despite the garish crowd. It was nearly noon, and the market was in full swing. Markets always made him nervous, teeming with noises and bustling tenants. The crowd was the perfect hideout for ruffians and cutpurses.

"One conversation with the librarian should suffice to convince you Caer Lon does not exist anymore and tomorrow, we will ride north."

He chose to consider her glower was due to the reek coming from the next shop, the acrid smell of stale fruits assaulting his nose. Sacha fumed more than ever.

"You have planned this ridiculous exit all along."

Derek glanced at her quickly while they reached the packed place. Sacha was looking around with a beguiled expression in her eyes. Her irritation was slowly easing. He grabbed her hand to take her away from a baker. They were not here to stroll.

"Every woman falls for a romantic story, especially one in which the young lovers need to fight to be together."

"We are not lovers. In love. Whatever."

She pouted, pulling her hand free from his. The haughty Lady of Haven thoroughly refused to be associated with him in any romantic way. His smile deepened as Derek thought about teasing her about it. Then he decided to hold his tongue. It was probably not a good idea to seed the notion in her lovely head. In addition, her repulsion at the idea was strangely disturbing. He was a prince after all, a fair knight and reasonably good looking. She should be… at least flattered.

Derek tried to focus on the matter at hand. While she got steamed up about their pseudo-pairing, she did not take notice of his denial over the mythic city of Caer Lon. He forced a short laugh out. He should be relieved that she was not interested. Whatever his mother and his friends insinuated, he was absolutely not ready to have marital knots tied around their wrists. She crawled under his skin too easily.

Derek jarred when Sacha touched his elbow slightly, forcing his attention toward the high shadow on their left. A four-storey building was visible behind the bell tower. He had been right about the monastery flanking the church. They would not need to go inside to ask the sacristan for directions. He regretted it, at least a little. Just to see Sacha jittering... Given her current state of mind, it was better to avoid the place entirely.

The monastery was not secluded and the monks allowed them inside. The presence of a woman into their walls made two of the older friars frown while three of the youngest skittered like rabbits. However, the friar librarian who joined them in the chapter room was pretty happy to have young people querying his expertise. He guided them toward the scriptorium, chatting openly about his devoted life.

"We acquire books as often as we can; we are lucky enough to produce honey and cheese so our resources are comfortable. Of course donations are always welcome..."

The allusion was crystal clear. Derek extracted a little purse from his jacket to present it to the plump little man trotting by their side.

"I trust this will secure future purchases."

"This is very generous, my lord; very generous indeed..."

The purse disappeared quickly into the large sleeves as the monk bowed, never slowing down. Sacha used his pause in front of a large double paneled door to explain bashfully.

"Friar Johan, we are passionate about history, and your library is so well known... We hoped we could use your extensive collection."

Derek recognized the suave inflection of her voice. She added just the right glint of innocence in her admiring stare. When did she begin to use charm to have her way with the male population around? He repressed a smirk. Her feminine tricks might have worked on him - once - she could not think it was going to be effective here, could she?

"Of course, my child, but only with my supervision."

The prince's narrowing stare went unnoticed.

"Oh thank you so much... You see, Derek and I had this little argument and maybe you can help me prove him wrong..."

Baffled, the prince shot a deadly glance at her over the tonsured head, but Sacha was smiling at her new friend, ignoring him. The monk patted her arm gently.

"I will do my best, of course. What is it about?"

She blushed slightly. Derek growled internally. *Blushing!* As if this was going to win the day! Baiting him - only once! - was one thing, but a monk!

"Well, we disagree about Caer Lon. Derek's family originated from Camelot, so he thinks he knows all about it."

Another blazing glare got lost. Her tone was deceitfully soft.

"He pretends the city is in the northern part of the kingdom, but I always heard it was in the south…"

He had never said north; he had said it did not exist! She would put the patience of a saint to the test!

They had entered a large square room with small writing desks covered with scrolls, some rolled and others flattened under stones. Ink bottles and quills were dispatched on each table. Friar Johan motioned at the entire room.

"This is the scriptorium. We copy our manuscripts here. You will wait for me here. Visitors are not allowed in the library itself."

Sacha looked at her new admirer with reproachful eyes. Her little moue was clearly designed to show her disappointment. Derek would have laughed, but he was too angry with her to do that. Oblivious of their respective turmoil, Friar Johan showed them to another larger table.

"Please have a seat. We have several documents about the Old City, at least two treaties and some poetry book, I think. The hours of Caer Lon's court, when the High Kings reigned over Camelot, were certainly a golden age." He sighed heavily, as if remembering times he was too young to have lived himself. "I think another book…"

The rest of his sentence rebounded on the closing door when he disappeared into the library. The nice little man, engrossed in his lecture, had probably forgotten he had ordered them to stay put.

Sacha sat and exhaled slowly, visibly annoyed not to be allowed to venture between the bookshelves herself. Derek ignored her arranging the folds of her skirt to check the documents spread on the table. The two bibles were uninteresting. There was a treaty of some sort. His mother would have loved it. The leaves of various plants were beautifully drawn.

The young woman started playing her fingers on the hard surface, impatient. Derek jumped on the occasion for a little payback.

"You should be ashamed of yourself, Sacha. Flirting with a monk, really…"

"I was not flirting."

She frowned while his smile grew.

"Oh no? What do you call the fluttering of lashes and the simpering?"

"I certainly did not simper!"

Boy, he enjoyed seeing her temper rising. Her eyes shone like green gemstones when she was unable to control her emotions and passion overpowered her. Derek dismissed her protest with a flip of his hand.

"Anything you say. Your little act is providing us the information to get back on the right tracks so I am not complaining."

Maybe he was a masochist; he suffered the tantrum, just for the pleasure of cracking that shell of perfection she erected around her like a shield.

"I *know* I am right about this Derek! Why do you refuse to believe me?"

Her voice shattered slightly. That, and her forceful reaction confounded him. Derek took a proper look at her. She was fisting her skirt so hard her knuckles were white. Her eyes glittered with tears more than rage. He bit back a retort and glanced away, vaguely ashamed. He just wanted to tease her. Upsetting each other was never part of their games, as far as he was concerned. He was not *that* insensible, whatever she thought of him.

The silence lengthened awkwardly. Derek rolled his shoulders backward, vaguely wondering how long Friar Johan would be. Staying inactive never suited him. Even in the heart of winter, he needed something to do. If there was too much snow to access the training yard, he would use the vast 'Salle d'armes' for sparing with Sebastian or Elwyn, or helped the blacksmith to check on the weapons and shields in the armoury.

Unable to stay still, the young prince was pushing on his feet to visit the other writing desks when Sacha's clear voice cut through the silent room. Her voice was deadly calm this time.

"You want to pursue another direction. I understand. You are free to go as you please of course."

Derek froze, glancing back at her. Sacha was seated impeccably at her side of the table, her head straight and her hands quietly crossed on her lap. Her impassive mask was into place once more. Her eyes were fixed on an icon on the opposite wall away from him. She dismissed him like a queen relieved a guard from her service. Derek scowled, shaking his head.

"This is out of question. I gave my word I will come with you. I am not taking it back."

If he had not known better, he would have sworn the flash in her eyes was relief when her finally gaze fell on him. Her words were less amiable.

"You are as stubborn as a mule," Sacha grumbled.

So they were back to their usual pestering. Why he was so satisfied about it eluded him. Derek smirked.

"It takes one to know one, doesn't it?"

Friar Johan chose the moment her cheeks were coloring in anger again to finally show up, his arms full of old scrolls. He had a spider web hanging from one ear and perspiration moistened his forehead. His load hit the table with a loud *thunk* when he let it down.

"Here. There are two more books, but you can start with that."

Derek mumbled under his breath when Sacha chose the heavier volume and pushed it toward him with an angelic smile.

Chapter 9

Elwyn blinked and groaned. The swell around his eye had deflated enough for him to see properly, but it was still painful. He guessed the contusions made him look like a raccoon. After being in and out all afternoon, waking up each time to feel his body hurt, he totally understood the animal's irascible mood.

He rubbed the last vestige of sleep from his face, hissing when the movement of his arms stretched the bandage around his chest. Fillin had his ribcage strapped so tightly he could barely breathe. He didn't feel like complaining too much about it. The wrap held his broken bones into place so the pain was almost bearable when he moved.

Elwyn straightened up stiffly, testing his strength, and sat. The canopy stayed over his head instead of reeling sideways, which was a good thing. Feeling no vertigo, he balanced his legs off the mattress precociously. So far, so good. The young man stood slowly. His knees buckled dangerously under him. He clenched his jaw as cold sweat ran down his back, but remained on his feet. His body protested, forcing him to grab the bed pole before he fell forward.

After a long minute, his muscles stopped screaming and reluctantly accepted the torture of functioning again, so he let go of his support, savouring the little victory. Carefully stepping away from the bed, and ready to take hold on the furniture if needed be, he approached the window on wobbly legs and took in the lands surrounding the place.

A grey mist covered miles of dense, dark green forest. Daylight was dim, though he could not tell if it was due to the weather or upcoming dusk. Save for the endless carpet of trees, he saw absolutely nothing. No clearing, no villages, no road. He barely distinguished the sky from the foggy earth.

The young man pressed his face to the glass to look down. The drop was vertiginous. Unless he grew wings, he had little chances to escape this way. Vaguely depressed by the sight, he tumbled back to his bed and sat again with a relieved sigh.

Fillin had left a pitcher of her strange beverage on the nightstand and he poured himself a cup. The bittersweet liquid calmed his thirst. Elwyn wondered once again why the taste was so familiar. It reminded him of lemonade, but it was not that, not exactly. The light acidity was something he was unable to place though he thought he should. The memory floated in the back of his mind, heavy, like a tight knot refusing to untangle and threatening to turn into another headache. He drained the last of his cup and clicked his tongue. Whatever it was, the drink was refreshing.

The young man lied back on the pillows, trying to figure out a course of action. Fillin was very sweet but he guessed her influence on his gaoler was limited. She had not been able to help Sebastian and he doubted she was more than a maid herself. Maybe she was a prisoner, just like him, and *the Enemy* granted her a little freedom so she could serve the household. He wished he could put a name on that faceless menace, a shadow hidden behind in pain and screams. At the same time, he was not in such a hurry to confront the foe. His arching body still held the marks from their previous encounter.

Elwyn closed his eyes. Sacha would know what to do. She always did, or at least she knew how to dragoon him into finding a solution to his problems. He missed his sister, and his friends. He certainly did not want Sacha anywhere near him at the moment, but he missed her nonetheless. At least she was in Haven, protected by the fortress walls and his father's guards; and Derek. He could count on Derek to keep her safe, even if he grouched to no end about doing so.

But were they cautious enough? No one but Sebastian and he seemed to have survived the raid. If so, by the time the duke got wind of the attack, the Enemy would be stronger and could benefit the surprise effect again… Elwyn straightened up looking toward the window again. He needed to find a way out of here, and some way to contact Sacha…

The liquid started to darken and solidify, until it reached the sombre grey color of tarnished tin. Satisfied, Wolfryth bent over the basin and murmured some words in a language Fillin didn't understand. Suddenly, the now-hard surface began to glow, and the young woman felt heat rising from the metal-like matter.

Her father rarely allow her to assist him and she held her tongue instead of asking the multitude of questions she had, keeping her mouth firmly shut while she observed the powerful magic at work. He had yet to explain what that precise spell was for, though she suspected it had to do with his obsession with Derek Pendragon.

"Look carefully. Influencing dreams is one of the most advanced spells when one controls the Spirits."

Fillin knitted her brows in concentration. She had yet to control the different elements, Air least of all. She was a natural with Water, but of course her father refused to acknowledge that. She glimpsed at the basin, wondering if she was to finally discover what the infamous prince looked like. But the surface was just reflecting light from the spell at work, and nothing else.

"Fillin."

The blonde stepped back quickly. The one condition for her to observe while her father worked was to avoid interfering. She was interested in Magic. The consequences were of little concern. Once she mastered the spells herself, she would have plenty of time to play with the results.

Wolfryth touched the surface again, visibly displeased. Fillin tiptoed to watch at the tin-like material from afar. It had stopped glowing and the color was clearing again. Her father's thumb pressed against the substance left a mark into it. She dared a question:

"It was solid gold, last time, wasn't it?"

The frown on the large forehead deepened. The man grabbed the basin with both hands and moved his face toward the mellowing surface. His hair slipped forward, nearly touching it, and he jerked backward.

"Father?"

She recognized the dangerous growl and was already retreating to the door when Wolfryth ordered "Leave me."

The door closed behind her and he concentrated on the recipient again. The large bowl of stone was filled with some silvery liquid once more. He cleared his mind to reach the power within him and bade the sorceress to yield to him: "*Pantswa nekem marzenia.*"

The liquid gurgled and greyed quickly, densifying.

"*Pantswa nekem marzenia.*"

The boils turned more violent as he focused on the spell. Wolfryth repeated his incantation a third time, forcefully:

"*PANTSWA PLON NEKEM MARZENIA DINE TO!*"

The effervescence ceased abruptly. The petrified matter began to glow again, the lead color giving way to copper and radiating. Wolfryth grinned, satisfaction twisting his scar into a horrible grin. Then the light vanished completely and he retained a cry of rage.

The sorcerer raised one hand over the basin and the liquid transformed into pure water. The image reflecting showed a young blond man, his elbow set on a table and his chin pressed on his wrist, reading. Pendragon. The shadow in front of him was blurred. With a new flip of his hand, the water turned back into silver goo.

His magic was not to blame. The controlling spell had rebounded *on the other side.* Somehow, the seer blocked his intrusion into her mind. Wolfryth snorted. With or without his *help*, her visions would push her forward. He could not fail.

oOo

The mirror was not doing her justice. Fillin pouted. The old surface refused to reflect the shine of her blond hair, and the incredible blue of her eyes. Her skin looked wan, instead of young and attractive.

She took a handkerchief and tried for the hundredth time to wipe out the stain. The reflecting surface gleamed for a second, and darkened again. She scolded. This place was impossible. Mirrors withheld fair play, some doors remained stubbornly closed. If by some miracle she managed to convince (coerced) the staff into cleaning one room, it was dusty and grim again the next day.

She sighed. Her father insisted they stayed here until he had found 'the Source', as he called it. And given only the blood of the dragon could open the way to that source, she had to wait for that stupid witch to bring Derek Pendragon to Caer Lon.

The blonde arranged her hair, smiling at her deformed image, unable to decide what smile suited her best. If only that stupid mirror could work properly…

How a girl with such powers could be that naïve? Her father manipulated her dreams for weeks now, and the seer had not doubted her visions once. She was too eager to prove her friends she *knew*. Predictable idiot.

The gold and blue dress fitted her perfectly, Fillin decided. It flattered her hourglass figure and enhanced the color of her eyes. It didn't matter if the spell had not worked today; the seer was already doomed. It was probably that despicable place playing tricks on them again. She could not wait to be back in Camelot's Court, with a crowd of efficient servants instead of those frightful natives or those halfwits guards her father called Jutes. This place was horrible. Waiting for an idle sorceress, barely able to control her powers, to bring her lover to them was excruciating. She stamped her foot. She hated this!

Everything was that so-called Sacha's fault. Her father had finally conceded to teach her, and because of Sacha, she had been cast out of the room and she had no idea when he would grant her a new lesson.

A gush of air made her skirt swirled beautifully, and Fillin chuckled as if the wheeze had cleared her mind. Even under the citraurantia's effects, Elwyn could explain how to use spells. He had magic too. She pirouetted happily. Yes, Elwyn was going to help with her magical education. All she needed was her book of spells, and to accept a kiss or two.

Chapter 10

The scroll she was painfully going through listed every single village in Camelot's kingdom, down to the smallest farm. Sacha repressed a yawn of boredom. Some notes about Caer Lon were made here and there in the text, mostly as travel length references. Unfortunately she had never heard about the other places. She covered her mouth again, her eyes burning under the effort. It was fair and good to know it took three days to go from the capital to Eld Leigh, as long as you knew where Eld Leigh was in the first place…

Abandoning the useless scroll, Sacha sighed and glimpsed at Derek on the other side of the table. She half-expected him to be fast asleep given that no groan or other loud sigh of impatience had escaped him since she had pushed the biggest book toward him more than two hours ago. Incredibly, he was wide awake and totally engrossed in his reading. He turned one page, one hand fisting in his hair to make it spike between his fingers. His nose crinkled in concentration.

Sacha gave a small smile. He looked like a cautious rabbit coming out of its burrow. She could nearly see bristles shivering.

"Did you find anything?"

In the quiet room, the monk's voice echoed loudly and she jumped, embarrassed to have been caught staring.

"Unfortunately not yet, Friar Johan."

"I am sorry to hear that. I brought you some tea, but I have to ask you to take it outside. Accidents, you know…"

The tray was on an empty desk near the door, with two cups and a plate of honey cakes. Sacha gently bowed her head and smiled in gratitude.

"Yes, of course. You are very thoughtful. Thank you very much."

"You are most welcome. I will come back for you before Vespers."

The monk grinned back and then disappeared into the library again. She guessed their plump little friend meant they were to leave with his next visit. The young woman sighed again. She needed a break; and honey cake was definitely tempting…

"Derek, do you want some tea?"

"Sorry, what?"

Her exchange with the friar librarian obviously had gone completely unnoticed. It intrigued her. Derek was constantly alert, vigilant like a sentinel on everlasting duty, and the last person she expected to fall into a book. That was more Sebastian's style…

Now that she had the prince's attention, Sacha repeated, "Do you want some tea? Friar Johan brought us some, with cakes."

"Yes, please."

The answer was polite, and definitely absent-minded. She insisted, "We cannot eat or drink in here, Derek."

"Hum hum…"

He wasn't listening to her, still deeply involved in his reading. Sacha reached over the table and put the taps of her fingers on the book, pressing it down gently. Her companion's expression changed into the impatient frown she knew so well, before he pushed away from the table.

"Very well."

She stood and moved to the door, picking up their snack in her way. Derek had no choice but to follow.

They found a bench in the convent, not far from the door and she settled there, putting the tray by her side to serve the tea.

The beverage was steaming hot and Sacha blew on its surface before taking a tentative sip, looking for something to say. All a sudden, she felt restless, unable to bear the calm that surrounded them. Making small talk with Derek seemed kind of absurd, however. They never really talked except to argue, until one of them gave up or their friends interfered. The only common ground she could think of was their current search.

"Your book seemed fascinating."

Derek swallowed a bite of cake, before he said curtly.

"It talks about the High Kings and their lineage."

She heard the rebuff, loud and clear, as he looked away. A book about Camelot High Kings had to talk about his family from his father's side. The topic of William was hurtful for Ylianor, and Derek never mentioned it, least of all to her. Sacha renounced conversing to concentrate on her tea and her piece of cake.

"The name Pendragon evolves from *'kin of dragon,'* the son of the dragon. One of my ancestors served with the XXIV legion, the 'Draco' Roman legion. He settled in the country after the war and married the daughter of a local warlord. Their son was nicknamed that, 'kin of dragon'. His first name was Acturus; Arthur."

Sacha glanced back at Derek, genuinely surprised by his long explanation. She was used to his haughty tone and sullen attitude. Curiosity and pride sparkled in his voice, unsettling. She answered softly, "I did not know that."

Derek shook his head.

"Neither did I."

His answer was tainted with regret. Sacha wished she knew the words he needed to hear. Maybe there were none.

A gush of chilly wind whipped the floor around them and she closed her arms around her, quivering slightly. The air still had to warm up, especially in late afternoons. April was fools' spring; she should have remembered that before leaving her cloak inside. Sacha swiveled around to protect herself from the cold breeze, the gesture conveniently hiding her trouble.

The prince drained his cup and pushed onto his feet, his forbidding mask back into place.

"It is interesting, but irrelevant. We need information, not old tales. Let's go back inside."

Sacha noticed this time he had not protested against finding the City. She followed him inside the scriptorium and they retook their places on each side of the table. Derek delayed taking back his book, so she presented him with her own *pensum*.

"This treaty is a tax-payment list. The collector wrote down the amounts he retrieved from each village, and how far it was from Caer Lon. I do not recognize the names, though. It was a long time ago and they probably changed."

"I will have a look."

Sacha scowled. He had little chance to know the forgotten names better than she did. Derek was peeking at every piece on the table except the book telling about his family's history and he had yet to make a move to take hers. He seemed torn between curiosity and the need to distance himself from the emotions it arose inside him. His hand lay on the open book in front of him, immobile.

"May I peruse yours?"

Sacha's query seemed to awake him. His answer came out as frosty as the wind outside.

"Be my guest."

Derek motioned her to take the book and picked up hers in exchange. Sacha grimaced at the top of his head and pulled the heavy volume toward her.

The writing was neat; the ink had reddened with the passing years. Talent copyists or the author himself had decorated the margins with beautiful bestiaries, flowers and landscapes. Sacha marked Derek's page with her index, and turned the pages to discover more delicate drawings.

Running water was a recurrent topic with the illustration: fountains and lakes were drawn every few pages. The few waterfalls were incredibly vivid. She was admiring an exquisite and strange fish with a long beak and a hole on its forehead when Derek interrupted her thoughts.

"I know that name."

Sacha lifted her head up.

"Gwel Caer; that's where my mother comes from."

"Gwel Caer? Are you sure?"

The young woman was quite certain Ylianor had never used that name. Yet the queen rarely talked about her past. Derek nodded impatiently.

"Yes. It is called Gwelgaer now. I have to talk to Friar Johan."

"Derek, this is not enough to… We need to… Derek, wait!"

He was already marching toward the Library door. Sacha stood up rashly, pushing on the table (and the book) for leverage. Her palm rubbed on the fragile surface and the unmistakeable noise of paper tearing up filled the room. She jumped with a little cry of despair. Derek turned his head swiftly, horror written on his face.

Mortified, Sacha looked down to assess the disaster. The pages she was examining had been severed by the middle. The wax-binding had partly cracked to reveal old yellow wires.

She sat back down with a sorry shadow on her face. She caressed the wounded book slightly, hating herself for the damages. How would Friar Johan react to the news? He had trusted them with his precious volumes and…

Her fingers froze and she moved her nose inches from the binding for a closer look.

"Derek, can you give me your dagger?"

"What? Why?"

He stared at her blankly. Sacha held out her hand.

"I need something sharp. Hand me your dagger please."

He walked to the table and presented her with the blade. The bell rang the first call to Evening Mass.

"Watch the door."

Sacha did not wait for him to protest and use the sharp tip of the knife to clear the remaining wax, opening completely the binding between the pages. The opening revealed a small scroll tightly rolled, no longer than her palm. A swift flick of the blade dislodged it from its hiding place and it landed on the table without a sound.

She was about to pick it up when the knob of the door turned. Derek pushed her aside and murmured "Smile," before he retrieved his knife and flipped the enormous book closed, just as their guardian appeared in the frame.

"Friar Johan, I want you to make a copy of that book for me. It is absolutely fascinating."

Derek shoved the heavy volume into the stunned monk's stomach, winding him on the spot. The poor man tried to catch his breath and grunted, "Well my lord… It will take time to-"

The prince gave him no time to recover before he cut in.

"I will pay generously for it of course. I will see you tomorrow about the details. Sacha, we have to go now."

Without waiting for a reply, Derek saluted the librarian and offered his arm to Sacha, urging her to take it with a meaningful glare. Speechless, she was left with no other choice but to let him guide her out. She flashed a quick smile above her shoulder to Friar Johan before exiting the room, using the second he closed his eyes and bowed his head in return to risk one glimpse toward the table. The mysterious scroll was gone.

oOo

"Can I try?"

Elwyn tried not to grumble and pushed the bowl toward his 'apprentice'. He hoped the snort that escaped his lips sounded more charitable than he truly felt. He had never missed with that spell before. Stirring water was a basic spell, he had done it for years. Water was his element. How could he have missed?

He probably was more exhausted than he thought, that was all. He needed some rest, and this whole 'lesson' thing was a very bad idea.

A childish chuckle erupted in the air, just before fish-shaped water splashed him in the face. *Beginner's luck.* Elwyn wiped his face with his sleeve and frowned, letting his annoyance show for the first time.

"Try not to dampen my bed, at least."

Fillin laughed and clapped. Elwyn's frustration evaporated. Her smile was contagious; it was next to impossible to stay annoyed with her when she looked so pleased.

"Teach me another one!"

Elwyn sighed.

"You know, there is not much you can do with only a bowl of water…"

The pretty blond sulked then plunged her incredible bronze stare into his.

"Please Elwyn…"

His mind started to gallop, racing to find something that could amuse her. Her hand slightly caressing the blankets between them was distracting. He gulped. What spell did he know that required only a bowl of water? Fillin really had fascinating eyes, that golden gleam… *Ah yes!* Elwyn smiled broadly.

"Well, there is the mirror's spell. It is advanced magic so…"

"Let's do it!"

He sighed again and began to teach her the ancient words to create an image of other people in the water. Sacha called it the 'spy' spell because it allowed a magician to see other people's actions, without them knowing. He preferred to refer to it as a 'mirror'.

While Fillin repeated the formula by herself to master it without tumbling on the complicated syllables, Elwyn closed his eyes briefly, falling back into his pillow as tiredness finally got to him.

If only his powers had not been exhausted, he would have been able to see his sister, and make sure she was alright; maybe he would have witnessed a silent argument between her and whoever contradicted her today, their father or Derek... It had to be something, to enjoy the tempest without being caught in the middle…

"Are you tired?"

Fillin's question brought him back to reality, Sacha's image lingering in the back of his mind.

"Just a little."

He nearly expected her to withdraw and suggest they tried it some other time. Fillin flicked her hair, playing with the long blond strands expectantly. She eyed the bowl, eager to test her new knowledge. Elwyn forced himself up again and grinned.

"All right. Concentrate on what you want to see. Form a picture in your mind. Then imagine you see it in the water."

"Uri deite arostand hudar skivat."

The magical words blew on the water. Elwyn's eyes widened when he recognized the figures forming in the bowl.

Chapter 11

To Sacha's credit, her usually so expressive mouth stayed mute, though her full lips parted slightly either in surprise or guilt. Derek silently appreciated her reaction, or rather the lack of it while he dragged more than escorted her out.

The young woman freed her arm as soon as they reached the now empty square in front of the church. The doors of the monastery banged closed behind them. Even then, it took her a full second to find her speech.

"How did you…-"

The prince shut her up instantly.

"Mind if we discuss our businesses elsewhere?"

From the shadow that covered her delicate features, he could tell the exact moment in which her temper chased away amazement. Derek ignored her glare, and started walking back toward the inn without waiting. Surely she could see the danger of talking about their findings in the middle of the street. He was not going to lose time to reformulate just to soothe her offended feathers.

Surprisingly, the proud lady held her tongue again and followed him quietly. Derek nearly shook his head in bewilderment. Women, particularly this one, were a mystery to him.

The sun had just set and the buzzing activity of the market was long gone. The shops were closed, save for a shoemaker who was clearing his stale and farther, a potter leaning against the doorframe of his shop. The man yawned with boredom, probably waiting for his last batch to harden. The few people still remaining outside were already hurrying either to church for mass, or to the peace of their homes.

As they progressed up the street, Derek noticed the quietness growing as the darkness slowly invaded the space between the tall buildings. He regretted that his jacket did not conceal his movements as a cloak would have. Walking with his hand on the hilt of his sword was ridiculous or very likely to bring up suspicion in the peaceful neighborhood. But his hand kept coming back to his belt, over and over again. He wished he could associate the feeling of prickling on his neck with the tiny scroll he had removed from the library, now safely hidden in his pocket.

A door squealed nearby. Derek automatically reached for his weapon again, his pulse racing. The impression of being watched grew, disturbingly acute. Derek knew if he turned, he would face only shadows and mist. Yet he could not shake the feeling.

Sacha tugged at his sleeve, "Can we walk faster?" She paused, visibly looking for an excuse to disguise her own discomfort "I'm cold."

Derek instantly accelerated his pace, yet instead of taking the lead again, he fell into steps with her. When his hand touched the cold metal of his sword again, it rested there.

Minutes later, the door of the 'Wild Boar' inn opened to offer them shelter against the blackness. Sacha almost welcomed the appreciative stares that followed her graceful walk, as she crossed the main room toward the stairs, Derek on her heels.

Candles had been lit in their room. The soft glow and the balmy air comforted her immediately. Sacha took off her cloak and used the extra time to compose herself, before she turned to face Derek, one eyebrow up in a mute question.

He grinned and that complicit smile achieved to settle her nerves. Derek plunged one hand inside his jacket and extracted the tiny scroll from it, before he discarded the garment.

The young woman lifted their prize carefully in her hands.

"I never saw you steal it."

Derek corrected her instinctively, looking at her kneeling on the floor in front of her bed, using the flat surface to unroll the precious document.

"I just borrowed it; just as you borrowed my mother's potions. What does it say?"

The old parchment was covered with a very small writing. Sacha frowned in concentration, narrowing her eyes to decipher it.

"This word is *'prayers'* I think. And this one is *'guide'*. It is written in a very old form of the language."

"Fascinating. But can you read it?"

She neglected to answer his sarcasm, giving all her attention to the illegible words. The handwriting was incredibly twisted and she had trouble making out the letters, especially since she did not understand the meaning of the words they formed. The first line seemed to be half finished, a title maybe. After a while, she announced: "I think this means *'prayers from the truthful hearts.'*"

The wood comb holding her hair felt heavy on her neck and she took it off, letting her long curls fall in her back. Derek pushed away and unsheathed his sword, swirling it in the air in front of him.

"Do you think you can unravel it fully?"

Sacha sat on her cot and pushed some rebel strands of hair off her shoulder. The abandoned scroll rolled up with a soft noise.

"I suppose. But it is going to take time."

The young man shrugged and finally put his sword away with a sigh. Silence fell between them once again. Sacha fiddled with her skirt. Her desire to talk with Derek unsettled her. Usually, she welcomed silence more than pointless chatter. She shook her head. Why did she feel so uncomfortable near Derek these days? They had grown up together; surely she should be able to remain serene around him, or if she *desired* to chat, to think of something else than their current quest to start a conversation. She did not feel that agitated with Elwyn or Sebastian or the rest of their friends. Of course, Elwyn was her twin and Sebastian her cousin, and neither treated her as carelessly as Derek did, but...

Sacha looked up to find him examining their bags and asked, "Is anything missing?"

He finished his task and stood up before he answered, "No; I don't think so. I am going down. I will have something brought up for you, unless you feel like coming?"

Sacha failed to assess if his sentence held an invitation, or a warning to stay put. She chose the latter and glanced back at the mysterious parchment. Derek took the hint, and walked out of the room without another word.

He chose the same table near the wall, which allowed him to scan the entire room at once, without having to guard his back. The waitress that had welcomed them in the morning hurried to serve him. Derek returned her smile absently.

"May I help you with anything else, Sire?"

Her slippery tone came with a peep toward the bar. Their hostess was watching her clients, her brows frowning from time to time, when men became too familiar with the servants. Derek returned his attention to the smiling woman in front of him.

"What is your name?"

"Gisela, Sire."

Her smile grew and she bent down a little, offering an impeccable view into her bosom. Sacha would bristle like an angry cat at the display. The prince went on without acknowledging her bow.

"Gisela, you have to be careful about the *services* you offer. You have a good job here; make sure to keep it."

Surprised, she blinked and straightened up. Derek pressed one coin in her hand.

"I have letters to write. Bring me some paper, quills and ink."

Gratitude painted on the maid's face before she bowed deeply again, and went on to carry his orders. He pushed back against the wall, and took a mouthful of mead, looking at the eclectic crowd above his cup.

His nervousness had faded as soon as the door had closed behind them, but the feeling was still there, lurking in the back of his mind. Derek wished he knew where the impression came from, and then dismissed the thought. He was better off enjoying the calm while it lasted. Sacha attracted trouble like a magnet. With her around, he would have his share soon enough.

The waitress came back with the writing material he had requested. She nodded at him graciously and asked if he needed a meal to be taken up for his lady. She insisted on the last two words. Derek agreed and ordered his own diner, repressing a smile. The named lady was probably going to flog the poor girl if she dared to address her that way.

He pulled the paper toward him and started writing. His smile stayed in place. For once, he would not be the one to be dashed.

oOo

Aetynan se onhæle bemeldian se door to Caer
O Hlæfdige
Gehlystan mín bén
Gif I ge cwyctan, gedælan tear
Ond forelæ me turh mín óht
Gif I áfeallan ahlepan me astandan
Ond en ur rihthand álæccan mín
Me cleanheort; me sorthword
Éadmédian to u
O Hlæfdige gehlystan mín bén
Ond aweglætan en Caer Lon

oOo

The young woman woke up in alarm, her breath laboured and her heart thudding. Air hissed through her lips as she tried to calm down. She could not tell if it was still dark, or if dawn had broken already. She felt queasy.

Sacha wanted to push onto her feet, and she realized she was lying on the floor. Standing asked too much out of her, and she fell back on her knees with a little cry.

Her eyes adjusted to the dim light, and she started noticing her surroundings. She crawled on her knees and hands, unable to straighten up, and reached the facing wall, and the body crouched against it.

Dried blood and dirt had formed a crust in the stubble on his chin under her fingers. His left wrist was clung to the wall at a bizarre angle. The left was bandaged with a rag she recognized to be a piece of her shirt.

Sacha sat near the prisoner and touched his forehead gently. She felt pain, unable to tell if it was his or her heart bleeding. Derek winced when she brushed the cut on his temple. His skin was cool under her fingers. Or maybe it was hers that was too hot. She did not know. Sacha took her hand away, and nestled against him in the semi-darkness. Her head came to rest on his shoulder, as if it was too heavy to for her alone to bear. Tears tingled in her eyes, hot as they glided on her cheeks.

"I'm sorry…"

His free arm came around her gently, and she drifted off again.

oOo

His face had the color of wax, pale and unhealthy. She recognized the high cheekbones at once, and the full lips, too red and plump for a man. He always complained his mouth was too feminine, but she had forbidden him to grow a beard, pretending it itched when she kissed him.

Sacha grabbed her long skirts, preparing to join her brother, when he turned to face her fully. His eyes were the same cornflower blue, warm and kind. She called, but Elwyn did not react. Maybe he was too far away to hear her. She called again and waved, but his stare stayed fixed above her head. Why didn't he see her? She was just in front of him; *Elwyn!*

Sacha moved forward then broke into a run, but the distance between them refused to shorten. *Elwyn! Elwyn, I'm here, look at me, Elwyn!*

His head turned toward her again, and she stopped running. He looked surprised. He held one hand up, testing the air. A frown shadowed his handsome features. She stared as he put both hands up, palms wide open in front of him. His brows knitted in some mute effort, as if he was pushing at some invisible wall. His hands fisted into balls and he punched at that glass she could not see.

Suddenly Sacha felt something pulling her down, crushing her lungs in a ferocious seize. She gasped and Elwyn took one hand to his throat, then the other. Her heart started pounding, hammering against her chest painfully. Air burned in her lungs. Her head fell backward and she panicked, unable to breathe. *Elwyn! Elwyn, please help me! Elwyn!*

Her brother was battering frantically at the barrier that kept them apart, his mouth opening in a call she could not hear. Sacha tried to breathe. She was cold. Her vision blurred in a maze of brown and green. So cold. She opened her mouth to scream. Something crawled between her lips. Her stomach revolted. She could not breathe. She jolted, trying to get rid of the suffocating grip. Her fingers grazed her throat, finding nothing. *Please…*

Chapter 12

Sacha fought to escape the claws of her dream. Her body protested against the merciless grasp retaining her. Still unable to breathe properly, her eyes firmly shut, she wiggled and jerked to break free, gasping for air.

"How… Calm down. You had a nightma-"

"Don't touch me!"

Her hysteric cry was more effective than her physical attempt to shove Derek off. He released her wrists at once.

She wanted to take her blankets up her chest, but his weight forbade it. Sacha tugged at the cover harder. She felt ill. She was freezing. She wanted to curl into a ball and be warm again. Her mind was still confused, unable to reconnect with reality; it refused to associate the impressive frame of the man seated on her cot with the prostrate form of her visions.

Sacha gave another pull on the sheets. Panic spread inside her; she had to get the sheets, she needed to be warm…

"Get off! Get off!!"

The shriek echoed dangerously in the silent room. Derek pressed one hand hard over her mouth to silence her. Attracting attention in the middle of the night after stealing from the library was low on his list of priorities. Her fright was starting to affect him as well. He felt powerless in front of her anguish and hated it.

"Sacha, be quiet… Everything is fine, it was just-"

Her teeth grazed his palm and he swore, taking his hand away instantly.

"What the hell?!"

The young prince stood up, giving up on comforting her; not that he had been very good at it in the first place. Once she could move under her blankets freely, she stayed immobile, her hands clutching the fabric anxiously. Her pupils were dilated with fear, never leaving him.

Indignation added to frustration at the idea that she was terrorized because of *him*. Furious with her, or with himself for frightening her, Derek made no effort to lower his tone.

"I was not forcing myself on you, for Christ's sake! What do you take me for?!"

He started pacing the room, certain her eyes followed each of his moves despite the darkness. He had just wanted to comfort her. His wandering took him to the opposite wall, then back to the beds and to the wall again. He should have been able to comfort her.

His failure aggravated and embarrassed him. He wished he had more space to give her. Obviously, his very presence added to her distress. It was too late in the night to go down to the main room for even a short moment. Maybe he could pretext some biological urge and leave...

"Please Derek... Elwyn needs me... Please help me..."

Lost in his thoughts, he had not heard her approach him, and he jumped at the contact of her hands on him. Pride exploded inside his chest at hearing her beg so desperately for his help. He longed to prove himself worth of her trust. Her skin felt icy cold through the fabric of his shirt.

Shaken by the conflict both ideas aroused inside him, Derek retreated behind his usual coldness, unlocking her fingers from him.

"I am here, aren't I?"

Her head fell on his chest when his words drained away the last mists of nightmare, as if she had finally regained full consciousness and was too weak to stand by herself. Derek straightened her chin up to look at her face. In the moonlight, her eyes were impossibly clear, nearly transparent. He pushed her long hair off her face gently, brushing the soft skin of her cheeks.

"You are not alone. I am here with you. Come back to bed now."

Sacha let him guide her to her cot. She picked up her comb and secured her hair with it. The gesture, so naturally feminine, was something reassuring in her disarray. She cuddled on her side, her knees to her chest. Derek tugged the covers up to her chin. The gesture reminded her of tucking in a small child. She felt just as vulnerable as one.

When his bed squeaked under his weight, she closed her eyes to concentrate on the sounds the young man made in the dark. His breathing was calm and steady. The peaceful rhythm, almost hypnotic, cradled her until her taut nerves relaxed and her own breathing fell into pace with his. She imagined the regular rise and fall of his chest as he drifted back into sleep. His strong presence created a shelter around her, even if he was several feet away. She felt protected near him, at peace; the feeling intrigued her.

Sacha exhaled slowly and the warm air rebounded on the sheets to caress her face. She buried her nose in the rough fabric, trying to remember the sensation of Derek's touch on her cheek. It was foolish to see anything but a comrade offering solace in his gentle gestures. In the morning he would be his usual self, contemptuous and infuriating. Now, he acted like he cared.

"Do you want to tell me about your dream?"

The murmur startled her and her cheeks grew hot. Sacha was grateful Derek could not read her thoughts. She'd been so sure he was sleeping. The wood of his bed cracked. She supposed he had turned on his side. She took a few more seconds before she realized she *needed* him to know.

"Elwyn was in a cage of some sort... I could not see it, but I know he was trapped... And when I tried to reach for him, I... drowned."

Another sound followed her confession and Sacha felt her mattress dip under his hand before he found hers to squeeze it.

"I will not allow any harm come to you."

She believed him. Then she remembered and inhaled sharply.

"You were hurt... We were prisoners and..." Sacha paused, as she understood the terrible truth. "You are going to be hurt because of me."

Hot tears threatened to well. Derek pressed her hand again.

"I consider myself warned, then."

He had to be grinning in the dark. The smile reverberated in his whisper.

"And so should you. No more reckless venturing and no luring me so I do your will blindly."

Sacha took away her hand, taken aback by his light tone. The bed protested again as Derek turned once more before he added.

"I was just kidding, Sacha."

He teased when she was opening her soul, revealing her secret fears to him? And she did not lure him into doing anything! Well, maybe once...

Sacha scowled, gratitude and freight a foreign souvenir.

"Your sense of humour is dreadful."

"You are the one to complain."

"Probably because I am the one who cares."

She realized too late the double meaning of her reply. She could nearly see his blue eyes sparkling and waited for the kill, her fragile nerves tensed to a breaking point. But Derek thankfully held his tongue, ignoring the open door.

When he talked again, the topic was completely different, and on safer grounds.

"Did you decipher the text? You were already asleep when I came up, I did not have the chance to ask you..."

"Yes, I did. It is a prayer, addressed to a goddess of the Old Religion. The prayer is a demand for her mercy and her help to let the supplicant into a High City. Derek..." Excitation bubbled in her voice, her previous annoyance forgotten. "I think it describes the way to enter Caer Lon!"

His bed complained again and a few seconds later, the candle's light blinded her. Derek came to sit on her bed again and he handed her the scroll, urging her to read. Sacha pushed up against her pillow and unrolled it carefully.

To the truthful hearts only
Open the secret door to the City.
Oh White Lady,
Hear my plea;
If I cry, share my tears,
And guide me through my fears;
If I fall, help me stand,
And in your right take my hand;
My heart is pure; my word is true;
Humble I come to you;
Oh White Lady, hear my plea;
And let me in the High City.

When she finished, his eyes had the same deep blue shade she had found so fascinating in the afternoon when he told her about his family's history. Light framed his silhouette, growing brighter and clearer by the second.

Sacha struggled, unsure if she was strong enough to resist the aura enveloping him, unsure what would happen to her if she decided to touch it. She saw the soft glow so clearly, defining his head and his shoulders, gliding around his chest. The light was irresistible. She brushed her palm over the gold dust, unable to stop herself.

The touch astounded them both. Derek caught her wrist in midair and her pale cheeks turned the delicate pink of those wild roses she loved so much. He was close enough to whiff it on her skin. The young man released her arm, ill at ease.

"We should go back to sleep."

Sacha nodded, avoiding staring at him while he moved to his bed and blew the candle. Even in the dark, a fine line of light defined his figure, fading very slowly as sleep claimed her.

One day earlier...

The door opened silently and the young woman glanced quickly both ways before she tiptoed down the corridor to another door. She knocked furtively, jolted by the sound. The authorization to come in gave her another jolt, even as she was expecting it.

The room was brightly lit, though the fire and the numerous candles failed to bring a joyful atmosphere around the brown-haired woman seated at the hairdresser.

"I did as you ordered, my lady."

"And are you sure no one suspects the changeling?"

"Yes, my lady. I took out the rest, so it will be the only option."

"Good."

The young maid curtseyed and was to exit the chamber when she hesitated.

"My lady? The Lady Sacha will be fine, won't she?"

The woman glanced at the worried girl in the mirror.

"We did what we could to help her Agnes. You did well. Leave me."

The maid bowed again, and exited the room.

The smile reflecting on the silvery surface vanished. She had done what she could to protect Sacha from herself. All depended on Derek now. She prayed he was simply strong enough to save them all.

Chapter 13

Derek concentrated on his tea. The porridge rested untouched by his elbow. In daylight, the events of the previous night had faded to become fragments of a strange puzzle he had trouble fitting together. He had stayed awake a long while after exertion finally caught up with Sacha and she fell asleep. This time, no bad dreams came to haunt her, and she was granted a peaceful rest. He yawned. His own sleep had been really too short for his taste.

"Good morning."

He pushed onto his feet to pull her seat, the gallantry an automatic gesture, before he remembered about the benches. He waited until she was seated nonetheless. Sacha smiled at him and thanked their host for the tea and steaming bowl of boiled oatmeal.

She looked fresh and in a far better mood than he was. Derek sat in turn and glowered at his breakfast. The beige mixture did nothing to cheer him up. He despised porridge.

"Why don't you ask for something else?"

The prince glanced up and met stirring green eyes. Her good mood annoyed him. Derek rumbled stubbornly, "I can do with this."

The soaked oats slithered down his spoon like a colorless slug and fell down into the bowl with a distasteful thump. He forced himself and took a mouthful of porridge, swallowing as fast as he could before his tired brain realized what he was putting into his mouth. The texture was abominable. Sacha's smile deepened at his grimace.

She sampled her own food in turn and declared, "This is absolutely terrible!" before she put her spoon down. Pushing his bowl aside first and then hers, she gestured the tenant for something else to eat. At last, Sacha returned her attention to her companion.

"Are we going back to the library this morning?"

Derek glanced at his former breakfast, grateful to be spared the torture, and amazed by her behavior. The day before, she could barely talk to him. And now she organized his meals and entertained the morning ritual with a casual composure of which their old teachers would have been proud.

Her conduct suggested she did not remember anything of the previous night. He wished he too could forget the disturbing feeling of her hand in his hair as easily. Did he conjure up everything, the nightmares and the following quarrels? Whatever had put her in such a pleasant mood, he was not going to complain anyway. Her expression brightened the space around her. Derek sipped his tea without answering.

"Derek?"

Sacha was still staring at him, so Derek gurgled some uncommitted "Yes." Then, given that she was still looking, he felt obliged to give a full answer.

"We need a map. You gave us a key to translating this thing, but we still need to find the door that it unlocks."

Gisela approached with a tray. The waitress smiled at him when Derek nodded his thanks, then bowed quickly and left. He helped himself to bread and cheese, and finally noticed Sacha's happy grin was gone. Derek presented her with the bowl of early berries.

"Do you want some?"

"I am fine."

He quirked a brow, surprised by her mordant tone. One moment she was joyous, playing house and chitchatting agreeably, and the next second she was frowning. How could he hope that they work as a team if she made a point to mislead him all the time? She was looking above his shoulder, her lips pursed into a thin line and the food untouched in front of her. Maybe going on an empty stomach would help taming her character a bit.

Derek swallowed the last of his share, and pushed onto his feet.

"Let's go then. I want another look at that tax collector's list."

The young woman stood gracefully, abandoning her intact breakfast and moved to climb up the stairs leading to their room without a glance back. Derek sighed and walked back to the table to cut a piece of bread, and folded it with a clean cloth before he thrust it inside his belt's purse. He preferred when she smiled and took care of him, of his breakfast that was. They really were too old to act like pouting children.

oOo

Friar Johan bowed deeply in front of Sacha, before he led the way to the library once more.

Taken aback by the excess of politeness, she brushed invisible dust from her sleeve before she followed him, and wrenched her neck to Derek. His satisfied grin alerted her. Sacha asked softly "Did I miss something?"

"Well, it seems that our new friend is impressed to the serve the Duchess of Pemfro."

Surprise and annoyance fought an even match on her regal features.

"You did not…"

"I did. We need more cooperation from Friar Johan. He is obviously more than willing to-"

"He was helping!"

Derek motioned her to speak lower.

"He just brought us books he probably knows by heart. We cannot afford to waste any more time. The Abbot received an official request for a copy of those chronicles yesterday evening and another for full-time assistance from the librarian; both services will, of course, be generously acknowledged."

"What do you mean an *official request*?"

Derek took out a small object from inside his jacket. Sacha recognized her personal seal.

"You took it from my bag yesterday!"

So that was why he was searching their bags while she scrambled through the scroll. She glared, holding her hand toward him.

"It is mine, hand it over."

Derek took her hand to wrap it around his elbow, as their friend was waving at them from the door of the scriptorium. The seal had disappeared in his pocket again.

"It is too dangerous to let anyone find it."

She extracted her arm from his, pouting, and lied: "Agnes must have put it here without me knowing."

He laughed.

"Sacha, it was actually a good idea you brought your seal. Now, be your gracious self and explain to your devoted admirer that we need a map of the kingdoms."

Sweet memories of the comfort he had offered the previous night dissolved completely. He was absolutely irksome. She was her father's daughter, and then what? He should at least have had the courtesy to ask for her permission before using the seal, and to tell her of his plans! Instead, he took her off guard and… and…

Sacha snarled internally. She was not some idle girl he had to woo by showing off some supposed strategic skills! Damn him!

"My lady?"

Sacha covered her anger with a radiant smile, looking daggers at her companion from above the bald head of the monk. Derek was obviously very pleased with himself, and laughing up his sleeve at her embarrassment. *Fine! Last to laugh always laughed harder.*

"Friar Johan, I am so grateful for your help… I need your skills, I assure you. He…" - she cast another dark look at the amused prince - "is still pretending he is right about Caer Lon's location. Yesterday, I found a list of names with distance to the High City…"

The monk nodded vigorously.

"The tax collector's diaries, of course, of course…."

"Unfortunately, the names are foreign to *us.*"

She insisted on the 'us'. Derek smirked. Sacha did her best to keep her tone even and soft. She wanted to behead him.

"Do you think a map could help in locating those places? So we can spot Caer Lon at last, and prove Derek wrong."

"Oh, absolutely. I have one somewhere, I think. Please take a place. I will be with you in a few minutes with the appropriate charts."

The large table was empty except for the documents they had examined the previous day. In a corner, a skinny monk was copying a thick book she recognized instantly.

Derek unrolled the list of places and glanced at it quickly before he looked around for some writing material. Curious, Sacha forgot she was annoyed with him and asked, "What are you doing?"

"I want to write down the names by distance order. We need to figure those, too. One day on horseback is not the same than traveling by cart."

"A tax collector travels with wheels; doesn't he?"

"I suppose."

He was already falling into his task, ignoring her. Derek frowned at something on his page and stopped scribbling. Sacha sighed.

"Let's hope he used only one form of transportation."

"What did you say?"

His distracted tone irritated her again. She repeated impatiently "I hope he used the same transportation mode, whatever place he visited."

The young man rubbed the ridge of his nose, looking back down at the original list. Then he beamed.

"You are brilliant."

Sacha felt her cheeks grew burning hot, all annoyance gone magically. She wished she could read his mind, just this one time, so she would not have to disgrace herself asking *why* he was so pleased with her. Derek bent over the table, calling her attention back to the copy he had abandoned, and the original scroll.

"Look. The collection is in chronological order. The first entries are always marked within a day or less off travel. The next ones are farther, two, three days. Gwel Caer is noted after a five-day travel."

"So he could have gone on horseback at first, then used a wagon afterward."

"My thought exactly."

His broad grin was contagious. Sacha's lips curved, matching his winning smile. His eyes flicked down an instant then came back to hers.

Sacha froze, mesmerized. The sparkles swirling in his stare fired a crown around his head, nearly blinding her. She jolted back in surprise.

"Sacha?"

The flames were devouring the air around Derek to engulf him completely. She gasped. Darkness now fought the light, nibbling at the glow, slowly, quickly, more and more aggressive. Light was merely a golden circle; darkness was nearly touching him…

"No!"

The young woman fell forward. Derek caught her in time before her head hit the hard wood of the tabletop. One knee on his bench, he steadied her at arm's length, then carefully helped her back to the seat.

"Sweet Lord!"

Friar Johan dropped his load of maps on the floor and Sacha snapped back into reality.

"I am fine."

Neither man looked convinced by her bravado.

"I assure you… I am simply light-headed."

Her confused eyes begged Derek to help with the pretense. Her cheeks were terribly pale. He looked desperately for an excuse to explain her swoon. The prince suddenly remembered about her skipped breakfast.

"Here."

The bread was scorned and held the mark of the knife he had used to cut it. Some crumbles fell on the table. Friar Johan mewled, torn between his duties toward the fragile lady and his beloved charges.

The shock from her vision rushed back making her tremble, but Sacha smiled bravely.

"I can't eat in here, Derek…"

"The hell with-"

"My lord!"

His swearing finally bested the monk's hesitation. The little man trotted toward them to help her stand.

"Please, my dear. You will take some fresh air while I look for something sweeter than dry bread for you."

The glower Friar Johan gave Derek got lost as the prince escorted the pair outside, watching Sacha like a hawk.

Settled on the stone bench in front of the scriptorium, Sacha sampled her bread, now covered with creamy butter and honey. Derek walked back and forth in front of her. She took a sip of milk and sighed.

"Derek can you stop? You are making me dizzy…"

"You are dizzy because you skipped breakfast."

Derek stopped pacing. It was his fault. She hadn't eaten because he had selfishly declared they go once he had finished while she was still poking at hers. He did not even remember why it had seemed a good idea to do so at the time. She was already tired, fooling him with brio, as usual, and he had pushed her too far. She too had slept poorly and she was so slender… Idiot. He growled, furious with himself.

"I am adding a new rule. No more skipping meals."

"You may want to write them down. There are so many I fear I cannot remember them all…"

And now she was making fun of him. Derek started pacing again, his annoyance changing targets.

"This is not funny, Sacha."

"No, no it is not."

Her retort clamped his mouth shut. The beautiful lady shook her head, her luminous eyes capturing his.

"I saw you entering a fire. Then darkness attacked and you…"

Her voice broke. It never occurred to him to question her vision this time. She was scared. For him? Derek felt his anger melt away.

"And where were you?"

Was she safe, at least?

"I… I don't know."

I was looking at you embracing death.

Sacha bent her head. Her hands rested on her lap, her fingers closely knitted together. Following her stare, Derek noticed she was shaking. He wrapped his own cloak around her, rubbing her arms up and down swiftly. Somehow, he doubted the ice in her veins came from the cold breeze swirling around the courtyard.

The angst in her stare burned into his stomach to a point he wanted to roar. Appropriate words seemed to elude him as always, and as always he wished he had kept his mouth shut as soon as he spoke.

"It won't happen, Sacha. Even you cannot drive me so insane that I throw myself voluntarily into the flames. Eat."

Why did he always manage to sound so bluntly arrogant? He saw the storm brewing on her face as the last words were out, chasing away the doubts and the fright. Sacha opened her mouth, ready to give him a piece of her mind, so he took refuge behind the plate, with his best imitation of Elwyn's coy smile.

"Please?"

The mimic blew out a good part of her tantrum. Derek could tell she was still annoyed with him, but he caught a flash of amusement on her face despite her stern expression. His blue eyes twinkled with relief. Sacha took the plate, suddenly highly interested in her food.

Chapter 14

To My Lord Guardian, greetings,

Our journey goes eventless. We had hoped to find our friends in Saint-Stephen, but unfortunately they have already moved to their summer residence. We will thus resume our travel shortly to join them. Your daughter is very anxious to see her brother again.

I hope this letter will find you all in good health. Please assure my mother of my faithful devotion.

Yours truly,

A

Geraint pushed the short letter away with a grunt. He resisted the urge to crush the paper into a ball to throw it into the fireplace. Ylianor would certainly want to read it herself. It was tempting nonetheless.

The note did little to reassure him. Derek had encrypted his message in a way that only few people could understand it. Camelot had been called the Summer Country when the Pendragons ruled the Kingdoms. And if he was not mistaken, Saint-Stephen Monastery was in a small town about half a day from the frontier that separated Pemfro and Camelot.

The middle-aged man straightened up in his seat, his back tensed against the furniture. The queen - he would never accept to think of her as any less than such - had arranged for everyone to believe Sacha was in bed, in theory fighting a strong fever. Only he, Jeffrey, Ylianor and the maid Agnes were allowed to her chambers. At the same time, two of his men had been sent to the north to check on the advance positions there, and officially, Derek had gone with them.

So far, the lies were holding, but it had been only two days... He had been edgy ever since they had discovered Derek's and Sacha's getaway, unsure about the feelings whirling inside him.

He worried about his children, including Derek, whom he considered a son. He was angry at his reckless daughter and her hot-headed prince. He hated himself for waiting all those years, witnessing how Wolfryth plundered his neighbours' lands, without being able to stop him for fear of attracting attention to the duchy and the royal family. Maybe Sacha had had a point; he should have stood up for what was right a long time ago.

Being right did not make up for her disobedience, or Derek's. Those two had spent years snubbing each other, harrying everyone around, and the one day they decided to pair up, it only attracted more trouble. He snorted.

Geraint reread Derek's message, trying to decipher more from the cryptic words. Yes, they were safe and sound. But no, they were not coming back.

Ylianor entered the room, her royal stance masking the worry he knew was agitating her. He pushed onto his feet instantly.

"My lady."

"I am sorry to disturb you, Sir Geraint, but I heard that a courier arrived earlier…"

"Yes. Please; this comes from Derek."

Ylianor walked to the seat he was offering her before she allowed herself to take the letter. She read, her blue eyes caressing the paper as if it were her son she was coddling. When she was done, she took a careful breath. Her hand trembled slightly when she handed back the missive, the quivers quickly controlled.

"They are alright."

Geraint nodded silently, looking for a way to tell the anxious woman his deductions from Derek's implies. She preceded him, however.

"They are going to cross the border, aren't they?"

"I fear so."

They fell silent, both parents crushed by the significance behind the news. As the rightful heir to the throne, Camelot was the most dangerous place for Derek to be. The dangers he encountered would extend to whoever traveled with him; namely, Sacha. No one could predict if they would find help in their quest, or threat. Years under a madman's tyranny could transform the most faithful supporter into a desperate traitor. Not to mention that Wolfryth would be free to attack the prince at his will...

Geraint broke the heavy silence first, standing to face the fire.

"This is madness... How on earth did they come to the conclusion that Elwyn is in Camelot's territory?"

Ylianor bowed her head an instant, getting her bearings, before she explained about Sacha's dream. Speechless, the duke took another minute to digest her story. For him, his children's gifts were never a cause of doubt, only of worry. Another cause of worry.

"She might be wrong."

Ylianor gave a tight smile at the man's feeble attempt to push away from reality.

"I dread she is not, dear friend. It is very dubious Sacha opened up to Derek about her visions. She knows full well how he is most likely to react. They must have found another clue leading to Camelot."

Geraint sighed, and then stepped back.

"I am sorry, Ylianor."

The blond woman nodded slightly. Now there was little they could do but wait, and pray for the better.

oOo

The short rasp on his door woke up Sebastian and he did his best to straighten up. Any effort to use his arms left him drenched in sweat while his entire body burned with pain. He ground his teeth and tried to present a calm face to his visitor.

"Come in."

The woman who entered the room was probably the last person he thought would pay him a visit, and she was certainly not Agnes.

He had not seen the little maid since her confession. Another servant had brought his meals and whenever he asked about Sacha's maid, the man explained with a sad movement of the head she was taking care of her mistress, who was apparently harassed by a terrible fever. Sebastian had frowned the first time he heard the tale, but kept his mouth shut. Visibly, the castle was supposed to think his cousin was in her chambers and Derek… God knew where. He had hoped for Ylianor or even his uncle to come and explain, but none had showed up. Some explanations would have been great though, especially given who his visitor was.

"Lady Sonia..."

The brown-haired woman smiled and nodded in return to his greetings.

The Countess of Gosharling, Sonia's mother, had been a close friend of the late duchess of Pemfro. She had sent her daughter to Haven the previous year, when Elwyn and Derek had been knighted and Sacha officially made her debut.

Sonia's allure and manners had instantly attracted attention. However, in spite of some light flirting here and there, she discouraged all potential suitors the same way Sacha did, sometimes more coldly, if ever possible.

In spite of that common trait, the two maidens had never really gotten along, probably because rumours said the only man likely to interest Sonia was Derek. The prince knew that and avoided her like plague, except of course when Sacha was around… De facto, neither Elwyn nor Sebastian dared to approach Sonia of Gosharling. Sebastian shifted in his bed, uneasy to find himself alone with his cousin's nemesis.

His visitor stopped inspecting the various phials and bandages set on the table and came to sit near his bed, on the chair Jeffrey had used earlier to examine the nasty cut on his left arm. She smiled, and Sebastian smiled back, surprised.

"I thought you could use some company, since your best friends are out of the Castle and your cousin is not well…"

Her honeyed tone changed surprise into suspicion. What did she know about his friends? He made an effort to keep doubts out of his reply "That is very gracious of you, Lady Sonia."

Her smile still in place, and warily friendly, she gestured at the display of medicine.

"Sir Jeffrey is obviously using a complete panoply on you. I trust his methods are efficient?"

"I do hope so, my lady."

The chitchat was misleading. What did she want? He could not help but think of a feline hunter playing with its prey. Sebastian winced. The role of the mouse was never to his liking. The young woman stayed quiet for a few seconds and he used the silence to observe her more closely.

She was indeed attractive, in a glamorous way. He had to compare her to Sacha, though he knew the comparison would probably irritate the latter to no end. Like her cousin, the Countess favoured long gowns which sculpted her willowy figure. Both had gracious faces, with high cheekbones and delicately hemmed lips. However the similarity stopped there. Sacha had green eyes, shining like clear jade, while the other woman's stare was as dark as obsidian.

Those dark eyes had returned to him now, and he struggled to adjust his posture in the bed, grunting when using his damaged arms triumphed over his stoic poise. Warmth ignited her eyes an instant and Sebastian stared the fire spreading there, fascinated, as she helped him up against the pillows. Her hands were blissfully cool through the fabric of his shirt. A blue-green mark impaired the inner side of her forearm, intriguing.

"I never saw anything like this…"

"Only my family is allowed to wear it. It's a protective rune."

The burn in his tortured muscles decreased significantly. He sighed in relief and looked for a new position in the bed.

"Thank you."

"You are badly hurt, my lord. Will you ever be able to wield a sword again?"

Her question echoed the doubts that assaulted each of his conscious moments, when the effect from the drugs Jeffrey served him started to fade. Sebastian closed his eyes an instant to find a suitable answer. When he opened them again, Sonia had already moved away and was walking towards the door, apparently having taken his silence for a dismissal. Sebastian obliged himself to voice his own fears out loud.

"I do not know."

Sonia nodded, thoughtful.

"I use to have great respect for the men of the bow."

Then she smiled once more, and left. Sebastian let his head fall on the pillow, exhausted and wondering what to make of her last comment.

oOo

When Ylianor entered Sacha's quarters, the girl was seated at the table, sewing. She jumped onto her feet and bowed clumsily in her haste, not daring to straighten or even look up.

The former queen glanced around the otherwise empty room. To her satisfaction, Sacha's chambers had every aspect one could expect for an ill person. The curtains were half-drawn, as if to protect the eye from the afternoon light. A basin was set on the bedside, with clean clothes piled next to it and another one was torn on the rim. The sheets were messed up in such a way Ylianor would have sworn the young lady was resting, if she had not known better.

She turned to the maid.

"Did anyone come to inquire about the Lady Sacha's health, Agnes?"

"Yes my lady. Sir Lot sent his page, as well as Sir Hadrian. The Lady Caroline came herself, and so did Lady Ashley. I did not let them in..."

The maid fidgeted nervously, twisting her fingers in her apron. Ylianor frowned, pondering about the visitors and Agnes quickly looked at the floor again.

The men's visit she had expected. The two nobles were still hoping to gain Sacha's favour, despite her blatant indifference. Caroline and Ashley were the worst gossips at Court, and their coming was not much of a surprise either. Surely rumours were spurting already about Sacha languishing after her brother, or even better, Derek.

Ylianor nodded internally. As long as everybody thought her son was on a mission up north and the lady in her bed, their true whereabouts would remain hidden to the world and the anonymity would hopefully grant them extra-protection.

However, one person was missing in the picture. Ylianor addressed the girl again, making her jump a second time.

"Did Lady Sonia visit you?"

"Oh no my lady."

The maid's chuckle had the queen's heart pounded harder at once. Sonia was very likely to come over, if only with the purpose of annoying Sacha. Geraint' daughter acted like a jealous she-cat around her, to the countess' never-ending amusement. The more disdainful Sacha was, the more Sonia sought her company with patronizing smiles and poisonous jabs. Ylianor frowned... Sonia should have come to visit...

Agnes blushed under her stare, then paled and suddenly burst into tears.

"My lady, I did it to protect my mistress! She... The countess said no one would discover it was a charm... My mistress was having such terrible nightmares and then Lord Sebastian was found and my lady decided to go to find Sir Elwyn with Prince Derek and Lady Sonia seemed to know all about it and she told me to put the comb in her bags and..."

Ylianor felt her blood freeze in her veins. She grabbed the crying girl by the shoulders and Agnes squealed in fret. The queen instantly released her grasp, breathing deeply to regain her calm. She pushed the maid into a chair, gently but firmly.

"Sober yourself Agnes... Calm down, and tell me everything, from the very beginning."

Chapter 15

Derek stretched and ruffled his hair to ease the itch the immobility had created in his shoulders. They had spent all morning studying the map and the list, comparing names and discussing issues about distance and locations. Each identified caption felt like a victory that Sacha celebrated with dazzling smiles. Every time her laugher pearled out loud, it urged him to push forward.

They started with Gwel Caer. This place they spotted easily, thanks to Derek's recollection of his mother's origins. Then they extended their research to neighboring areas. Soon, they confirmed that time-close entries were equally close geographically. The problem was that not all the names were charted; far from it.

Friar Johan hypothesised the missing villages were not represented on the map because they were too small. Sacha pointed out the amount collected at each stop was dutifully reported in the tax collector's log. They could use it to sort the places by their size, considering that small villages could pay only little money. Derek proposed that they make a copy of the list while eliminating the lowest prizes, on which both his acolytes agreed.

However, things got sour when they had to decide what should be considered as a minimum.

"We cannot afford to miss one place. We have to look at all the entries save for the smallest amount, and proceed step by step."

"This is going to take ages, Derek! We could not find anything near Shaftesbury so the taxes at this place are our minimal target."

"You cannot be sure about that Sacha. The map is not scaled, so maybe they did not put all the names because there was not enough space to write them down."

"This is the most ridiculous argument you have ever served me! You just cannot expect to be outspoken and..."

"My lady, I think Sir Derek is right."

The monk's interference brought a cocky grin to the prince. Sacha nearly growled in frustration. She glared at Derek while he folded his arms across his chest, triumphal. Friar Johan looked at them in turn and sighed. Neither seemed ready to abdicate first. The bell saved the poor librarian from the hostile silence.

"I have to assist Mass... Please excuse me."

The other monk was already out of the room. Sacha repressed a disdainful snort when the door banged on their hurried little friend. Derek grinned, "Your pouting scared him."

Piqued, Sacha scowled again.

"I am not pouting. You are-"

"I would prefer if you use 'charming' after that verb. Anyway, Friar Johan confirmed in this case I am right, so..."

"So you admit you are not right *all the time.*"

"Sacha..."

Her name hissed between clenched jaws as his temper started to boil. Only the sight of the unrolled map and the task at hand stopped Derek from adding some unkind remark about 'know-it-all' ladies that would certainly have pushed the growing argument into a full-scaled fight. He took a deep breath and gestured toward the papers spread on the table.

"I would love to pursue this conversation; unfortunately one of us has to be reasonable. Do you want to copy the list, or shall I do it?"

Her eyes dilated dangerously at the sarcasm. Sacha clamped her mouth shut so hard he thought he heard her teeth thump.

"You started it."

Her grouch could apply to either their 'discussion' or the illegible scribbling he had begun hours ago. Derek picked up the quill and resumed his work.

Already on her feet, Sacha decided to put some distance between them so she could regroup. She felt so furious that tears burnt her eyes, and it enraged her even more. *Don't cry Sacha, he would be too happy...* No, not happy... He never looked happy when she was upset, she had to give him that. Derek always acted the same with her, careless and without particular interest. She made it easy for him; she reacted within the second each time he teased, giving him the pleasure of seeing her make a fool of herself. She was worse than a capricious child. *She* was the one looking for his approval, and acting stupid because he refused to give it. She shouldn't. She wouldn't.

Her steps took her to the desk where the other monk was copying the fat book Derek had fallen in love with. Looking for a distraction from her confusing thoughts, she bent over the illustrations. The soft colors, cobalt blue, sparkling gold and pure white created the illusion of movement in the stream of the waterfall. It was vivid, and incredibly beautiful…

"Sacha, could you come over here?"

The question broke through her contemplation and she obeyed, surprised to realize she was calmer. Calmer, but not forgetful.

"Yes, Derek?"

Her glacial reply met a stunned blue stare. Sacha felt her face warmed. However heated their arguments were, Derek rarely nursed a grudge afterward. He always showed more forgiveness than she did. She softened her tone.

"What is it?"

He indicated one name on the map.

"What do you make of this?"

"Laean Astethan."

The name spoken out loud sounded familiar.

She recognized the shoreline not far from it, the hard cut, the creeks and the straight coast of her native area. Haven was not on the map. Maybe it was too small or it simply did not exist when the chart had been drawn. Sacha directed her attention to the spot Derek was tapping with the end of his quill: midway between the west coast and Londinium, closed to a large label marked Dark Morte.

The young woman looked up to the prince, who was already nodding to answer her coming question.

"Here?"

"I am quite sure Friar Johan will confirm it. Now look at the corresponding entry."

She executed herself eagerly.

"One day. Derek, this means… This means Caer Lon is close to Lann Stephan!"

Sacha beamed and clapped in joy, nearly knocking down the inker in the process. His lack of enthusiasm cooled hers instantly.

"You are obviously thrilled by the news."

The prince met her stare quietly, not at all bothered by her sarcasm. His blue eyes were unreadable.

"I am wondering. If the High City is so close to civilization, why has it been lost for centuries?"

The possible meanings behind his question finished to sober her up.

oOo

Friar Johan chose to answer their question with facts, and a legend.

"The High Kings ruled from Caer Lon for hundreds of years after the Roman Empire declined. The king and his knights ensured peace and justice in the Ten Kingdoms, so it was said a virgin could walk without fear, *A Mari usque ad Mare,* with a gold tray in her hands. All were free to observe their practices, and lived in harmony with each other whatever their beliefs. The Court welcomed bards and scientists, commoners and nobles alike. Chroniclers called it the Golden Era of Albion. It sounds idyllic, doesn't it? Well, I suppose it was. Until, of course, human greed destroyed the equilibrium. The High King was betrayed by his nephew and his own sister. A terrible battle opposed them, which none of the armies survived. The king died in battle, as well as, it is thought, the nephew. The king's brother-in-law Caid, despairing over the treason of his wife and son, refused to take the High Throne, and abandoned Caer Lon. He left with his daughter and settled in the future city of Camelot, farther north."

Sacha glimpsed at Derek. He was listening carefully. She wondered if he already knew this story. Maybe he had read it in the book. His face was calm, free from the amazement of the previous day. His stare was a little clearer than usual. Sacha heard the sting of an edge in his voice when he said, "This explains how the kings departed Caer Lon, but not why the City became completely forgotten. It is apparently less than a day from here. It seems impossible that no one knows where the ruins are."

The young woman frowned at the word "ruins." Derek touched her hand, and she realized she had wrapped her fingers around his forearm. Friar Johan continued with his explanation. She took her hand from under Derek's.

"The House of the Dragon's decline and King Caid's choice to leave are history. The disappearance of the High City belongs to bards and myths. Truth is, nobody knows for sure how the way got lost. It is said that Caid refused to put his traitorous wife to death, for he loved her still. He handed her to the Faerlings, a Druid Covent, because she was born 'gifted'. Living with them, she realized what she had done and grieved. She learnt about magic, devoting her days to the People and redemption. From here the stories are even more confused. All agreed that at some point, she travelled secretly to Camelot. One legend says she never returned to her covent, and the Faerlings, furious to have lost their High Priestess, cursed the city or let the forest swallow it. Another version claims the king forgave his wife and went to the High City with her. Together, they performed an ancient ceremony which sealed the doors to the heart of Caer Lon and it will open with the blood of the Dragon, when he returns."

A shiver ran down her spine. Sacha had heard similar words in her dreams. *Hand the son of the Dragon.* She pulled away from Derek and turned her head slightly, buying time to mask her trouble before she faced him again. The rasp in his voice felt like a deadly knife in her stomach.

"What was the woman's name?"

Friar Johan sighed.

"I think it was Eileengail of Shareling. People also called her the White Lady."

Oh White Lady, Hear my plea

Sacha felt nauseous, her head heavy and the world spinning fast before her eyes. The monk finally noticed her distress.

"Are you unwell my lady? You are very pale…"

She flipped her hand so as not to move her head, certain she would lose her balance on her seat if she did. Sacha hoped her voice sounded as normal as possible.

"Do not worry. I am fine. Thank you for telling us these stories. They are wonderful."

She smiled, sure it looked like a grimace and fooled no one.

Derek reported his attention to the map, his eyebrows knitted. After a full minute, he pointed at a caption.

"Here."

Curiosity beat her queasiness and Sacha unwillingly bent to read the name.

"Alynnfaid? Why there?"

Derek pushed away from the table to pick up his cloak, readying to leave.

"Call it an intuition."

The name sounded too much like 'Eileen's faith' to be a coincidence. The fact it, too, was within Camelot's border.

oOo

The wind had finally brought dark clouds over the town to give the late afternoon the gloom of a cold, stormy winter night. Mist was already licking the roofs. They heard thunder rolling as soon as they stepped out of the library. Derek hoped the weather would hold until they reached the inn.

The constant roar in the sky covered the noise of their steps on the pavements. They hurried through the large place, but the rain outran them and started to fall before they reached the street heading to the Wild Boar. The first drops soon became a curtain of water, dampening everything.

Derek saw Sacha skid on the slippery pavement and he settled for a more conservative pace. They risked twisting an ankle on the uneven wet stones.

Their hoods were useless in the storm, endlessly pushed back by the fierce wind. The prince finally renounced keeping his in place and let the tempest plaster his hair to his skull. Rain was running down his face, so he had to blink constantly to clear his vision. The storm made it impossible to see farther than three feet ahead.

He avoided the first blow by chance, forced to move sideways to avoid tripping into a puddle. Derek blocked the second hit, grinding his teeth in pain on the impact of the hard club with his forearm. He lunged to avoid a third swing and the hilt of his sword collided with his adversary's throat, crushing the men's trachea.

Derek twirled. Slowed down by his cloak, he barely deflected a knife aiming for his side. Another pivot and he slashed the other man from the waist to the opposite shoulder in one swift movement. The ruffian wobbled backward and fell.

Panting, the prince looked for a third attacker, but the rogue had chosen an easier prey. The attacker squeezed Sacha's throat, choking her. Derek saw the gleam of her dagger hitting the ground through a fog of anger and rushed forward. Steel bit into the exposed flesh of his upper wrist and hand, draining blood. The prince switched his sword from hand to hand and thrust, killing the man with a vengeful grunt. He reversed his grip on the hilt without pausing, using his sword like an oversized dagger in the back of the last aggressor.

A hiccup escaped Sacha when the dead body fell on her. She pushed away frantically, nearly tripping in her haste to escape. Derek steadied her by the shoulders, quickly checking her for injuries. Air rasped and hissed through her lips as she tried to retrieve her breath, twisting his insides into knots. Derek crushed her into his arms, craving the slaughter of the beast that assaulted her a second time.

Her skin was cool against his cheek, her scent spicy with fear and relief. His body, fuelled by adrenaline, claimed carnal dominance and a more intimate embrace. His free hand closed on her neck to take her closer. Sacha mewled in pain. A nasty mark marred the fair skin of her throat. Shaken to the core, Derek pushed away to grab her hand, his mind still fuzzy with lust and anger.

"We cannot stay here. Come."

"My Llord!"

The young man spun on his heels, fetching his sword again in the general direction of the call. He lowered his guard when he recognized the silhouette signalling them inside a small house.

"Quick! There are four more men. I saw them split earlier. They must be waiting for you up the street."

Gisela closed the panel behind them and barricaded it, before she made sure the windows were covered.

"Who are they?" asked Derek.

"The Guild. A gang of thieves and mercenaries, obeying no one. You probably attracted their attention, paying for small services so largely."

The young man rattled in discomfort. It had never occurred to him his generosity would get them the wrong attention. They needed quick answers and... Gisela added softly, "Some say they obey the Sorcerer-King of Camelot..."

Sacha moved in his back and his stare automatically sought her out. She had approached the chimney, apparently fascinated by the small fire. Derek saw her hand moving toward the logs, yet he did not really notice. If Wolfryth was after them... The need to have her close raged in his stomach again, potent.

Suddenly his mind reconnected with his eyes and he bawled in warning. Lightning ripped the night and the sky exploded above their heads. The outside chaos burst into the house when the fire detonated. Gisela jumped back with a yelp of surprise.

Slowly, the flames decreased to their normal size.

"You control fire!" the servant said in marvel.

Sacha turned her head to the other woman, her stare abnormally bright.

"Yes."

"I knew you had magic." Gisela said before she pointed at Sacha's dark hair. "Holly wood is a powerful charm."

Stunned, the lady stretched her arm to touch the comb, but the maid stopped her.

"No! You must wear it, so it protects you."

Derek cut in, bringing the conversation back to more urgent matters.

"We have to go back to the inn. We need our-"

"You can't!" Gisela cried "It's too dangerous!"

The young man racked his mind for solutions. If he went alone, he could outrun… Sacha was quicker than he.

"Gisela, do you think you can bring back some of our things?"

The blond woman nodded fiercely. Sacha stepped toward the door.

"Perfect. I am coming with you."

Derek seized her arm when she passed by him.

"Out of question."

"There is no need, my lady. A servant can go unnoticed…"

Gisela smiled at Sacha, then at Derek, before she moved away to prepare for her shift at the tavern. He was grateful Sacha did not insist. The dark-haired lady had escaped his grip to walk back to the fire again, her face revealing nothing of her inner thoughts.

The young man approached and held his hand up to smooth the argument he was sure was coming. The wound scorched painfully at the movement and he could not repress a groan. Sacha turned to him instantly and gasped. "Derek, your hand!"

The gash had reopened, and fresh blood was soaking the rim of his sleeve, running down his fingers. He pulled his hand away with a grimace.

"It's nothing. Just a scratch."

Sacha glared.

"Of course it is. I tend to make a point of fussing over silly things. Sit down so I can have a look."

He took a step back.

"I told you, it's-"

"I will not let you bleed all over Gisela's house. Sit."

Derek sulked but obeyed, and lowered himself on the stool at which she was pointing magisterially.

"You are worse than my mother."

Sacha knelt in front of him with some clean clothes and a bowl of water to wash the cut. Her smile suggested she considered his protest a compliment. Maybe it was.

Chapter 16

The kiss fluttered across his mouth, delicious and tempting. Her lips brushed and teased, hesitating between softness and pressure. The caress blurred his thoughts, erasing the memory of another tantrum.

The delicate fingers curled against his chest, fisting his wet shirt. Elwyn shifted in discomfort. Fillin straightened up and her movement put more weight on his broken ribs. He hissed in pain. The pretty woman covered her mouth with her hand, blushing.

"Oh, I'm so sorry, I forgot…"

Every breath was a painful fight.

"…Alright."

Elwyn wished his groan was enough to persuade her. He was tired. His chest and back burned. As much as he liked the company, he wanted her to go away. She had used him for magic. And she had used kisses to make him forget she sent their practice bowl flying with a flip of her hand after another attempt at the sublimation spell failed.

Her last outburst targeted Sacha when he tried to explain that even he barely managed the difficult enchantment without his twin by his side. *I certainly don't want to hear anything about* her. Fillin's retort nagged at him, its cold sting holing in the pit of his stomach. Sacha was his sister and he missed her; of course he wanted to talk about her. Just like he wanted Sacha to meet Fillin. She would, once they escaped. He would free Fillin and take her with him to Haven…

The young woman chuckled. Did he say that out loud? Why was she laughing? Amusement sparkled in her eyes, a brief flash of gold across the polished bronze stare. Within the second, Fillin was playing with his shirt again, distracting him, reminding him it was dampened.

"You have to take it off before it gets your bandage wet, Elwyn…"

He had never noticed how she mouthed his name to make it roll on her tongue, like she enjoyed its form on her lips, swallowing the last of it with a small thud of the tongue. The syllables bloomed in the air, light, spreading to create a different call, some beckoning sounds he had to possess. They surrounded him, playing on his skin and in his hair, humming inside his head to creep down his spine until he could no longer retain a shiver and a low growl.

New words compulsively bounced in his head, foreign at first, then crystal clear. *Narijt droch Forra, kilten den Forra.* The Source is to be found. The Source is to remain sealed.

The sudden cold nearly froze him. Rain bit at his tensed body like a million of angry bees. He held tight, grinding his teeth in the effort. Ice hit his left hand but the enraged scream disappeared in the curtain of water and thunder. Blood beat loudly in his ears, his heart about to explode in furor. Breathing was strenuous.

"Elwyn?"

Air abruptly entered his lungs again and he focused on his companion. Brow furrowed, Fillin was observing him and the look on her face was something he had never seen before. Predatory; distrustful. He looked for an excuse, unable to wrap his mind around what just happened.

Flames danced in the hearth, eagerly licking the logs. Sparks erupted and disappeared with a bang. The fire grew brighter and it roared when the storm forced a gush of air down the chimney. A chunk of wood exploded loudly, creating more sparks; Elwyn jumped to his feet.

The silhouette in the doorframe cast a formidable shadow inside the room. Elwyn pushed on his feet. The scar on the man's face twisted horribly when he smirked. The leather bind retaining a mass of grey hair added to the general impression of savagery radiating from the visitor. Elwyn stepped back. He stumbled on his chair when he wanted to put the heavy piece of furniture between them. He gripped the back to regain his balance, resisting the urge to crouch behind it.

Confused images of that ugly face and pain flooded his mind. His body felt like it was shrinking to flee the memories of torture.

The yellow stare weighted him, with the same impatient look a wolf gave to a rabbit venturing out of hiding.

He wished the giant would say something, yet he dreaded hearing its voice. Who was he? Why had he attacked them? What did he want? He had to protect Fillin. Where was Fillin? The pretty blonde seemed to have left the room; at least she was safe…

The other took a couple of steps toward him and his questions vanished. Who cared about the how and why? His limbs betrayed him, already weakened by the effort of the day. For a moment, he felt his legs turning into cotton and feared he would collapse. Elwyn started to shake uncontrollably. He grasped the chair harder, praying his arms did not give way, too.

The man sneered again and flipped his hand negligently. The chair began to move sideways. Elwyn lost his footing for good, and fell on his knees with a yelp of pain. His torturer laughed. The sound rolled dangerously until a log in the fire split with another eruption of sparks. The terrifying laugh died. Elwyn's anxiety climbed up one more notch, as images started invading his head once more.

oOo

Wolfryth entered the main room to find Fillin comfortably installed in front of their supper. He sat on his chair and helped himself to a large piece of turkey. The sorcerer gestured toward the wine, and the jug floated toward him to fill his cup. He gulped a mouthful of his food before turning to his daughter.

"Your magical pet needs to learn not to resist me."

The blonde looked up from the chicken leg she was skinning.

"Please tell me you did not play with him again… I put so much effort in bringing him into a useful state..."

"I want that witch and her princeling here now! The Guild fails to explain what is delaying them. Derek killed four of their men tonight. I saw their pitiful attempt to capture them. Useless pawns."

Fillin glanced up before she continued taking gravy away from her meat, unimpressed by her father's anger.

"Why don't you simply bring them here, father?"

The yellow stare shone with impatience.

"They have to enter Caer Lon freely or the Source will remain hidden."

Fillin bobbed her head, already bored by the overused explanation. A growl of thunder echoed her lack of interest. She tried to keep her voice clear of sarcasm when she asked, "Do you think Elwyn's calling for help again will be enough?"

A flash of twisted pleasure bolted through Wolfryth's face.

"Oh, this time it will be a different call... Anyway, your little sessions with him are coming to an end. The citraurantia's effect is waning. "

"That's impossible!"

She pursed her lips right after her protest. No one could fight the 'magic sleeper' plant, and Elwyn was so weak he could not even manage a simple metamorphic spell... On the other hand, if he recovered his use of magic, he would be far more efficient at teaching her... Her pensive pout did not go unnoticed. The sorcerer put his cup back on the table.

"You will not visit him further, Fillin. As soon as our guests arrive, the warlock is going back to his cell."

She changed the subject rather than insisting.

"Will you teach me tomorrow?"

Wolfryth laughed.

"Yes, my eager daughter, unless I have to prepare for the final step."

Fillin accepted the answer more or less gracefully. The seer and Derek Pendragon had taken their time so far. Maybe she could hope they delayed further.

oOo

His tired arm trembled when he fetched the blade up to look at it. Its steel gleamed like thirty torches, blinding him momentarily. For a moment, he hesitated. More than a fine weapon, this was the symbol of Caer Lon, the symbol of the High King's powers. The High King was dead. His hand fell down his side, still gripping the topaz-adorned hilt. He had been asked to keep the kingdoms safe.

How could he? He was not a Pendragon, not by blood. His wife was. His wife had betrayed him. She had betrayed her brother and king, for powers beyond her reach. Eileen was gone too; the people would watch over her. Excalibur did not belong to him, neither did the High Throne. He wanted none.

The middle-aged man lifted his arm once more to clash the sword on the altar in front of him with enough force to break it, quickly turning his head when a chunk flew by his face. He felt blood pearling at the cut, running down his cheek. Or maybe was he crying over all that was lost? Reluctant, he glimpsed at the former weapon and gasped. The sword was intact. The stone barely held a scratch. How could the metal resist such a blow? This was impossible! He struck again, with all his will, this time keeping his head straight despite the sparks which erupted around him. His second attempt failed, and the third. The hits reverberated up to his shoulder in throbbing drifts. The more he tried to break the magical blade, the harder it seemed to become.

Out of breath, he turned around the massive cut stone to find another angle. He couldn't afford to let the Sword be found, and he had no desire to keep it. If he could not destroy it, he had to find a way to protect it. Something had to be done, something, anything. No one but the truthful king could use Excalibur and the powers it unleashed.

Caid held the heavy Sword one last time, the hilt high above his head, and closed his eyes. The Kingdoms had to be protected. He had promised. He stabbed the altar one last time.

oOo

Elwyn curled up in his bed, his arms around his knees; his head hurt. Now he was alone, yet the images kept spinning madly before his closed eyes without his being able to isolate one. He wished he could distinguish just one, so he would know that he was still sane.

He recognized the magical mind bonding, though he was too weak to push it away. The sorcerer had forced so many images in his head he was sure his screams were deafening. The visions had come before the magician. Did they come from him?

The torture had lasted for hours; then again, maybe just minutes. He didn't know. He had lost any notion of time. It hurt. Images pierced his mind, again and again, driving him mad with pain and sorrow. He felt the pain in the fighter's body. His heart broke with the man's sorrow. The man of his visions was not the one fighting in the rain, though he was the same. The man in the rain looked like Derek. The man with the sword looked like Derek. It couldn't be. They were one. They were numerous. Elwyn wanted to scream again, and yet he did not remember screaming at all.

The spiral of colors and shapes was endless, pulsing, drilling into his brain until he could hardly tell if he was human, or a living ball of nausea. Where was Sacha when he needed her?

Chapter 17

The water felt cold on her skin. Sacha cupped her hands to wash her face once and then again. She was trembling. She didn't know how to stop. She wasn't trembling before, when she had to push her magic into the fire. It was consuming her, ravaging her insides. She had had to get rid of it before it burnt her alive. She wasn't trembling then. Her hands were also steady when she was tending to Derek. She could not have cleaned his wound and knotted the bandage properly with shaking hands. So why was she trembling now?

The gash on his hand was not too deep, though it had bled profusely. So much blood... She rubbed her hands under the water. Derek's blood stained her hands. *No... No, please no.* She couldn't... She had to stay calm, she had to... *Don't panic. Breathe normally. He's fine, everything's fine...* It hurt when she breathed. The back of her throat was burning. The water was so cold. There were waves of nausea in her stomach. She was going to be ill...

One hand touched her shoulder and she jumped upright.

"My lady, let me help..."

Gisela guided her gently toward the stool Derek had deserted. The maid used a fresh cloth to dry her hands and face, then she untied the long dark curls to brush humidity away from them. The smoothing helped Sacha's frantic pulse to decrease slowly until comfort finally sank in.

"Thank you."

The maid returned the timid smile and finished braiding her hair before she clipped the hazel wood comb into place. Then she turned to Derek:

"My lord, on Fridays the market is always frenzied so tomorrow you should be able to leave the city undetected. With all the coming and going from the merchants, none can possibly notice..."

Derek bowed his head thoughtfully before answering:

"It's a good idea."

"I have to go now. I will bring back everything I can. Please help yourself to anything you need."

Sacha smiled again at the blonde woman, which returned it with friendliness. Gisela gave a quick bow to Derek, and then disappeared in the rain.

Derek cast a quick glance toward the windows to make sure the gush of wind escorting the servant out didn't disturb the curtains protecting them. In this weather, the chances of anyone watching the street were nearly nil, but Sacha understood his caution.

Now the aftershock was gone; she felt empty and weak as a kitten. Even walking to go lie down on the bed in the opposite corner seemed like a colossal task.

The small room was very simply furnished. The table was paired with two stools, including hers, and a small bench. A dent in the wall covered by a roughly cut cloth served as pantry. An old chest, probably full with Gisela's more precious possessions, lay half hidden under the bed.

The last and only adorned piece in the room intrigued her. The dark wooden cradle was carved with birds and trees, tarnished iron circled its belly. Forgetting about fatigue, Sacha approached it to run one finger on the metal, fascinated. The material vibrated under her touch, breaking into a soft song. Her heartbeat adjusted to the peaceful rhythm of the baby carol. She recognized the air; her mother used to sing it when she was little, a light and happy ballad. Sacha hummed the song softly.

"Sacha?"

Derek's call pulled her out of her trance. Blushing, she turned and noticed his surprised stare. The song had been only in her head. It felt so real...

"It was hers... His father made it as a bridal present for her mother. They were happy."

"You can't possibly know that."

She tried to explain the images pulsing in her head. A man built like a bull carving the wood; a blonde woman cradling a baby girl with a tender smile. It was so clear... Love had nestled in the cradle, and left its print in the wood. Gold and pink spiralled in her mind, brushing over her stomach. She flinched despite the gentleness of the caress.

Sacha pressed one hand to her stomach, surprised. The air scintillated before her, sparkling with joy and hope. The child in the cradle had blond hair with the warbling smile of healthy babies.

"Oh, he's so pretty…"

Her green eyes swiped over Derek's handsome face, unable to conceal his features with her vision.

"He's yours!"

"What?! Of course not. I didn't…"

Blushing furiously, Derek took his hand away from the crib. Sacha bowed her head to hide her embarrassment. She had seen Derek's son, she was sure of it. The baby was adorable, and she… The young woman shook her head to clear the last bits of magic from her mind.

Looking for her composure, Sacha looked around once more at the mantle, then back to Derek. Her gaze grazed his hand, immobile along his side.

"Does it hurt?"

Awkwardness rose another level. Derek folded his arms across his chest, hiding the bandage from her sight.

"No. Now if you don't mind, I have to think about our getaway tomorrow."

She furrowed her brows at the harsh reply, unable to overlook it completely.

"It depends a lot on what Gisela will bring back… Let's hope she will think about some of my clothes… This dress…"

Sacha trailed off. The cloth itched her skin and after two days of wearing it; she refused to think about how it smelled. In no way she was going to admit that to Derek, though.

"With proper clothing I can hide your sword and your cloak so…"

"I beg your pardon?"

She grinned at the shock in his voice and eyed his outfit.

"You can't hide the fact that you're a knight when you carry that sword. And you have to admit, Derek, red is not discreet…"

"They're mine."

A dangerous gleam flashed in his stare. Sacha held his gaze and her skin started to tingle again. The fire burning in his eyes was spreading around him already, just like it had in the library. She broke the eye contact and swallowed. She understood his meaning. His colors, his sword, were a part of him; his birthright.

Her breath caught when her hands closed on his folded arms. She didn't remember approaching him. Under her palm, everything became clearer. He was proud, yes, but more than anything he longed to prove himself; he had such a strong heart...

Derek gently unclenched her fingers from his sleeve.

"I really wish you would stop doing that."

Sacha looked up again, surprised and slightly ashamed by her momentary lapse.

"Doing what?"

"Manipulating me into doing your will."

"I am not-"

He interrupted her denial, which was just as well because her cheeks were growing embarrassingly hot.

"I am a reasonable man. If you suggest something sensible, instead of shrewdly trying to bend me to your wishes or to boss me around, I am going to listen."

Reasonable? Sensible? She seriously doubted that. And she never tried to manipulate anyone, let alone giving him orders, he was damned to stubborn anyway! Sacha took a deep breath to calm down before she said something she would regret later.

"So; does it make sense to you to try keeping a low profile, and avoid showing you are Prince Derek, the captain of Haven's knights?"

He answered her sulk with one of his best sneers, which she was one heartbeat close to whip off his face with a slap.

"Yes, actually it does."

oOo

Sacha sighed discreetly and moved a little to find a more comfortable position. The night's events kept bouncing back at her; the attack mixed with her visions were denying her of a much-needed rest.

She shifted again on the bed. They had stayed up late, waiting for Gisela's return, and afterward assessing the options their belongings offered.

For a good part of their vigil, she and Derek had argued about their next moves. After a while, they had fallen silent, maybe realizing the bickering was fruitless, or seeking comfort in the silence and each other's company. At least she was; she could not tell for Derek. Sometimes, she had no means of knowing what was going on inside his head.

She turned cautiously to avoid disturbing Gisela who was lying next to her, and opened her eyes. Derek had deserted his own narrow bunk to resume his watch by the fire. He was probably reviewing each step of their escape plan, one by one.

Derek had his chin on his good hand, his elbow resting on his knee, and his left arm along his thigh. For an instant, Sacha thought about joining him but decided against it, preferring not to disturb his rest, if it was one. Even in deep thoughts, he looked powerful, and reassuring.

The idea intrigued her. She had seen him calm and wistful more often in those past four days than she had in her entire life. Sacha wondered if she simply had forgotten to pay attention. Warmth rose in the pit of her stomach at the thought, uncomfortably pleasant.

"Derek is a good man."

Gisela's murmur at her back gave Sacha a turn.

"Yes, he is."

"And rather handsome. Are you two betrothed?"

Sacha blushed, and she felt grateful to have her back to her curious new friend.

"Good Lord, no!"

Her exclamation echoed in the quiet room Sacha anxiously peeped at the shadows on the wall, alarmed Derek might have heard her. None flinched and she concentrated on Gisela's next question.

"Why not? You obviously care a lot about each other."

The notion might apply to her, Sacha thought. She did care about the man seated a few feet away. She generally avoided defining the feeling, but it was care; maybe even tenderness, with a hint of jealousy and a good portion of annoyance. And desire, if she was perfectly honest. Her feelings toward Derek were definitely a strange mix, but...

"Derek never showed... He does not regard me as a potential princess."

Nor did I ever admit I would consider him as husband material, did I?

She turned to face her accidental confidant, looking for an answer to her mute question on the other woman's gentle features.

"A princess?"

Sacha felt her cheeks warmed once more against the rough fabric of the sheet. They had taken care to keeping Derek's true identity from Gisela, and with one slip of her tongue, she had blown his cover. Stupid, stupid, stupid. She was just useless. Her head drifted into ridiculous fantasies and she acted like those idiots drooling around Derek she couldn't stand. No wonder he thought so little of her! She tried to sweet-talk her way out.

"Yes, a princess, like in bard's tales. The brave knight turns into Prince Charming in those, doesn't he?"

Gisela chuckled, probably reading through her obvious lie.

"Life is not a bard's song, Sacha." Late at night, nestled under the wool blanket, titles and formal addresses were overrated. "If you find a man that suits your needs, don't wait for declarations of undying love and minstrel's nonsense or you will wait for a long time. If Derek is what you want, you should act upon it. I'm sure you know how."

Sacha fell silent, looking for something to retort. This conversation started to look a lot like Ylianor's "vinegar versus honey" lectures. Sleep would have been a great excuse to divert the topic, but it still eluded her. She could not even yawn. Her neck yearned to turn for another glimpse at him. Granted, not to revel in his appeal; no, of course not. That would be disgraceful, just...

"You have an amazing gift."

Magic was far from the best subject as well; yet she found it safer than the uncharted romantic territories.

"I see fragments of possible futures. Sometimes it is just a sensation, like this evening. I… I had a vision about a baby. Derek's son." *Why was everything taking her back to him?!* "I wish I could describe it for you. It was warm and brilliant, and so wonderful… I liked it better than my other visions."

She thought of the nightmares, of her panicked awakenings, her heart bouncing madly to escape her chest and her throat so tight it hurt. Magic didn't seem amazing then. Sacha changed the subject once more.

"Do you think we will be able to exit the town without being seen?"

"Yes."

The affirmation came from behind her, loud and indisputably male. She blushed furiously. He heard! What else had he caught of her secrets? She feared turning around and meet his mocking stare.

"You should rest."

His voice was quiet again, slightly tired. Sacha risked a glance above her shoulder. Derek had not moved from his former position near the hearth, and was not even looking at her. Maybe he had not heard that much.

"So should you."

For once, she managed to keep annoyance out of her reply. Or not. Derek exhaled noisily.

"This is not a contest over who can best resist exhaustion, Sacha. Try to get some rest."

Should he had shown concern instead of patronizing her, or simply added 'please', she would have tried to preserve the fragile truce they had achieved during the evening. But he didn't, and Sacha instantly forgot about tenderness and understanding.

"You are the wounded one; not I."

Derek stood abruptly and walked back to his corner to lie down on his cot.

"Here. Happy?"

God he *was* insufferable.

"Very. Good night."

Temper boiled in his snort and her pride purred.

Sacha turned to lay on her other side. Gisela's amused smile greeted her. She glared. The other woman's smile widened, but she said nothing. The lady closed her eyes, and finally dozed off.

Chapter 18

Morning was already half gone when Derek finally agreed to leave the small house. The crowd had grown so much it was nearly impossible to see more than four feet ahead. They had to negotiate their way through a compact forest of stalls and peasants. The more they progressed through the crowd, the more nervous he felt, though he couldn't pinpoint why; the market's frenzy provided the perfect cover for their getaway, should the powerful Guild still watch.

Derek swore loudly when a passing wheel forced him to jump aside. *Bad idea, waiting.* They should have gone the previous night. The hell with the rain. They should have gone as soon as Gisela came back with too few of their possessions: merely a change of clothes, and the assurance that Mistress Marion would look after their belongings and the horses.

The few words he had gathered between the servant's chuckles and the beautiful Lady of Haven's constant blushes had been sufficient to get the basics. The innkeeper obviously assumed they were retiring to the monastery, and now she was expecting the pair back in a day or two, blessed by a priest... He would have laughed if it hadn't been for the spectre of Sacha's reaction. This was going to be awkward, at best.

The prince twisted to avoid being stamped by a cow and growled when the cowman's stick hit his back. He pulled angrily at the bag he was carrying to free it, dismissing the peasant's apology with another grouch. It took an effort to dismiss the suspicion of attempted robbery. Of course it wasn't. The guy simply didn't pay attention to anything but his herd. Derek tried a deep breath to settle his nerves, scanning the surroundings, and swore. Sacha was dancing around like she was enjoying herself; in a minute she would stop and negotiate a bunch of flowers or a length of fabric. He cursed again, more loudly. Apparently, her awareness evaporated in daylight.

Derek pulled the musing lady behind a cart more or less gently. Glimpses of silver and red mocked him through the opening of her cape. Couldn't she at least be discreet? He barked, "Stop wagering. Keep your head down and close that damn thing!"

The cloak he could do without, but the lack of steel by his side perturbed him. He was incomplete without it. Useless. Exposed. The crowd was faceless and unfriendly. Men were carrying sticks as thick as his arm. More clubs than sticks. *Dangerous things, those. Could crush the strongest man into a pulp...* Were those two Hercules marching on them? They could be looking for a generous knight and his sidekick.

Derek grabbed Sacha's wrist to urge her forward. She grimaced, probably because the long blade bumped into her legs with every stride. He had advised her to wear it sideways, but of course she hadn't listened. She never listened. And now she was going to bruise, or get them caught if anyone noticed the blade, and if they needed to run...Derek squeezed her shoulder, and the hard crush made her yelp.

"I'll take it back."

Sacha shook her head with a sharp "Out of question." and weaseled out of his reach to slip between a cart and a mule harassed by its load. Derek gritted his teeth, glancing around for an easier path to follow her. The two bullies spread out above the flow of heads. He bobbed his shoulders and hurried behind her. Fighting their way upstream was stupid. They were too damn noticeable.

The bell banged ten blows and his heart boomed with each clang. His sleeve got caught, and he jerked, reaching instantly for his dagger. His confused mind took in Sacha's light rose perfume one heartbeat before he struck his assailant in the heart.

"This way."

He released his grasp on the blade while she steered him into a side alley. Carrying the sword didn't seem to bother her now she was free to zigzag between the women holding half-empty baskets. Derek strode to keep up with her.

"Sacha, wait, we don't even know where we're..." He crashed into her back when she stopped "...going."

The narrow alley opened onto a bigger place, and the eastern city gate. The carts were pouring in through the opening. Another line had formed of merchants who had completed early business and waited to exit the town. Once in a while, guards interrupted the incoming tide to allow a couple out. Derek groaned. "This is going to take hours."

Hours, in an open area, where the enemy could spot them. Oh, that was bad... He wiped his hands on his hip, where his weapon should have been. They needed another plan. The hair on his neck prickled. The crowd was circling them, threatening. His pulse was shooting discomfort down to his hands, another reminder he was sword-less.

Derek pushed his pack into Sacha's hand.

"Hold tight."

"What? Why?"

Without waiting, he circled her waist with one arm, and swept her off her feet. Sacha fretted.

"What are you doing? Derek!"

She gripped his shoulder when he started toward the garrison. Her cloak started gliding but she managed to keep it into place somehow.

"Sir! You can't-"

"It's my friend. She doesn't feel well..."

The soldier examined Sacha's pale cheeks. She had closed her eyes and looked in shock. Maybe she really was. Derek hardened his hold.

"Please. She needs space. Crowds tend to overwhelm her..."

The sword was moving along his side. He could feel the weight of steel against his waist. If the guard didn't buy his story, they were in for a lot of trouble... Sacha jarred in his arms and moaned, pulling onto the weapon. His muscles started to heat uncomfortably in the effort. *'Come on...'*

"Let them pass! You! Can't you see this girl is unwell? Give way! Let them pass!"

"Thank you, Captain."

The private dwelt on the title and nodded with a poor imitation of a commanding air. Derek didn't wait and quickly marched under the portal.

He stopped a few yards from the wall, quitting the swarming road to put Sacha on her feet. She leaned against a tree while he sucked in air.

"I don't see why you had to put on such a show."

Derek's attention jerked to the beautiful woman on his right. She was sulking, lips slightly pursed, annoyance already blooming in her green eyes. She couldn't be serious… He sneered.

"Oh really. Didn't you see the two clubs about to swing at us?"

Sacha glared. He gave up arguing. "Please hand me back my sword. I want to put some distance between us and this Guild sometime today, if you don't mind."

The emerald stare flickered dangerously. He had taken them out of the monster's den. What the hell was her problem now? Sacha faced him, one hand on the belt near the hilt of his sword, the other fisted on her hip. If she continued to delay them for nothing… Derek snapped, "I don't have time for this" before he stepped forward. Sacha scowled, daring him to put his hands on her. He was very tempted to grab her again.

"My sword, Sacha."

Her eyes blazed, but she slowly untied the scabbard from her waist. The sword was heavy for her to hold at arm's length, yet he did not rush to help. He would probably earn himself a ferocious slap if he touched her now. Her arm trembled when she handed the blade defiantly. Derek held her stare as he belted it.

Neither had backed up, so they stood only a few feet away from each other. A different pull started to taunt his stomach. Her pale cheeks were pink, her lips parted to show pearly teeth he was sure she dreamed of using to rip his throat apart. She was clearly furious. God only knew why. Alright, maybe his tone had triggered it somehow. He rose to the bait every time she took him off guard. But he just… enjoyed the banter. She was fuming, and beautiful.

Derek slipped his thumbs into his belt, hesitating between more teasing and a prudent retreat. Sacha did not leave him any time to decide. She stepped back first.

"Now that you feel whole again, maybe we can go?"

She spun on her heels, ready to hit the road. Derek grabbed their pack and followed her.

Outside the town, the road quickly cleared of traffic. They came across a couple of late shepherds, untiring dogs trotting by their sides, then nothing at all. With fields on left hand and compact copses on their right, their progress quickly grew boring.

Sacha strolled in front, trying very hard to ignore Derek's gaze on her back. His eyes had taken a deeper shade earlier, so blue it made her heart race.

"It's too bad that Gisela left our map behind."

Derek appeared by her elbow, close enough to touch. She bit into her lower lip, fighting the heat coming up her neck.

"We don't have your mother's potions, either."

Staring at the horizon was a good thing. He couldn't notice her trouble if he didn't catch her eyes...

"What's wrong?"

'Could he?'

"Nothing."

"Come on, Sacha, you're not that unreadable."

Really? When did that happen? She used to do a good job at feigning indifference. She sulked.

"I am fine. Now be your usual self and ignore me."

Derek choked.

"May you repeat that?"

This time her cheeks turned crimson. Oh no. She didn't mean for him to hear that. Oh. No. Without a proper answer, he insisted:

"You scold me every chance you get. You can't really expect me to stick around to be flogged."

Sacha kept her mouth firmly shut. He took hold of her arm, forcing her to stop and face him.

"You started this. Don't walk away from it. Being honest won't kill you."

"Oh, you want honesty? Fine! You ignore me. You refuse to acknowledge I am an intelligent woman, that I can be useful." Derek's eyes widened; she was too far gone to notice his temper was dissolving into astonishment. "I am not one of those idle girls who faint with a whiff of your alleged irresistible maleness and purr around you like cats in front of cream!"

His eyes had turned a different blue, teasing.

"A wildcat, maybe…"

Sacha's hand shot up so quickly he almost missed his catch. Derek tightened his grab when she brawled to get free, hissing like the angry feline he had just compared her to. Her eyes were cold enough to freeze Hell. Maybe not his best move…

"Is there a problem here?"

Both jumped, startled by the strong voice interrupting their face-off. Derek released her to reach for his sword. The intruder had stopped his carriage a few feet behind and glanced back and forth between the contenders. Derek let down his hand. Sacha kept her gaze on him an instant longer before she turned her head to greet the man.

"No, we were just exchanging different views on social behaviour."

The newcomer seemed old enough, though a life in the fields could age a man beyond his years. His beard was greying above the navy blue scarf around his neck. The rest of his clothing was neat, if not brand new. He nodded with a small smile.

"So I heard."

Derek stepped forward before the man simply resumed his travel.

"We are going to Alynnfaid; is it in your general direction by any chance?"

"Yeah, you can climb in."

Sacha took the offered hand to settle on the front seat. Derek shoved the bag and his sword on the back platform before he jumped.

"Thank you."

Their new companion made the reins snap and the cart started down the road.

"Your tongue is singing when you speak. Where are you from? The name is Baul."

Derek grinned. Baul meant snail in Camelot's peasant dialect.

"I'm Derek and this is Sacha. We're from the western coast."

Baul considered his answer then shrugged, slashing the reins again.

"You're a long way from home. Going to Londinium?"

Sacha stared at Derek, at a loss for a plausible lie.

"Hell, no. We heard about Alynnfaid, so we wanted to have a look."

"Ah, yes, the waterfall is something one must see at least once. You're lucky. This year it's particularly beautiful."

The High King's manuscript was illustrated with vivid streams... Her eyes connected with Derek's above the back of her bench. By the spark in his stare, he remembered too. Her anger dwindled in the deep blue eyes fixed on her. Why was it he always managed to overcome her defenses so easily? She couldn't stay mad at him when he had this *win-it-all* grin on him. Sacha swallowed, unable to look away.

"So we were told."

Baul bobbed his head.

"That's a long way to come to see a waterfall."

This time, Derek was the one seeking Sacha's help silently. She offered her best innocent smile.

"I love books with a passion. Saint-Stephen Library is so well known. I had to visit it. Today's sightseeing is my thanks for Derek's patience with me."

And here she was, flirting again with a man twice her age. Derek frowned when her sweet act earned her a fatherly smile. Baul returned his attention to his animals and abandoned his questioning.

Chapter 19

One glance in the mirror convinced Ylianor there was little she could do to cover up the signs of angst on her face. Too little rest and even less appetite had left their marks. Small wrinkles circled each side of her mouth as the smoky shadows under her eyes made them shine like gemstones.

Her hands trembled slightly when she picked up the small phial of perfume Derek had offered her just weeks before. Not on a special occasion; *just because,* He'd flinched when she pressed a kiss on his cheek in thanks and mumbled that he thought she'd like it. The floral scent caressed her nose. A thoughtful gift from a loving man. William had been just as attentive, or touchy when she displayed too many thanks for his liking.

She gave a small smile to her tired image. Her son looked so much like his father. She had never gathered up the courage to talk to Derek about William. She thought she was protecting her son; that she was offering him a chance to create the man he wanted to be, instead of mimicking a ghost. Truth was, it was too painful talking about the one she had loved and lost, and loved still. She had missed him every day, every hour, for the last fifteen years.

She refused to lose her son, too. The proud woman breathed in carefully, and put the small bottle back on the dresser.

Sonia rose on her feet when her host entered the winter garden. With the clear days of spring upon them, the small greenhouse was otherwise empty. Ylianor's invitation to join her here had come sooner than she expected. The young woman smoothed her sunny dress. She hoped it hadn't come too late.

"Lady Sonia."

"Your Highness."

Annoyance flashed in the cornflower blue eyes. Ylianor took a seat and waved at her companion to imitate her.

"I am not longer a queen, as you know full well."

The young brunette bowed her head briefly, maybe in an apology as she held the glacial stare. Ylianor might refuse her title, but she still acted like a Royal.

Pushing the thought away, Sonia focused on the reason that had brought her to Haven. There were alliances to revive, and time was ticking away fast. The young woman recited: *"The Dragon's blood sings, rise the Power to life; watching are the Faerlings, until needs its wife."*

Ylianor scowled. She was being given more riddles by a child, when she needed answers... The lady barely kept her tone regal, almost a snap.

"Spare my patience and tell me why you forced Agnes to betray her mistress. What do you want with my son?"

Sonia lowered her gaze to mask her surprise. Under the icy words, she felt fear, and it troubled her. Ylianor was a mother deeply worried for her only child, but the queen also knew the significance of the poem. She had to. She had been raised by the Elders to marry a Pendragon. She couldn't ignore...

Sonia allowed her eyes to brush over the fingers clutching the armchair, their knuckles white in wary. On an impulse, she covered the cold hand with hers, offering comfort. Ylianor pulled abruptly away from the touch. Sonia resigned herself to using words for reassurance.

"My lady, my family was always meant to protect the Blood and its legacy."

"I don't understand."

Sonia hissed under her breath. In their grand scheme, the Countess of Gosharling and her counsellors had overlooked minor details, such as making sure the most important pieces on the chessboard knew their roles and the risks. So it relied on her to explain...

"My mother is a descendant of the Faerlings; we are the last of the Forest People. When Caer Lon fell, we took an oath to King Caid."

"It's a legend."

"With all due respect, Queen Ylianor, it is history."

The title casted a shadow on the weary stare, though this time Ylianor let it pass unuttered. Sonia went on.

"Caid not only entrusted us with the late High King's sister, he left something else to our guardianship: Eileen's price for her treason. I thought you were aware of that, you were taught by the People…"

"I heard your poem before, but it means nothing to me."

The older woman had regained some part of her composure. Sonia repeated reverently, *"Watching are the Faerlings, until needs his wife."*

Ylianor stood. She knew the words. She didn't understand them but she needed to. Her voice quivered when she wanted it to stay firm.

"Please, Sonia, this is not the time for word games. Derek's life is at stake, and ours too. You must tell me… What does the poem mean? What did you do to Sacha? Did you put a spell on her?"

Sonia seemed not to hear the questions or the anguish behind them.

"We guard Excalibur's scabbard."

The older woman sat back down slowly. The scabbard had a legend of its own. It was said High Kings couldn't be defeated while they wore it. It was also said only the Worthy could wear in battle it without its soul being sucked into the magical item. Only the legitimate Blood could hold the Celestial Blade, and resist its deadly spell.

"Why now? Why Derek?"

"My mother is a Reader. Elementals talk to her. She governs none, but all speak to her."

Sonia's voice hushed.

"The night Derek was born she saw the four elements become one. Fire fell from the sky and when it split the Earth, Water changed its course to reveal what was hidden."

It made no sense; nothing in the last days' events did. Ylianor shook her head.

"Sonia, if you know something that can help us, you have to tell me. Please…"

The young woman bowed her head in apology.

"I'm sorry. I'm forgetting you are not aware of our prophecies. My mother witnessed what we, the Forest People, believe are the signs of the rise of the next High King. But let me finish, I hope it will make everything clearer."

A cloud masked the sun, dimming the light inside the garden for an instant.

"So the Signs were acknowledged and we began to prepare for the King's return but-"

"Camelot fell."

Sonia went on, dismissing the interruption with the shortest nod.

"Yes; my father was instructed to take you to Haven, the only place where we would still be able to follow Derek's upbringing."

"Your father?"

Ylianor remembered the dreadful night when she had lost so much. She had tried very hard to bury the memory deep inside her heart, to no avail. She had never forgotten the terrible noise of the walls crumbling down; the yells of agony. The horrid smell of death... A desperate ride in the woods until dawn broke, Derek clutching her waist; one dark-haired man bowing before the five year old boy and herself, when a small group of knights welcomed them at the southern frontier of the kingdom. And that man had turned his back to safety, and returned to fight for his lost king.

"Hector... Sir Hector was your father..."

Now the queen recognized the onyx stare, and the determined chin, inherited from her late husband's second-in-command. It seemed each step, each one of her actions had been under scrutiny for years. Ylianor shook her head, unsure if she was annoyed or grateful for that 'protection'.

"In Haven, Mother was able to watch Derek through the Seer's dreams."

The royal blue eyes narrowed. Sacha's true feeling and thoughts about her son were hers, a private place, her refuge... How dare someone observe-

"You spied on Sacha and used her to watch us?"

Sonia held her hands up in peace offering.

"We simply kept an eye for your well-being, my lady. As it is our duty to do. Of course, we had a biased image of the King-" Ylianor's stare hardened at the smirk in the young woman's comment. "But it was better than nothing. Then, last year, Sacha's visions blurred somehow."

Sonia arranged her skirt around her, smoothing the fabric on her lap.

"Mother sent me here to discover the why, if not the remedy."

The brunette grinned mischievously.

"I admit I was curious... I heard about Derek Pendragon all my life. When I met him, I knew. His blood sings."

"Sacha did misunderstand your interest in Derek."

Bitter amusement spiked in the otherwise sober tone of Ylianor. Sonia's mouth twitched.

"Did she? I wish I had managed to befriend Sacha. If we had got along better, maybe I would have noticed the mark sooner..."

"What mark?"

Sonia looked away, studying their surroundings, then stared back at the queen.

"When a sorcerer puts a spell on another magical being, the enchanted core reacts. That reaction leaves a mark. Sacha avoided me so efficiently it took weeks before I recognized it and alerted my mother. By then-"

Ylianor interrupted once more:

"What is it? That spell Wolfryth put on Sacha, what is it?"

Her heart vibrated dangerously. Sacha was enchanted. Sacha had convinced Derek to go to Camelot straight into the beast's den... Ylianor forced herself to swallow, already loathing Sonia's answer. The younger lost no time denying Wolfryth was responsible.

"He apparently used a controlling spell."

"So he could alter her visions, or rather 'channel' them."

The queen folded her arms across her midsection. However hard she squeezed, the chill grew inside her, colder and colder.

"Sacha's nightmares worsened this winter."

"Yes. She saw only what he wanted her to see. We interfered, but we were late and Wolfryth is incredibly powerful. I never encountered a charm so strong before. Of course it had to be, to make Sacha submit. Her Seeing is the most potent since…"

Ylianor tensed; the discreet gesture tugged Sonia back to the main topic.

"When I finally identified the curse, mother was able to use a counterspell to stop him watching. We hoped that without the sight, he could not influence her. It worked, more or less efficiently, until the patrol was attacked."

Sonia stopped, eyeing the glass door. Sunlight poured inside again, untouched. However, she felt something, like someone looking over her shoulder. Sonia pushed onto her feet, inviting Ylianor to imitate her.

"Would your Highness walk with me?"

They got away from the bench to approach the trees the gardeners had still to put out. The rose bushes already showed buds between the tender spring leaves. Ylianor mechanically tore out some weed growing at the feet of an orange tree, and then another. Sonia's account seemed to be coming to an end and with it the fragile clasp she had on her emotions. It was too much, aimless. She had lost her husband, might lose her only son and the lovely girl she considered as a daughter; all this sorrow and abandonment for what? In the name of obscure prophecies and the greed of a sick man? Why? Hadn't she suffered enough? Hadn't her family given enough? What gods could desire so much pain?

The sliver of grass escaped her in a quiver. Ylianor winced as she noticed blood pearling from the cut. The throb washed away part of the anguish burning her stomach. Calmer, she faced her companion again. She knew she risked blowing up the cover they had so carefully put into place, but she had to ask.

"If Sacha were outside your reach, could *he* control her again?"

Sonia admired the queen's poise, her woe so evident just a moment before.

"I convinced Agnes to use a holly wood comb with her hairdo as often as possible. Holly wood grants protection and strength. As long as she wears the comb, Wolfryth won't be able to touch her, wherever she is."

The knowing, suspicious smile disclosed that the younger lady suspected Sacha was not quietly resting in her chambers. Ylianor heaved out a breath, not at all reassured by Sonia's answer. Even out of Wolfryth's grasp, the beautiful enchantress rushed headfirst to wherever her passionate heart led her when nightmares struck. She believed she could save her twin brother; what would happen if... There were so many ifs, so many things left to treacherous chance. Sacha might lose the comb, or simply buy another band; she preferred wearing her hair plaited rather than tied up...

And Derek... Derek couldn't stand Sacha's magical outbursts or how vulnerable they left her. Ylianor could only pray their conflicted emotions toward each other wouldn't magnify the danger they were facing.

"The Forest People will do whatever is necessary to protect the King, my lady. However, when the time comes, he will have to find his way by himself, to prove himself worthy."

Ylianor reported her attention back to the brunette by her side.

"How will you know that he is?"

Though she asked, her heart already knew the answer. Derek had to survive. He had to live to legitimate his claim.

Chapter 20

The wheel rolled over a pothole and his head hit the wagon's rim. Derek groaned, brawling to straighten up, still groggy with sleep. Sacha turned to him, and her smile sent warmth down his chest to curl in the pit of his stomach. Vaguely disquieted by the sudden urge to pull her close for a snugger nap, Derek yawned, hiding behind his hand. He tried to chase away the last bribes of daze to no avail. Her smile swayed back to their guide, her eyes abandoning him. He realized the cart was stopped.

"Thank you for the ride, Master Baul."

Derek reached for the purse at his belt, only to be stopped by Sacha's arm stretched over her seat. His hand fell back on his lap, useless. The farmer nodded, "It was nice having company for once; my house is about two miles down the road, in case you want to stop for the night after your sightseeing."

"We will remember that. Thanks again."

Derek was glad she took the initiative. He yawned again, numbed and confused by his lack of energy. He never had trouble waking up. He always snapped out of slumber sound and keen. Sebastian compared him to a catapult's spring while Elwyn complained about it every occasion he got. At the moment, he had no energy whatsoever and his head pounded disagreeably.

The young prince noticed the peasant was looking at him expectantly and finally jumped down the platform, hauling their belongings behind him. His legs protested in the impact, joints hard and hurting.

Sacha moved to help him recovering his balance. Derek shrugged, "I'm fine."

Her jaw dropped for a second before she pursed her lips, something undefined flashing in her sea-coloured eyes. Derek regretted his rebuff. All his body was stiff and sore, as if he had spent days in bed harbouring a strong fever.

"I'm good, Sacha, just…"

His voice bent into an apology and he shut up. What would he apologize for? Maybe he *had* a fever.

Reins snapped too close, making his heart jump up to his throat. The cart slowly set into motion. The high-pitched shriek howled through his brain. Derek shut his eyes tight one second, fighting the feeling of being right below a bronze bell in full swing. When the ring dimmed, he secured the bag on his shoulder to mask his shaking.

"Derek..."

Her call had him tumbled. It enveloped him like a second cloak, drawing him back to her. A headache drummed madly on his temples. He wanted to rest his forehead on something smooth and welcoming, so the pressure building inside his skull would ease. Something soft and fragrant, like her shoulder...

"The path is this way, we..."

"Derek, there is no path."

She spoke so softly he wondered if he had dreamt her nonsense.

"Of course, there's one! Look!"

It was right under their feet, a small trail going straight into that breach in the curtain of trees, toward the rocky hill behind. Sure, it wasn't a Roman-paved road, but it...

Her stare shifted from pale jade to deep emerald, the light in them flirting with all the green shades in between. Torn between fascination and another wave of dizziness, Derek shook his head to clear away the thought. His mind was too full of her since he had woken up.

The pounding in his head decreased slightly as he stepped away from the bewitching lady. Another step and the pulse sank in his chest where it belonged. His head and neck hurt, slowness glued to each move he made. She stared at him with a small smile he had trouble defining, amusement or concern. His vision blurred. The world started spinning so fast around him that he staggered.

Sacha reached forward, her hand looking for his arm to steady him. Derek reeled back instinctively, worried to see her accept his rebuff with only a sigh. She never missed an occasion to berate him. Why not now? Thinking asked too much of an effort right now.

He walked away from the woods to approach her. Fireballs exploded behind his temples. The pain almost brought him down. Did he moan? Sacha's arm rested around his waist as she helped him to sit on a boulder under a tree.

Her fingers were glacial on his skin. While he was sitting immobile in the shadows, the fog which threatened to swallow him an instant before didn't seem so menacing. He struggled to stand, satisfied that he felt steady enough to move his head without immediately needing to gag.

"It's alright. Let's go."

"Maybe we should wait..."

She trailed off under his glare. He could hardly remember one time when he shut her up without causing her ire to flare. Was he that pitiful? Derek flexed his fingers and winced, quickly taking his hand away when Sacha wanted to have a look.

"I told you, I'm fine."

"Right. You were about to faint, too."

Her tone was more like her this time; biting; cold. He preferred the gentleness. The part of his brain that was not focusing on the throb in his hand recoiled at the thought.

"I didn't faint."

"Oh, really." Her hand left her hip to point out the heavy clouds above their heads. "You were resting your eyes from this blinding sun, maybe?"

First her care disturbed him, and now she was furious, he regretted her tenderness. He was definitely unwell. But at least he was feeling more... Less... Whatever. Derek picked up the forgotten bag, starting between the trees.

"Absolutely. Shall we?"

Derek didn't wait for an answer to enter the forest. Under the canopy, the trail was faint, but still perceptible. Hurried steps at his back confirmed she was following him. He just wished he could overcome his headache as easily.

"This way."

"How-"

Sacha clasped her mouth shut again as the prince changed direction to follow the rock wall.

After nearly an hour of Derek randomly taking her through the woods, Sacha was getting anxious. She followed him out of heed, letting him lead the way. She trusted him; of course she did... Mostly. When they knew where to go; when he showed he knew what he was doing. But at the moment, following looked more like a leap of faith. Derek was acting so beside himself it spooked her.

She jogged to remain abreast of him. Derek's left hand was clenched on the hilt of his sword. Sometimes, he grimaced when the metal pushed into his palm, stretching the skin of his backhand. She was quite sure the wound bothered him, but given his sour mood, he would refuse to let her take a look if she suggested it. Despite his protest, he had nearly passed out earlier. And he babbled about roads when the only things there were dirt and half-rotten leaves. What was she supposed to do when he dismissed her concern or neglected to explain himself? She worried about him, for God's sake!

Sacha stopped dead in her tracks and counted up to five to see if Derek noticed. Lost in his own imaginary world, he didn't stop.

"I am not going anywhere until you answer my questions."

She expected him to spin around and scold her. Instead, he arranged the bag on his shoulder, barely slowing his pace. She wondered if he had heard her at all. He would not go on without her, would he? Sacha resisted the urge to run after him.

"Derek, we need to TALK!"

She stiffened as he finally turned around to face her. Red circles ringed his eyes, the pupils alarmingly dilated. His breath was harried, coming out in raps yet he didn't even seem to notice. Derek opened their bag to pick up a gourd. She watched as he took long gulps before he handed it to her without a word.

The earthy taste of the water grazed her tongue and she forced herself to swallow before handing the flask back. Derek reached for it at the same time and their fingers touched.

oOo

She had never seen a room this huge. The ceiling was so high she felt dizzy with her head pulled backward to look at it. The wall on her right was bare stone, with the exception of three massive shields. The sun pouring from the enormous windows on her left prevented her from distinguishing the coats of arms on the weapons.

A murmur from the crowd gathered in front of the two-step stage drew her attention back to the throne. The chair beside hers matched the oversize of the armor and the windows. Its back towered nearly two feet above her head. The wood was dark and unadorned. The only concession to luxury or comfort was the thick crimson velvet of the arms and seat.

Another gasp escaped the people and she jolted as blinding steel bit into the shoulder of the dark-haired man kneeling a few feet below her. Her cousin winced. The deadly blade ripped on Sebastian's chainmail, aiming for the black swan embroidered on his collar. Her throat tightened, her hands clenched her skirt. His head fell forward in acceptance. Pain kicked viciously low in her belly.

oOo

Derek jolted out of his haze. He blinked madly for a few seconds before his eyes narrowed on the young woman tottered before him. He panted:

"What the hell…?"

Sacha stumbled on her feet, looking for his support when her legs wobbled. Derek swatted her hand away, only to grab it ferociously a second later.

"What did you do to me?"

"It's not me, Derek, it's you!"

"No. What did you do? How can I… Tell me!"

He choked half-finished questions, his incoherence scaring her as much as her lack of answers. His already too-strong grip was relentless, bruising her. Without warning, his eyes lost their focus again and her name bubbled from the back of his throat.

"Sacha…"

Heat irradiated from him, pulsing harder with each frantic heartbeat. No visible fire licked his form, yet the world simmered in queasy waves around him.

Kneel…

It was magic; she recognized its appeal, both irresistible and dangerous. It was magic and it came from Derek… The power was far stronger than anything she had experienced before.

Kneel…

It surrounded her, commanding, striking blow after blow in her soul to bend her will.

Kneel…

Her calves and thighs burned in the effort to stay upright. The power pouring from Derek crashed on her, weighting heavily on her shoulders, pushing her down until her knees hit the ground.

Kneel…

Her lungs tightened, refusing to function. Her heart burned, twisted and screamed in want and pain.

Kneel…

The word printed a scorching brand in her mind. Her stomach revolted, the pull torturing her core. Her abdomen squeezed atrociously.

Bow to your king!

Magic was everywhere, around her, inside her, choking, more vital than oxygen. And suddenly the voice disappeared leaving her shivering and out of breath on the leafy ground.

Derek helped her to sit, his hand fastened around her neck, stroking her hair. When her eyes opened he pulled away slowly, a little taken aback by their closeness, rescuing her comb when his sleeve caught into her mane.

"Are you all right?"

Sacha took a tentative breath. The pressure squeezing her heart shifted, the need to vow eternal allegiance vanishing gradually. Breathing exhausted her.

"Are you?"

"Yeah." Derek paused, perhaps wondering if it was wise to insist when she eluded his question. "It's gone. I…" He paused again. "What just happened?"

Bile clogged the back of her throat, bringing tears dangerously close to spilling. Her face felt damp with hot sweat, while her extremities burned with cold. Sacha checked in their surroundings, certain she was to heave if she moved more than her eyes.

The trees that confined them to semi-darkness formed a prison of vegetation. Elms, hawthorn, and ageless oaks boarded a small river. The gorge ahead was steeply sloped. The dark rock, wet with white foam, gleamed in the daylight. The forest breathed age and mystery. A gush of wind played with her cloak to uncover her arms and legs. Goosebumps erupted instantly on her skin.

Oblivious, Derek twitched his nose, his senses alert once more.

"Tell me you hear that, too."

The low roll echoed ahead of them; the grumbling of the waterfall was close.

Derek straightened up and offered his hand, the one that still clutched her comb. The holly wood item looked very small and fragile in a man's hand. Sacha hesitated, remembering Gisela's advice. Holly wood guarded its bearer against evil magic or angry Elementals.

Her fingers quivered slightly when she closed Derek's hand over the strange little trinket.

"Keep it, it will protect you."

He smirked, his good hand landing on his sword, claiming he had all the protection he needed. One delicate brow arched. Derek pocketed the comb quickly before he hauled her up to her feet.

Chapter 21

Sacha followed him into the small gorge formed by the narrowing rock walls. The deeper they ventured into the fault, the more strenuous the path became. They progressed slowly into a roofless tunnel of black granite so smooth it would offer nothing to hold on to if their feet slipped in the potholes time and water had carved within the stone. The foam sprayed the rock face so it gleamed like polished glass.

The forest behind them appeared completely silent, the occasional bird song drowned into the rumble of the river. The water boiled and jumped in its bed, assaulting the overgrown grass on the banks.

Derek helped her up another boulder, then leaned against a rotting root to catch his breath. The brambles nearby welcomed her with hard thorns as thick as her thumb, making it impossible to rest against on the occasional fallen tree. Grateful for the break, Sacha inhaled as deeply as she dared, instantly rewarded with a batch of nauseous waves deep in her throat, residue from the rush of magic inside her. Her stomach lurched again when she tried to take another profound breath, her tired lungs cloyed by humidity and putrid smells. The effort and lack of oxygen made her dizzy. Blood hammered so loudly in her ears that she nearly missed Derek's complaint.

"Those damn things grow everywhere."

He was playing with the bandage around his left hand, scratching and rubbing. She was about to advise him to let it be when Derek peeled it off impatiently and threw the ruined cloth in the river, where it pinked suspiciously before sailing away. His hand was bruised, the wound raw and stained with dried blood.

"Derek…"

The young man discarded her concern with a frown, pulling his cloak off to shove it into the bag. "We're nearly there. Let's go."

Sacha wished he had granted them five more minutes of rest when her head spun, forcing her to close her eyes. Then the world went black.

oOo

The night was dark; as dark as it becomes just before dawn. Tomorrow, a new moon would be born, but tonight, even the stars seemed to sleep. The torches and fire pits in the courtyard failed to cast more than a few feet of light around. When the sentinels stirred the brands in passing, the sparks in the pits died as quickly as they appeared. The King turned away from the window to resume his pacing in the empty corridor.

Farther west, a shadow moved deep in the forest, hiking silently along a forgotten path which bordered a ditch in the ground, an ancient river bed. The white hawk on its right shoulder squirmed and spread its wings with a high-pitched cry. The shadow, a woman, calmed it with a stroke.

"Quiet, my winged friend. Listen, the world is changing."

Silence cloaked the forest again; the woman resumed her climb.

oOo

Sacha jerked upright with a gasp. Derek propped her up, helping the flask to her lips. She tried to swallow some water and coughed.

"This is foul…"

"Only you can be picky in the middle of nowhere. Can you stand up?"

"I think so."

It was more bravado than real strength that bolstered her legs. Sacha looked around, surprised to realize it was still daylight. The nausea was gone; only a vicious burning sensation remained in the pit of her stomach, threatening to fold her in two. Her head was pounding so hard even the small splash of water on the banks was painful.

The lightning bolt ripped the sky apart, leaving a trail of blinding light behind it. Instead of the odour of sulphur which always accompanied the fury of storms, the air sprinkled with freshness. Another fireball shot through the night, then another. The dark velvet was strained by a shower of white and yellow dashes, as if some hero from an ancient era were fighting his gods, slashing and gashing furiously. The battle raged for several minutes, an eternity, before the rain of fire hail ended, darkness taking over its right to the night.

Quiet and shadows prevailed once more, smoothing, cradling the world into oblivion, when a gigantic explosion shook the earth. The blast was followed by another, a dozen, a hundred more, each stroke followed by a stronger one. Panicked, the hawk squealed and took off, flying in circles above its mistress, as high as the forest canopy allowed it. The ground swelled madly, trees and bushes dancing in a wind that should not have been there.

Finally it was over, though the roll refused to dwindle, growing until thunder roared directly beneath the priestess's feet. Far east, a cry erupted, heartbreaking. The pain traveled through time and space. The woman jumped back from the rim, just a second before water rushed in.

oOo

Cobalt blue eyes welcomed her back. Sacha blinked a few times, trying to focus. She was lying on the ground, her head propped up against their bag. Her hand had fallen into a water hole and she took it out instinctively, sucking in air heavily.

"We have to move up. Take my hand."

His hand was warm on her freezing skin, strong and just a little calloused. She gripped it harder, the only solid anchor in the chaos fizzing in her head. Derek hissed in pain. Sacha gasped, easing her grasp instantly.

"I'm sorry, are you hurt? I didn't mean to…"

He refused to let go of her, urging her up.

"It's okay. Come on, we'll find some place up there for you to rest."

Blood dropped from the reopened wound, tainting her fingers. Sacha lost ground again.

oOo

The fire inside her was like nothing she had ever felt before. It ravaged her for an agonizing second, tensing her already weakened body to a breaking point, her bones crumbling into ashes. Out of breath, confused, she managed to open her eyes. Salty sweat burned the fragile organ and she mewled. One firm hand pressed on her waist, a move deep in her womb and the heat built again, inescapable, so wonderful and terrifying at the same time. Her hips angled forward to ease the discomfort.

oOo

"Sacha, stay with me. Look at me; no, no, don't close your eyes. Stay with me."

oOo

Charitable fingers brushed away wet strands of tangled hair from her face. Her nails clang to the sheets. The pain was too much to take. It hurt. Oh Lord, it hurt... Nothing could be worth so much pain...

"Another push your Highness. Breathe deeply... Now push!"

The cramp wrecked her feeble try at taking in air. She screamed to forget the pain, and groaned and screamed again when her body split in two.

An angry shout echoed hers, the noise drilling through her exhaustion. She wanted to turn to bring comfort; she needed to fight the terror she heard in that small voice calling for life. Her body betrayed her. Her stomach clenched again and the queen felt blood sticking on the sheets torn under her thighs. She wanted to cry.

Her arms were too weak to hold anything, yet she found enough strength to cradle a small package, a crinkled red face tugged up in white and gold.

"This is your son, your Highness..."

"A son... Derek..."

oOo

Shivering, Sacha inhaled sharply and exhaled a long difficult breath. She felt cold and hot, drained and exhilarated, as if she had given birth herself. Her back and legs were sore. Some muscles whose very existence she had ignored ached deep inside her. The twist deep in her stomach was torture. And yet, she had never felt so much love ever before.

Her eyes flustered open, looking for the man who was new born just a blink ago. Sacha pushed up on her elbows the best she could, surprised at being able to move at all. Derek was crouched between her and the river, filling their gourd with fresh water. He turned when she stirred, relief painted on his face; the emotion quickly passed.

"Here."

Derek offered the flask and retreated a few feet backward. She took a tentative sip. This time, the water was icy and delicious. Sacha tried to sit, still light-headed.

"Take it easy. Whatever affected me earlier, it's on you now."

She pondered over his statement and shook her head, regretting it instantly when rainbows flared in the corner of her eyes.

"No... No, those were normal, not..."

The *voice* hadn't been there this time, only images and feelings...

"Normal?" Derek bursted out straightening to his full height. His anger boomed over the crashing noise of the water on the rock. He seemed on the verge of hitting something. "You lost consciousness! You moaned and tossed so hard, I thought... Bloody hell, don't you dare say it's normal! Christ."

Worry cracked behind the swearing, sweet as honey. Sacha struggled to get up and approached him. His heart pumped hard under her palm, mesmerizing. Derek covered her hand with his, and she allowed the contact for a few seconds before she swayed back. Her legs wobbled dangerously.

"I am a seer, Derek, you know that... I have a hand on Elemental Air and Fire. Visions are part of it..."

His eyes flashed the dark blue-grey of winter clouds.

"You have dreams; when you are sleeping."

She couldn't help but grin a little at the childish retort.

"Yes, and sometimes they come when I am awake."

Daydreams of gold dust brushing his shoulders, or a crown of fire around his head.

"You cannot *not* have them, can you?"

Sacha gave a tiny smile. The storm was gone, replaced by a sheepish glint in his stare, a gift when his mouth stayed so serious. She spoke softly, "Magic is a part of me, just like the sword is a part of you."

Derek grumbled, unconvinced.

"I think I saw your birth," Sacha offered, "and how much your mother loves you..."

"Why?"

The question puzzled her. She always saw fragments of the past and the future, pieces related to emotions or fitting in a bigger picture she rarely understood. Nothing she could think about made sense here. Her brain was too weary to really try.

"I don't know. Maybe it means you are linked to this place. I saw a fight in the sky, and the Earth opened in two. Sometimes the images do not make sense."

"Most of the time, you mean."

Sacha pouted and Derek swallowed a chuckle. Having her sulking at him again was reassuring, compared to how cold and pale her cheeks were when she fought in his arms a few minutes ago.

"I want a closer look at this waterfall. Stay here while I-"

"I am coming with you."

Derek frowned, but chose to keep his mouth shut, silently allowing her to follow.

The water came down more than seventy feet. The rock had curved with the centuries to allow an almost vertical fall. The stream glittered in the downing light until its striking white hit the pond below at full blast. There, the diamonds dissolved into an aggressive blue-green colour. One side of the pond was inaccessible, the cliff edging directly into it. On their side, the narrow trail continued up to the waterfall to disappear behind the curtain of water.

A ray of light came through the clouds to caress the wet rock; golden spray cascaded on the water like blond hair on a bridal veil.

Sacha clasped her hands in wonder.

"It's so beautiful…"

Derek ignored her comment, walking upstream until the bank was only two feet wide, a slippery tongue caught between a curtain of gushing water and hard rock. The water crashed upon the rock table, threatening to mill anything falling in its way.

"Step back. The edge is not safe; there are cracks in the bank. I am not sure it can take both of our weight."

"What?"

Sacha cupped her ear, signalling she hadn't gotten his words. So close to the fall, the noise was deafening. He tried to cover the thunder.

"I said, stand back!"

Chapter 22

"**Where** is Elwyn?"

The woman flinched, resuming her search for dust flakes on the floor. Fillin narrowed her eyes, barely resisting the urge to grab the servant by the shoulder to shake a satisfying answer out of her. Surely her question was simple enough that even an idiot like this one could understand it.

She gritted her teeth. The woman *looked* stupid. Her fingers were clenched into her voluminous skirt; the psi-like tattoo on her left forearm made her another of those forest people her father kept enslaving. They were good for nothing; not cleaning, not cooking, and certainly not providing satisfying answers. The pretty blonde stamped her foot, and spat every syllable.

"The man who was here. Where. Is. He?"

She punctuated each word to drill the question into the halfwit's mind. A pair of violet eyes came up to meet hers, annoyingly empty; as empty as the maid's brain, for sure!

Fillin's temper rose dangerously close to the surface, forcing her heave in a deep breath. Anger always turned her pink cheeks to crimson, and red wasn't a color she found attractive on herself. Not that she had to worry about her looks now that Elwyn was out of her reach. Or before, mind you; she had barely had to flutter her lashes to have him jump at will.

"Oh, never mind. You will answer to my father later, I suppose."

The blonde spun on her heels, making it a point to bang the door after her. The yelp and the crash that followed her exit felt utterly good as it echoed behind the door. The torch on the wall flickered, making the darkness dance along the corridor.

Fillin glared, as the flame slowly reached a steady glow again. Oh, she really couldn't stand this place; it was full of secrets and shadows which refused to be unveiled. Whenever she managed to lift a corner to expose the mysteries of Caer Lon, another corner darkened; layers upon layers of ancient knowledge blocked her sight, each just within her reach, and all so far away that it enraged her. Knowledge was power; different from Magic, yet just as powerful, if not more. She wanted to know.

Fillin sneered once more, and arranged her puffing sleeves before she started down the stairs. There was only one place she could hope to find her teacher now.

oOo

The sorcerer walked back and forth before the stone basin. Twice in the previous days he had tried to reach for the Seer, and had been repelled both times. The fire beside him roared his disgust. How on earth did she manage to block him out? She didn't know how, or she would have done so from the very beginning!

Trying to get some answers out of her twin brother had been another waste of time and energy; the boy was so thick he had gathered nothing but images of a long-forgotten past out of his brain. Who cared now how a kinglet had tried to break what was unbreakable, and of course, achieved nothing but to trap the Source in the stone? The sword and its power would make him invincible, immortal maybe, and bring the world to its knees, bending before the greatest sorcerer of all times. He needed that sword. The flames licked the mantel, almost white in greed.

Wolfryth approached the bowl, catching his reflection in the silvery liquid. He frowned, yellow eyes gleaming, and the liquid cleared to become as transparent as water. He despised Water, such a weak element, just good enough to play tricks when one got bored. Yet it could have its utility…

Bending forward, he murmured, *"Uri deite arostand hudar skivat."*

His scarred face deformed when his breath troubled the delicate surface. Slowly, a glow came to life at the bottom of the basin, spreading light through the liquid, coloring it in tones of green and black. The ghostly shapes in the woods sharpened. A blond man was leading the way, one hand stretched backward to help the dark haired woman to reach near a white fog.

He snorted; Pendragon and his enchantress. So they had finally decided to stop lurking in that pity of a city, and progressed in their search of him... The woman tripped on the smooth flat surface, as if her legs were too weak to support her, instantly steadied by her companion. How chivalrous of him...

Wolfryth's eyes gleamed as he recalled the ferocious predator whose fur he wore as a cloak. The sorcerer wiped the image from the bowl with a backflip of his hand with a wicked scorn. The seer seemed exhausted; with her defenses low; it would be so easy to retrieve his grasp on her, almost too easy.

Wolfryth smirked in derision, both eager and disappointed. Her resistance was futile but it was so entertaining...

oOo

A squeal woke Elwyn up. His head weighed a ton, so heavy he didn't even bother to lift it upright. His neck had every chance of snapping if he tried. It also felt empty, thinking of it, now that the images had left him alone.

Unable to open his eyes yet, he used his nose to figure out what had changed around him. The floor was cool, just not as blissfully cold as it was when he passed out in his room. The stench was vaguely familiar; it held its own odor, spiced by sweat and fear, mixed with...

Elwyn opened one eye and moaned as he was rewarded for his effort by a flourish of exploding stars on a dull brown sky; a furry dull brown sky. When did the sky grow fur? With black whiskers?

His jolt instantly chased away the little intruder.

"And I'm back with the rats..."

Elwyn gave up on straightening up and carefully rolled on his back. The shackle bit into his forearm so he stopped pulling at it and finally sat, hissing when the upright position awoke the contest of the broken ribs in his chest. When the pain decreased from hellish to excruciating and he could breathe again, Elwyn lifted his head delicately to check his surroundings.

This cell had no window. The wall at his back was cut directly into the rock. The clasp was solid iron, the only metal his magical connection to Elemental Earth couldn't affect. He gave an angry pull to the chain. His try granted him another pang, which somehow turned into a chuckle.

"Oh Elwyn... You can't break these..."

Her whole being repulsed him, from her pale blond hair and angelic face to the smug on her sneaky little mouth. Just the thought he'd kissed her... Eww... He didn't bother softening his grouch.

"Lessons are indefinitely postponed, Fillin. Go away."

Breathing still hurt, but at least he had the satisfaction to guess she was glowering when she retorted, "There's no need to be disagreeable."

"Well, my lady will pardon me if I lack some manners. I think they disappeared when *your father* tortured me!"

Fillin snorted.

"There is no talking to you when you're so bitter."

Elwyn exploded, and so did the fireballs behind his lids, but he didn't care.

"Are you kidding me? You drugged me and you manipulated me so I would teach you magic and now I'm chained to the wall in a dungeon with *rats*! Did you think I would be grateful?"

She pushed a handful of silvery blond hair over her shoulder, glaring.

"You should be. After all, it's thanks to me that you were out of your cage in the first place. I talked my father into letting me take care of your wounds. And if you had told him what he wanted to know, we would still be comfortable upstairs practicing."

"I can't believe it..." Elwyn muttered. It had to be the plant she had made him absorb that made him fall for her; momentarily insanity; feverish lust; whatever. He was chained to a wall, beaten black and blue by her own father, she admitted she had voluntarily deadened him, and she still thought he would jump at her every command?

"Leave me alone."

"Pfff! As if your stupid little sister were going to save you. She can't even save herself."

His blood chilled.

"What are you talking about?"

Fillin rolled her eyes, or he guessed she did by the smugness in her reply.

"You don't really think you are *that* interesting, do you? You're just the bait, of course."

Elwyn held to the tiniest flicker of hope.

"Then you failed. My father and Derek would never allow her to come after me."

She laughed, and the sound turned his insides into a block of frozen stone, rippled by the icicles flowing in his veins. It was a lie, a trick, just another trick to use him...

"They didn't come; of course not. They saw through your schemes. Derek-"

"Oh, Elwyn, you're so naïve, it's sweet..."

Stone and ice morphed into a glacial need to yell.

"Shut up!"

He grappled to get up, his legs shaking under him; the iron around his arm seemed the only thing solid around him.

"Shut the hell up!"

The voices in his head awoke to scream their approval. His skin tickled. His free hand closed in a fist around a non-existent weapon. The words spilled out before he recognized them.

"Adjegy zibran egyver felhok."-

Then suddenly it was there, a spear conjured out of the moisture in the ground and the humidity in the dungeons, out of his blood, a deadly weapon he was free to use on his enemy. The transparent shaft took the glint of solid glass.

Fillin squeaked: "You can't! It's impossible! You don't have that kind of magic!"

Elwyn roared.

"I TOLD YOU TO SHUT UP!"

The pike flew through the air. In a daze, Elwyn saw it pass between the bars, slicing the air toward the vague silhouette in the other side of the fence.

"Legi skjold!"

The weapon broke in two on the invisible barrier Wolfryth created in front of them. Fillin backed against the wall, squeezing her hands, her voice trembling in disbelief.

"Father, he tried to harm me."

Elwyn confronted the wild stare of his enemy.

"YES! And I'll try again as soon as I get the chance! And this time I won't miss!"

"Legi angrep."

The low growl was lost in the terrifying noise of the abandoned spear crushed under the shield. Elwyn's knees gave way under him and he fell to the ground, affected by the annihilation of his weapon. He understood too late that creating it had taken a part of himself, his strength or his very own magical core…

Horrified, he saw those bits of him crumbled to merge with the sorcerer's creation, becoming a part of it, atrociously powerful. Wolfryth's eyes gleamed in pleasure.

"Kill him."

The renewed blade moved up from the ground and flew again.

oOo

Derek's shout widened until it hit the rock face; the sound curved, vibrated, reaching higher octaves, growing louder. It continued to inflate, unbearable, so empty, so sharp, wracking her bones, exploding in her heart… She backed with her hands over her hears, under the fall, away from the noise, it had to stop. *Please make it stop… make it stop… please, please, please…*

"Sacha!"

Chapter 23

In a second that seemed to last an hour, Derek saw her hair spread in the water like it was alive before it disappeared in the furious boils of the pool. He dropped his bag and his sword and dove. The water chilled him instantly. His body protested, his muscles clenching painfully at the assault. The simmers below the waterfall made it nearly impossible to see anything. His eyes burned from the turmoil and the icy cold water. He had to fight to keep his eyelids open.

Derek swam deeper, panic rising by the second. His lungs squeezed, begging for air. He couldn't see Sacha anywhere. He gave another stroke. She was here, somewhere, just within his reach. God, he was freezing. How to find grey among grey?

The lack of oxygen started affecting his senses. From now on, he would allow her to wear only bright colors. She took his breath away in pure white. His fingers were getting numb from cold. She was stunning in vivid red. He had to find her. Her eyes shone like the purest emeralds. His heart crashed against his chest, fighting for a way out. His whole being was screaming, urging him to go up for air.

Grey clouded his vision and he feared he was fainting. Derek threw his hands forward and grabbed the dark algae blocking his way. The wire circled his wrist, soft as silk. He pulled and the roots resisted. His eyes stung from the boil of the water. Despair renewed his strength. The young man untangled his hands from the floating mane to clench the ghostly form he prayed was Sacha. His foot hit the ground and he kicked, hoping the suction pulling them downward would yield.

For several agonizing seconds, he felt the silt collapse under his feet. The moving ground gripped him, swallowing his ankles. Derek searched for a better hold on the body against his and pushed. He would not give her up. Ever. He bent his knees and his arms closed firmly around her waist before he pushed as hard as he could.

His head broke the surface with a vital gasp, instantly drowned by the water falling on their heads. Breathing never felt so wonderful. Derek didn't take time to savor the blissful air intoxicating his blood. He swam to the bank with Sacha in tow, keeping her head above the water as best he could. He lifted both their bodies onto the muddy ground, then into the grotto he had glimpsed before her fall. Keeping her close, he looked for a pulse. Her skin was icy and slick under his fingers.

"You came this far, Sacha. Don't give up now."

It was dark below the waterfall, or perhaps the night had fallen upon them. Using only the dim light and his sense of touch, he found her throat. Kneeling, he rubbed one hand on her back and sides, his other hand glued to the minuscule proof she was still alive.

"I won't allow you to die on me. Wake up, Sacha. Wake up, please…"

His chattering teeth choked the last word. He wanted to yell at her. To beg. Anything, so back to him. Suddenly Sacha convulsed, her spasms worsening by the second; her stomach clenched violently under his palm. He quickly rolled her on her side before she choked on the water she had swallowed in nearly drowning.

Shaken, Derek backed against the wall while she coughed and spat, trying painfully to recover her breath; he kept his head in his hands, eyes closed. For an instant, he thought he had lost her, and the world had become empty and tasteless.

After a few minutes, he felt strong enough to face her and he watched attentively as her queasiness calmed down and she pushed, ungainly on her knees and hands, then straightened up to sit on her heels. Derek waited, not trusting himself around her.

Sacha batted her eyelids, a little dazed. Her head hurt and she touched her scalp, almost stunned to feel her hair wet and tousled. She pushed the locks from her cheeks, and noticed her clothes, too, were drenched. She was cold. She remembered praising the beautiful sight and moving closer to Derek to catch his speech. A warning of some sort, before the world broke under her feet and…

Her head really hurt. Elwyn was the one gifted with water and earth. Why couldn't the antic Caer Lon be in a desert? She hated being damped to the bone. Or freezing cold, for that matter.

Derek's attention was fixed on her and that, too, was unusual. He generally avoided looking at her for long. She glanced up, trying to adjust to the dim light, and realized he was wet too. He hadn't been when they walked closer to the waterfall, at least not to this point. He looked like he had taken a bath fully clothed and just stepped out of the tub. Just like she did.

"Did we…?" *Take a swim* sounded stupid. "Did we fall into the pond?"

Her question seemed to amuse him but not enough so that he would answer right away. The young man moved from his support with a grimace and walked to the entrance to retrieve his weapon and his bag. The ceiling was so low he had to keep his head bent forward. His frame filled out the opening completely. Sacha stood on tottering legs. Her own head brushed the stone above her. Instinctively, she looked for something to steady herself and she found his arm ready for her.

"Thank you."

The heartfelt words took him by surprise. But it lasted only a second, before he barked, "We need to keep moving or we'll freeze to death. Let's go."

Holding their packs at arm length, he started toward the dark cave in front of her. Sacha had no choice but to follow. Somehow, she was grateful he assumed she could walk. It forced her to fight the lassitude which was slowly invading her. If only she had not been so terribly cold… She didn't question his venturing into the cavern. Approaching the water again… Another shiver shattered her bones.

The small passage seemed to connect to a bigger cave. Fortunately, it went drier as they progressed farther from the fall. On the other hand, light was only a memory now. As darkness grew, Sacha felt her wet clothes become heavier on her shoulders, refusing to dry. She was unable to warm up, and she was sure her teeth were going to crack if they continued chattering so hard.

Derek was still going, towing her behind him. She had gripped his sleeve at one point, letting go off his arm but unable to free him completely. Her pride refused to ask for a stop. She forced one foot in front of the other, enduring the glacial sting cutting her bones. Her cloak tangled in her legs to make her trip. Her dampened boots made each step spongy and more difficult. In the dark, her labored breathing rolled loudly, reverberating in the silence around them.

Derek stopped, fidgeting while her chattering teeth tried to break her jaws. Taking her hand, he forced her fingers to close around a stick of hard wax.

"Can you light the candle?"

She tried to make sense of his request as the unbearable pressure crushed her temples. The words seemed disconnected from each other.

"Sacha, I know you are tired, but we need light. Please, try to light the candle."

She focused on the form in her hand, picturing the wick. The pounding in her head jammed harder. A small flame erupted, dangerously weak before it grew stronger. The effort to call on her magic exhausted the last of her strength. Derek instantly caught her when her legs gave way under her, helping her to the ground slowly.

The small gleam chased away the shadows around his face. She hoped she didn't look that pitiful. His hairs were half-glued to his skull, half spiking in every possible direction. His skin was glowing under the candlelight. His strong jaw was firmly clenched, probably because he was fighting shivers, as well. His shirt was nearly transparent and the bulge of muscles, strengthened by years of training, showed through.

Sacha tightened her cloak around her. She regretted it instantly, for more cold seemed to penetrate her bones. The heat on her cheeks was almost welcome in her prison of ice. Derek's voice floated toward her, so far away...

"You need to get rid of your wet clothes."

The order partly stopped the mad dance of her teeth.

"I a-am not di-di-dives-ti-ti-ting in front ooooof you."

Derek groaned and fixed the candle on the ground with drops of melted wax.

"I didn't pull you out of the water to see you die of cold. Here."

He handed Sacha a dry shirt he had extracted from his backpack, along with his cloak.

"It will help you stay warm, and modest."

Her fingers refused to release him. Derek gently unclenched her hand from his sleeve, brushing her skin.

"I won't be long. I just want a look around."

Free from her grasp, he put the cloak on the ground and pulled his shirt above his head. Sacha's eyes widened in – appreciative - shock. How long had it been since they played in the lake, children, unaware of the effect of bare skin? She swallowed nervously and shivered again. The play of light on his shoulder blades distracted her. Clearly, they weren't children anymore. Head low, Sacha started unlacing her shirt, and took off her boots, then her pants, fighting (blessing) the heat cramping up her neck and face.

The light flickered on the wall in front of her. She guessed Derek had taken up the candle to visit their shelter. Risking a glance above her shoulder, Sacha glimpsed his large frame. His back and his shoulders were bare. Her gaze moved down to his waist, locked on the display of skin and muscles which were very… really… She turned away with a muffle cry.

With her eyes firmly shut, she finished stripping off her wet clothes. Twisting her hair into a bun to wring it out the best she could, she unfolded the shirt. A sigh of relief escaped her lips when she slipped it on. The blissfully dry garment was large for her slender frame, and nearly reached her knees.

She wondered what Derek was doing. He had saved her life… She didn't dare look around, in any case her traitorous eyes ventured inappropriately again. Crouched with her knees to her chest, she relished in the scent of his shirt. It smelt of earth, and metal, and something peppery she thought was just Derek. The rough fabric was comforting; yet her body heat refused to decrease, as tiredness sank back in. Cold seemed encrusted in her bones, so her skin burned while her insides quivered. Her head grew heavy once more and soon keeping her eyes closed stopped being that hard.

His voice made her jump out of her half-doze.

"You can look now. I'm covered."

Teasing perked in his voice, too tempting to resist. Her eyes fluttered open before she could even blush. Covered was a manner of speaking. He had wrapped his cloak around his hips as an oversized towel. The shadows played an intriguing ballet on his bare chest when he bent down to pick up the bag. For a moment, she failed to convince herself that his speech was more interesting.

"There is an alcove up there, where the walls narrow."

Sacha nodded and stood awkwardly, unnerved by the feeling of her naked legs offered to his attention. One hand on the wall to steady herself, she took one step forward and tripped. Derek circled her waist to support her. She hadn't notice he was so close.

Her teeth started their crazy chatter again and she began to shiver uncontrollably. Pain shot through her legs with every step. His grip on her waist tightened.

"Just a little farther, Sacha. It will be easier to warm up there."

She could only nod. "Warm up" had the taste of wishful illusion. Tears burned her eyes. She shut them tight to stop them from welling, exhausted by the effort and the desperation of their situation. Their clothes were drenched and without a fire, it seemed impossible to dry them. They could not go on with only three candles, his cloak and the shirt he had given her.

"I'm sorry."

Derek stopped walking to look at her face, surprised.

"What for?"

"We were attacked and you got wounded; then I fell and you had to jump into the water to help me. Nothing would have happened if I hadn't force you to come with me."

"You didn't force me to do anything."

His tranquil voice contrasted with the riotous bounce in her chest.

"You asked, I agreed, and I'd rather be wet in this place than have you dead."

Her hug erased the fatigue; it was over before he even realized her arms had circled his shoulders but it chased away doubt and worry. She trusted him with her life, and it was enough to renew his strength. The ice of her touch when Sacha slipped her hand into his reminded him to take in air. The strange cave didn't feel that cold anymore.

Chapter 24

Derek looked anxiously at the wax in his hand. He had two more candles but God knew how long it would take them to get out of the tunnels.

Going back meant diving and swimming against the stream if the bank had totally collapsed. The idea had less than little appeal. But if they didn't find their way through the caves or if they reached a dead end, the third candle might be their only chance to walk back to the waterfall.

He made a mark with his nail in the wax; past this, he would blow it up. They could not afford to waste their resources.

Sacha was spreading their wet clothes on the ground the best she could, maybe hoping the air would be enough to partly dry them. He didn't dare to say her attempt was fruitless; with the humidity around the cave and the absence of a proper warm source, their clothes had little chance to dry.

Her face was marked by the trauma of her near-death experience. White circled her lips, which had taken on a worrisome dark shade. She tried to hide it - she always tried to hide everything - but he could see she was trembling again.

They had nothing with which to build a fire, basically no light, and they were possibly trapped inside a mountain. Derek punched the wall in frustration. Sacha glanced up.

"Derek, your hand is hurt!"

He grunted. Of course it was hurt, he had just hit a stone wall…

"You're bleeding..."

In the dim light, he barely made out the red color staining the ground.

"Don't worry about it. Sacha, we have some food in the bag. Can you-?"

"Come here."

Her order suited him better than seeing her desperate, as she had been earlier. He failed to swallow his smirk when she motioned for him to sit down.

Sacha gave him a reproachful glance and took his hand to check the sore skin; her fingers were so cold he flinched. Another cutting look shut him up before he protested. She abandoned him briefly to tear a band of cloth from her wet shirt.

While she knotted her pitiful bandage around his hand, Derek concentrated on their goods.

"We have enough for two days, I think, if we split it carefully."

Two days of food, for two days of light.

Sacha nodded, still occupied with her tending, and he went on with his examination. The bread was a little spongy and the dry meat, not that dry. He also found an apple and some brown sticks he supposed were sugar canes. Derek nearly added they couldn't afford to stay in those caves more than two days; but seeing her eyes watered when she yawned, he said nothing.

"We should put out the candle while we sleep. I can light it again later."

The wax had melted past his mark. Sacha was already curling into a ball like a cat, her eyes fluttering closed. Her features were strained with drain, greyish despite the gleeful candlelight. Food lost the little appeal it had. Derek blew on the little flame before he leaned backward slowly. The stone at his back didn't feel that cold; unless he was getting use to the chill. The cut in his hand pounded painfully under her tight bandage.

"Can we go out by the waterfall?"

In the dark, her voice stretched on a note a little too high to ignore the anguish behind her question. Derek tried to remember where she was and held his good hand forward, brushing something round and soft he hoped like hell was her shoulder. He told the truth.

"I am not sure. The bank partly collapsed."

Derek jolted when her hair wet his arm as she turned to face him. Sacha moved to push away but he wrapped his arms around her, bringing her to his chest. She stiffened at the contact. For an instant, he wondered if her shivers came from cold, or the intimacy of his hold.

A drop of ice glided along his hip, silencing the devilish voice in his head, which had started to detail the many ways to share and increase body heat, one by one.

"We'll find another way out. Take some rest."

A low, thankful sigh answered him. Derek wished he could believe his own words.

oOo

He kept his eyes close. Listening to Sacha's fractured breathing helped him concentrate. He couldn't sleep, though his body longed for the rest. His mind raced over that poem again and again, trying to make sense of the strange stances.

Derek mouthed some of the verses silently.

> *If I cry, share my tears,*
> *And guide me through my fears;*
> *If I fall, help me stand,*
> *And in your right, take my hand*

He had taken a wild guess, turning left each time the wall curved or split, because if the right hand was offered, then the escort would have to give its left. He interpreted tears as the waterfall, and the legitimate fear anyone would have at walking through it.

He could be wrong. He could lose his way in the endless maze of pillars and turns and lead them to a death of freezing and hunger. Maybe the prayer meant to take the right path and not the left. Maybe…

Sacha shivered and his eyes snapped open. His mind was so blurry it didn't shock him to be able to make out her delicate frame. The cave might not be as pitch black as he thought, or his eyes were getting used to the darkness. She stirred, her legs hunching higher under the garment, so her knees pressed hard into his flank. So much for the romance.

The tunic had slipped down her collarbone to bare the inviting swell above her breasts, more than decency would have normally allowed. Derek swallowed, watching the feeble light played on the landscape of her throat. Had her skin felt that soft under his palm when he thought she was an intruder in his chambers? It was only days ago; an eternity. It would be so easy to close his eyes and truly lay with her. It amazed him how different she was since they set off together. Unless she had always been like this, both defying and tender, and he had never taken the time to notice. Shaken, he forced his hand to withdraw from the curve of her neck.

Sacha sighed softly and Derek jerked back, letting go of her. He needed some distance, something to distract himself from acting like a lustful teenager. *Think about weapons. Foot play Training. Tournaments. Fully-armed tournaments.'*

His armour would have been great to wear at the moment instead of being barely covered near her: some cold, hard steel, thick enough to protect both of them. Unfortunately, his armour was in Haven. Humid breeches and shirt would have to do. Derek gathered his clothes as quietly as he could not to disturb her and started to dress. His elbow hit the wall behind him when he slipped his tunic on.

The loud curse echoed in the empty cavern. Sacha opened her eyes slowly and instantly gasped, reaching to the loose end of her bodice to cover herself.

"Derek!"

The young man searched his mind for a suitable excuse for whatever she might chastise him for: the improper touching, the swearing, anything, as long as she would stop looking at him with such a baffled look on her face. Then he realized her widened eyes were focused above his shoulder. His mouth clasped shut instantly as she babbled:

"The wall... It's glowing!"

If he had not been so keen on listening to his lowest instincts, he would have noticed. Maybe he had slept after all, and the day had broken again, dawn pouring into the cave from a natural chimney he hadn't heeded when scouting with only a candle.

"Yeah, I know," he lied cheekily.

Still protecting her modesty with one hand, Sacha tottered up to approach the opposite wall, touching the stone lightly in bewilderment.

"And it's warm too…"

She laughed. Her happiness pearled in the air, enticing, right before goose bumps attacked her once more and she inched closer to the seemingly hot wall, nestling against it, her beautiful smile chattering. Derek grumbled.

"Please, take it."

His cloak enveloped her from head to toes when he put it on her shoulders before he took a quick step back when Sacha flashed a grateful smile above her shoulder. She pulled the garment closed, briefly burying her nose in its folds with her eyes shut. Her cheeks flamed to match his cloak's crimson color at the indulgence.

Where had he gotten the idea that getting dressed would help? His tunic glued to his back. The pants seemed wetter now he had them on, and squeezed his lower body disagreeably. He jittered to get accustomed to the itch on his skin. Derek looked for another topic, finding none.

Sacha crouched against their wall again yawning as discreetly as she could. Derek perused their provisions. The apple didn't look that bad, maybe a little crushed on the side. In any case, it still looked better than the bread.

"Here."

She munched at the fruit, barely taking a bite before she put it away.

"I'm not hungry."

Maybe she wasn't. She looked paler than usual, nonetheless. Derek frowned.

"We may have light, but we still need to keep up our strength to get out of here."

Her snort was missing her trademark bristle at being patronized.

"You're not eating, either."

Derek lied again. It was a skill he had mastered around her, it seemed.

"I ate while you were sleeping."

Sacha scowled in doubt - alright perhaps mastered was an overstatement - but she said nothing, taking another nibble before she abandoned her apple for good.

"Can we stay here, just for a little while?"

They shouldn't. Deep within the cave, they should use every minute of light they could get to move forward. He detailed every reason they should move on in his head as her green eyes opened to fix onto his.

"Yes, of course."

Derek leaned into the wall, savoring the heat in his back through his shirt. Sacha pressed her cheek on her knees, nestled under his cloak. Uneasy, he grabbed his sword to check the blade. After a while, he couldn't pretend anymore.

"The light probably comes from some sky light I didn't spot earlier."

Sacha turned her head toward him and for a minute, he could only stare as her hair cascaded over her knees like ebony silk.

"Do you see how the wall seems to glow? I never saw anything like it..."

Her murmur finally got to him and Derek gulped. The wall *was* glowing; it radiated light from within. A gleam coming from a ceiling opening would not do that. It would break into a cone of light, dimming away from the source. What he saw was different; the light was everywhere. And the warmth... The warmth enveloped him, welcomed him like a lover's arms. It made him long for home and peace.

Derek snapped out of his thoughts to find Sacha's sea green gaze still on him, studying his face. He insisted.

"It must be you. This place recognizes your powers, or something."

Sacha took her time to reply, long enough for him to notice her lips had regained some of their natural strawberry coloring, as she slowly warmed up. Her voice seemed more assured, too.

"I am gifted with Air and Fire, Derek. What's happening here is different. It's difficult to explain. It feels..." She paused. "I don't know what it is. But I am not the one doing this."

Derek played with the bag strap.

"Who, then? Me? You suggested so before, but that's impossible."

"Why not? Caer Lon is a sacred place, the High City of the Pendragons. It is yours, by all means."

He shook his head. What she suggested was crazy. They were in a cave, not inside a long-forgotten city, and in no way could a bunch of stones react to a human being. The light, the warmth, they had to be a magician's doing. It was ridiculous to think a few drops of his blood on the ground could unleash all of this. She always went for the wildest theories, when there had to be a reasonable explanation, some fluorescent moss or…

Derek tried another approach.

"What about Elwyn? You're twins; you have a special bond. If we are getting closer, can you… feel his magic?"

Sacha frowned slightly in thinking.

"Maybe."

A few seconds later, her grin lit the air more surely than the strange glow coming from the walls.

"Do you remember when he animated the statue while King Ilar was visiting?"

Ilar had come with his son, a prat of about their age, who had plagued her and every other girl in the castle with unrequited attentions or insulting remarks until a growling gargoyle scared the hell out of him. Elwyn liked nothing more than show off his link to Earth. Derek bared his teeth in a fierce smile.

"Oh yes, absolutely."

They both chuckled at the memory of the yelps and fret; Geraint somehow forgot to discipline Elwyn. They all wondered if his royal visitor had asked him not to.

Derek gazed away first, pushing onto his feet.

"If you feel rested, we should move on."

Sacha nodded, and quickly gathered her clothes. She said nothing about the fact the strange heat had nearly dried them and he was glad she had dropped the subject.

Chapter 25

Sacha's clothes were stiff and disagreeably hard on her skin. Her cloak hadn't dried, so they decided to leave it behind. Her feet protested when they set off again, pumping into cold slushy boots, but she kept her mouth shut and followed.

Derek decided not to use their candles, for the glowing from the wall provided enough light to walk at a good pace, if they could consider the cautious progress they made along the corridors a good pace. The prince stopped each time the wall curved, motioning her to wait while he scouted a few yards ahead.

They didn't talk, save for some encouraging words or directions from time to time, mostly from Derek. Sacha preferred it that way. Their previous conversation had clearly upset her companion. As for her, silence was preferable to mentioning their sleeping arrangements.

A smile tingled on her lips. His arms had been closed possessively around her, more than a friend was entitled to do, even in a life-threatening situation. She wasn't naïve to the point she thought Derek had decided to put his humid clothes back on just because he was eager to get going. She suspected he found her desirable, and the knowledge felt surprising; confusing; amazing...

"I think I see a split ahead. Wait here."

The young woman watched his large frame blurred away, still smiling, and used the brief pause to look around. The unusual brightness sculpted the stone into the strangest shapes, impossible mushrooms or crystalline trees. Where the outside rock had been black as obsidian, inside it was strained with pink and light grey and freckles of silver gilt. The light seemed to come specifically from those, as though the walls sparkled from within.

But what truly fascinated her was the warmth. It pulsed gently under her palm when she touched the stone. Sparks ignited up her arm when she trailed her fingertips on the surface smoothed by age.

Sacha wished Elwyn was here. His gift would have allowed him to feel the power coming from the mountain. And maybe the man striding ahead to scout would have listened to his friend more than he listened to her.

Once again, Derek interrupted her meditation. He looked concerned.

"The corridor splits in three branches ahead. The right one is completely dark."

"And the other two?"

Derek took a swig from the jug he extracted from their pack.

"They are both bright. The one in the middle seems narrower, but it's hard to tell."

Sacha drank in turn, scrutinizing his face when she handed back the flask.

"It is bothering you."

Derek gave her a surprised glance before he confirmed, "Yes; I don't like it."

She waited. The young prince put the jug back into their pack. Their reserve of fresh water was limited, too.

"There's another hypothesis that we didn't discuss earlier."

"Which is?"

"What if all this-" he motioned to the walls surrounding them "-does not come from a friend?"

Her eyes widened in fright. Derek went on.

"Given we needed light and heat, we assumed they were a gift. I think we can't dismiss the possibility of bait."

Sacha heaved out a sigh. How could she convince him *he* was the source of the magic? That he had nothing to be afraid of? The vision they shared in the forest, the voice claiming her allegiance, the cavern brought to life, they all came from Caer Lon, reacting to his Pendragon blood. She opened her mouth to argue and stopped, suddenly suspicious.

"Derek?"

His lopsided smirk didn't reassure her.

"We'll go right."

She had a bad feeling about this. If she was right, his choice of a path meant that they stayed in the dark for a reason, a very good one. They shouldn't defy the High City, it was dangerous.

"I don't think it is a good idea…"

"I thought you would not. That's why you are staying here."

"What? No!"

Derek gently unclutched her hand from his sleeve to take a candle from their bag.

"I'll just make a quick survey. I'll be back before you have finished listing sweet names to call me."

His banter didn't amuse her in the least. Sacha crossed her arms on her chest and scowled.

"You're not going in there without me. If this is a trap…"

Derek stepped forward.

"That's exactly why I don't want you to come."

"Derek-"

Heat crept up her cheeks when he moved closer, his blue eyes diving into her green ones.

"I'll be careful."

Little flakes of light spiralled around his head, branding the air around them with gold. He was still holding her hand, and the contact became almost unbearable; yet she couldn't resign herself to let go. She wanted to hold him, hold onto him, until her heart settled back into a quieter pace.

A grin played on his mouth when his gaze moved down from her face to their fastened hands. Far away in the back of her mind, her pride jerked and tried to rebel, as she realized Derek was using charm to force her to stay put. She couldn't care less. His stare was a soul-binding navy blue.

"Thank you."

Sacha blinked. She had lit the candle he was holding without even noticing she was using magic. Derek bowed his head once, and strode away.

Sacha sit with her back to the wall. She closed her eyes to listen to his footsteps moving away. Was the knot low in her stomach what he felt when she cajoled him into obeying her? She failed to know if she liked it, or not.

oOo

One twist of the hand and the key turned in its lock to ensure Wolfryth he would not be disturbed. What he intended to do required a total focus. The spell would project its conjurer's memory into another magical being. It would open his mind completely, so any intruder would be able to gain an unshaking hold on his psyche, and even strip him of his powers. Dark magic always came with a price of blood, if one were taken off guard.

Standing in front of a full-length mirror, the sorcerer opened his hand. The metallic powder scintillated in his palm.

"Traiasca mijin eloben."

He blew on his palm and the mirror surface filled with gold dust.

oOo

The stomping in the corridor told her all she needed to know. A ferocious smile curved her lips. Frightened whines and panic gallop erupted from below. She didn't care. The wait was worth it. Finally the time had come. Tonight, she was going to conquer the Dragon's blood, and acquired its power.

The magician caught a reflection on the window. The full lips showed more carnal want than grace. The stubborn chin, callousness. The eyes, those eyes that once had been a very pale green, made the blazing fire which ravaged the towers look like a jealous little flicker of a flame. The long dark hair swayed in its leather band when she turned to the door.

"Sorcerer!"

She turned around, a mocking smirk on her face.

"Your Highness. I nearly wait."

The man's fear and grief at seeing his castle in ruins and his men dying swirled around his shoulders, delectable. She licked her lips, trying to catch a taste of it on her mouth. Yes; she perceived fear, and anger too. Her sneer twitched. William Pendragon was exactly where she wanted him. The King - or rather former king, she corrected automatically - took a step forward, blade held in both hands.

The sneer morphed into a hoarse laugh.

"You are no match for me. Legi pavirke."

A gust of air smashed into William Pendragon's back strong enough to make the large man stumble forward, still gripping his sword with both hands. Annoyance blazed in the wolfish eyes at his persistence, amusement gone.

"Lazar meld ild."

A tongue of fire snaked out of nowhere, darting toward the king. William Pendragon jumped aside, then dodged, groaning in pain when the heat licked his thigh. Desperate to strike back, he lunged, thrusting his blade upward.

Steel bit into her cheek, leaving a trail of blood and pain. Sacha hissed. How dared he? How did a ridiculous kinglet dare touch her! Fury erupted in thunder and flames around her. She wanted him on his knees and broken. She wanted him to beg before she sliced his throat open.

She had ravaged his kingdom. Now she was going to crush him to dust. She licked a drop of blood on the corner of her mouth, and snarled. Oh, how she was going to enjoy his suffering...

A snap of her fingers and the man collapsed on the floor, holding his elbow with a cry of pain, but he refused to drop his sword. Sacha allowed the wild beast holed up in her chest out in a dangerous growl.

Straightening the large frame she inhabited to its full height, she whipped the air with her hand. The man cried out loud, as more bones broke. Still he fought to stand up, using his blade as a crutch. His knees gave in a flip of her hand; then his ankles. He pushed on his arms, the sword useless on the floor, and she splintered his shoulders. He still refused to yield.

Sacha gritted her teeth, irritated by his stubbornness.. All he had was hers now, why bother? She didn't need Pendragon alive to obtain his power. She just needed his blood.

"Legi angrep."

William gasped when an invisible lance pierced his flank; his eyes widened in pain and with one final jerk, he was gone.

Finally! Finally she had overpowered the Dragon, and its power was hers! Her laugh inflated inside her; the twisted joy was *maddening. It rambled over her body and echoed forever in the empty room.*

oOo

Sacha shrieked in terror, desperately gasping for air. Her throat clenched hurtfully, forbidding her to take a proper breath. Oh God, what she had done? It had been so pleasant to torture the man, to witness his agony and add to it. Her stomach revolted and she fell forward to heave out non-existent bile on the stony ground. She had just killed Derek's father and took intense pleasure from it. Oh Lord, Derek...

Sacha jumped to her feet, one hand on the wall to secure her stance, and started down the corridor.

"Derek!"

She found the split and stalled, momentarily blinded by the brightness in front of her. Running into darkness to be comforted by the son of the man she had killed... How could she? Blood hammered in her ears as her heart tried to escape her chest, yet not so loudly that she didn't notice the rock's threatening grumble. Sacha broke into a run.

"Derek!"

One strong arm intercepted her, the ghost of William seizing both of her arms to immobilize her. She screamed, unable to look away from her victim's face, searching for twists of pain, a pain she had been so thrilled to inflict. The square chin and the masculine mouth were the same, yet untouched by death; the eyes were different, bluer, concerned.

"Sacha stop! The ceiling has partly collapsed up there, and I'm not sure about-"

The crash of falling rocks interrupted Derek. He leapt forward, pulling Sacha roughly after him.

"Quick!"

A crystalline bee gnawed at her arm; Derek didn't allow her time to massage the bite, but hurled her behind him. The candlelight flickered and died under a shower of gravel and cobbles. Derek accelerated. Her shoulder hurt from his pull.

Derek pushed into the main tunnel. After the darkness, the soft light assaulted her dilated eyes. Protecting his eyes with one arm, the young man refused to slow down until he reached the place where they had parted and he pushed her into the wall, covering her body with his. Thunder rolled, alarmingly close. She ducked before him instinctively.

William's bones had snapped with the exact same thud that a boulder made behind them. So easily; a twist of her wrist had been enough. Enjoyable, really... Forgetting about danger, Sacha fought to free herself from his grasp. Derek jammed her head back into his chest.

"Stay down!"

Sacha hiccupped.

"Your father... Please Derek, forgive me, I-"

The grip on her forearms hardened, bringing tears to her eyes, unless it was the guilt...

"What are you talking about?"

The rolling of falling rock drained away. Sacha muffled a sob before she uttered the horrible truth.

"I killed him."

Derek stepped back. Seeing the alarm and the shame in her eyes, he released her arms to take her face in his hands, forcing her gaze up. He said firmly: "My father died fifteen years ago, Sacha. Wolfryth murdered him, not you."

Tears wet her cheeks.

"But I saw-"

She bit her tongue, eyes darting away.

"Sacha look at me."

She obeyed, and let herself drown in the cobalt stare.

"You didn't kill anyone. It was just another nightmare."

The strength and the gentleness she read in his gaze brought more tears to her eyes. She swallowed them back, for him. Derek watched her face carefully, before he let his hands down her arms, and winked.

"Please don't read too much into this, but I should have listened to you about this tunnel."

Sacha snivelled. Her timid smile reassured him.

"Let's avoid dark entrances in the near future, then."

Chapter 26

Everything hurt, Elwyn realized. His back, his legs, his head, every part of his body yanked in pain. He feared he would start screaming aloud if he dared to move a lash. All in all, nothing really different compared to the past few days... Except maybe that his mind was crystal clear, instead of fuzzy. Yes, he remembered every single minute, from the moment he had called on powers he didn't even know he possessed to the spike piercing his stomach.

He rubbed the spot tentatively but took off his hand in the same movement with a loud groan. Come to think of it, the pain was awfully different compared to the past few days, about a thousand times different.

Elwyn carefully propped his back against the wall, panting and hissing. A squeak objected to his efforts, immediately followed by the rush of claws on stone.

"I wish I could weasel my way out as you do... Ow..."

The rat didn't bother to answer. Elwyn sighed.

He remembered everything; yet some parts of Fillin's spitting, he wished he could forget. Sacha was coming for him. She shouldn't. He couldn't begin to imagine what Wolfryth wanted from his sister, but she had to stay away. Nothing was more important than that.

"Please Sacha, for once in your life, don't rescue me..."

oOo

"Do you remember him?"

Surprised, Derek looked up to the woman cringing against the wall some feet away from him. They never brought up the topic of their dead parents, her mother and his father. In fact, before they started on this journey together, they had rarely exchanged more than ten words at a time, their sporadic attempts at conversation generally ending with one of them storming out.

She did not sound annoyed or angry now. Derek looked away, scratching the ground with the heel of his boot silently.

"My mother smelt of roses. Father says she used to sing ballads to lull us to sleep, but I remember only the roses."

Glancing at her, Derek noticed she had circled her knees with her arms, and pressed her cheek on the cradle, her favourite position lately. It made her look small, and fragile; approachable. It stirred something inside him, a need to protect and soothe, somehow deeper than the longing, or was that a part of it?

"Is that why you favour that scent? The roses?"

The subtle perfume always floated around her in Haven. Even here, after days of doubtful commodities, sleeping in a hayloft and a forced, fully-clothed bath in a muddy pond, he could still smell the roses when he leaned closer.

"I think so. Do you want some water?"

Derek shook his head. The abrupt change of topic was as unsettling as her choice of conversation in the first place. Was she shocked that he noticed her perfume? Happy? Unconcerned? Anyway, he was glad she changed the subject. He really didn't want to talk about his father. At the same time, he needed her to understand. The words were out before Derek even realized he was speaking.

"It still pains my mother to talk about him. And Geraint never really says anything, except that he was a great king and a good man."

"You look very much like him."

Derek chocked on his breath and coughed. She couldn't possibly know that. His mother had said so, once, after he had presented her with a small bottle of perfume he had found in the low-town market. But Sacha couldn't know what his father looked like. How he carried himself. How he fought. How he died...

She claimed she had seen his death. He didn't want to know. William Pendragon was dead, murdered by an evil man, and it was enough. She said she had lived it; maybe she had. It would mean her powers were increasing, this strange place acting like a magical reflector or something akin. Or it meant the threat was greater than they both imagined...

Derek fidgeted uncomfortably. Her serious stare caressed his face, yet he refused the eye contact. Talking to her seemed easy, all a sudden. Or at least, it was easier than letting her read in his gaze the path his thoughts were taking.

"Geraint is probably the closest thing I ever had to a father."

She considered his remark for a moment, then laughed. The pearl of gaiety chimed in the silence of stone, warming the air around them.

"What a horrible thought."

"I beg your pardon?"

The young man glowered. Had she coerced him to visit places of his soul he voluntarily ignored, only to mock him? It would be... exactly like her; the former her. The one she was back in Haven, when they disregarded each other; the one she was, well... before.

Derek returned his attention to Sacha, brows knitted.

"... Not what I meant. I have enough with looking after Elwyn and Sebastian. I have no wish to include you in my list of brothers."

"Sebastian is your cousin, not your brother." Derek corrected her out of habit "And last time I checked, you were hitting Elwyn on the head with his own socks. It is a strange way to look after him."

"He was refusing to listen to me."

The figurative cloud above his head evaporated and Derek grinned. The conversation was turning into their usual bantering, and perhaps he was more comfortable with that, after all.

"I didn't listen to you about the tunnel, either."

Among other things.

"Does it mean you want me to hit you with socks?"

She managed to remain absolutely serious despite the silliness of her question. The ghost of a smile haunted her lips. Derek was nearly tempted to search their pack for some, just to see if she would.

"Wouldn't you like it..."

Her mouth twitched when she laughed and Derek found himself unable to look elsewhere but at the soft curve of her mouth. After a moment, he succeeded in glancing up into her eyes. Jade danced in mischief. He cleared his throat, vaguely embarrassed to have been caught staring.

"We'll stay here for a little while. I will take the first watch. You should take some rest."

The husk in his voice made him shift uncomfortably. Sacha jerked up, muffling a yawn.

"I'll do it. I fear we will need your skills more than mine in here."

Her voice sounded uncertain, teasing gone. Derek wondered if she was afraid to have more nightmares. He bowed his head and moved to rest with his legs between her and the empty space in front of her.

"Wake me up when you are tired."

He suspected she would not obey. But it felt the right thing to say when she nodded firmly and smiled at him. He lov-... He liked her smile.

oOo

"But he tried to kill me!"

Unimpressed by the shrillness in his daughter's voice, Wolfryth continued eating.

"Yes. Hadn't I forbidden you to see him again? Maybe next time you will obey."

Fillin stamped her foot.

"But father-"

"I told you, Elwyn has his utility. When I have what I want, I'll get rid of him. Not sooner."

The blonde huffed.

"Yes, yes, I know, the blood of the Dragon unleashes a source of immense power. Well, I don't care! Elwyn attacked me and I want him punished!"

His fork slammed back onto the table.

"Enough! You're immature and impatient, which is exactly why I do not teach you magic. Now leave me."

The blonde pulled on her hair angrily. This was so unfair! What Elwyn had done was unforgiveable. He had tried to KILL her! After all she had done for him! She had tended to him despite her father's reluctance. She had befriended him and granted him an opportunity to share his knowledge! He wasn't even that good at teaching, but she bore it! And he was a terrible kisser. This horrible ungrateful disgusting *being* had tried to hurt her! And her father implied that it was her fault?!

Fillin's lips pursed in a thin line of anger. Well, they'd see. No one assaulted her and got away with it. Her father could have Derek Pendragon to play with, for all she cared. The Pendragon wasn't coming alone. She was going to punish Elwyn by taking what he cared about the most - his darling little sister.

oOo

She had never noticed how unsettling it was, not to know what part of the day it was. Day, night, it was all the same lost deep inside the mountain, and her brain buzzed, trying to get a grip on an impossible time frame. In the surreal light pouring from the rock, they had invented their own time frames: walk, rest, walk, rest. The lack of structure apparently didn't bother her companion, as Derek had dozed off as soon as he had closed his eyes, or so it seemed.

Sacha lost her battle against yet another yawn and shook her head to clear it. She had nothing to distract herself. Her fingers itched for something to do. She twisted her neck again, wincing when it cracked. If only she could focus on something - what awaited them once they found their way through the rocky maze, Elwyn, the source of the powerful magic affecting them; anything other than her dreams, or Derek. The dreams transformed her nerves into a tight ball lodged in her throat, suffocating. As for the sleeping man by her side...

He did nothing more than tease and stare. But those glances dispersed dandelion's seeds in her stomach to make her feel... soft. It intrigued and embarrassed her at the same time.

"I don't know what to do..."

"About what?"

Red crept up her neck to warm her cheeks.

"Nothing!"

Derek straightened up.

"It didn't sound like nothing. What's the matter?"

Embarrassment threatened to reduce her to a babbling pool of heated honey at his feet. She lied cheekily.

"My hair. It is tangled and I hate it, but I don't know what to do about it."

If he found her vain or shallow, then so be it. She hadn't really asked what he thought when he fixed on her lips like they were some mouth-watering (but forbidden) fruit, had she? Derek's eyebrows shot up, before he nodded.

"I think I may… Yes."

He patted his pockets, and pulled out her holly wood comb.

"Here."

Her hand trembled slightly when she picked it up.

"I'm sorry, I know it's ridiculous."

Derek rubbed his chin with a frown, watching absently as she started untangling the messy black strands.

"I think I can understand."

The two-day stubble shadowed his jaws and cheeks. He looked older, stronger, almost dangerous… The dandelion seeds were now dancing above her belt with hundreds of butterflies.

"You look different with a beard."

"Different good or different bad?"

She hesitated. His smirk invited more butterflies to join the circle.

"So there's something you like about me after all."

The blue stare sparkled with amusement. Sacha twitched her nose.

"I have yet to make up my mind."

Derek snorted, his glare balancing between "*I don't believe a word of it*" and "*you're not funny.*"

"We should go."

Sacha pushed onto her feet at once. The prince whipped his opened hand on his thigh before he secured their bag on his shoulder with an exaggerated pull and started toward the crossing once more.

oOo

The mirror turned a lifeless black. Wolfryth jumped back with a yowl.

"No!"

The fire belched forth white-hot flames, crushed down by a fiery, yet non-existent wind. A thin line appeared on the dark surface, almost as gleaming, and snaked up with the softest whisper; with every harried breath the sorcerer took, the line split in two, three, four, five-branched stars until it covered the entire once-silver area. Then the mirror cracked and fell into dust at the man's feet

Wolfryth took another step back to avoid being touched by the ashes. The spell had rebounded once more. He didn't understand. Only a minute before it had worked, distilling his own souvenir into the Seer's troubled mind, and now…

He snatched a goblet of wine nearby and gulped it down. For the first time in years, he tasted fear.

Chapter 27

Elwyn recognized the scenery.

He was standing in a field behind Haven castle, which sloped gently toward the seashore. They used to horserace each other along the small path to the water; he never won, with Derek and Sacha always competing for the lead.

The ocean's scent tingled his nose. He breathed in deeply, eyes wide open to savour the glorious day. Sacha was walking swiftly toward him on the beach. She wore breeches and a shirt that was too large for her. The wind had messed up her hair. Even in the distance, he noticed the signs of exhaustion on her face and her posture.

He started to walk in her direction and tripped. The ground bit harder than it should have. When Elwyn looked up, a second silhouette had appeared by Sacha's side. The large red cape swirled around her without slowing her down. Elwyn tried to stand. A yank brought him down again. Light dimmed around him. The sand under his hands gave way to a patchwork of stones. The sun was sinking behind his sister and Derek.

"Sacha... No, don't come here!"

The young woman lifted her head and beamed at him, breaking into a run. He yelled again at the top of his lungs.

oOo

Sweat glided down his neck, the salty moisture burning his skin. God, he was tired.

Derek ran one hand below his collar and winced. How could his fingers feel so hot when his breath came out in cloudy rasps? When he forced his lungs to work, the air he took in was painfully cool. Breathing was painful.

He extended his arms to support himself on the walls, nearly losing his balance when his hands missed their goal, stepping sideways to reach the rock. He would have sworn the middle tunnel was small when they took it. Now, his fingers barely brushed the gleaming stone.

With a quick glance above his shoulder to make sure Sacha was oblivious to his misstep, the prince took in another gulp of air. Pressure built around his chest, far too quickly. His vision narrowed on some very bright point at the other end of the tunnel. He stepped forward, ignoring the riot in his stomach. Sacha's light footstep in his back echoed like a thunderstorm in his head.

"Derek?"

The nausea attacked his throat when he turned his head to acknowledge her call. Derek forced himself to straighten up, praying he didn't faint like he had in the forest. The shivers were the same torture in his back.

"Everything's fine. Stay behind me."

At least this time, everything had the clarity of crystal, instead of the fuzzy glaze he couldn't resist in the morning. He made out each dimple and needle in the rock face when he touched it. He noticed the smallest irregularities under his feet when he walked. The freshness of the air on his face amazed him in this underground world.

The light in front of them changed, a minute ago just a flicker and now a straight line, broad as his thumb, maybe broader; several inches wide, really.

"Derek we should go back and take the left branch. I-"

Derek grabbed his companion's hand to unclench her fingers from his shirt.

oOo

"Take it."

The king had one knee on the ground, his formerly lustrous armour stained with dried blood and mud. The noon sun was spreading his formidable mark on the crushed grass. The battle had started before dawn, and it was lost already. The shriek of metal against metal continued to bristle in the air, but the moans of the wounded buried it more and more.

"Sire, I can't. This..."

"Take it Caid, and leave. You know what to do."

Light mirrored on the blade the king was holding upright against his thigh, his tired hand still gripping the golden hilt. The king brushed dust from his face with the crook of his arms, grunting when the motion straightened his shoulder. Caid noticed his arm rested against his side with an angle. His duty was to obey, but to leave his king without a weapon, at the mercy of traitors to his crown, traitors of his blood...

"I want you to take my sword, and fulfill your duty. You swore on the Dragon's Throne to obey."

"My lord..."

King Derek grabbed the offered forearm and stood with difficulty.

"I love Morgan, Caid, God only knows how much. But your son betrayed his vows and for this I will confront him. But I cannot risk he gets this sword. He is unworthy of Caer Lon and of its secrets; please, go."

The knight presented his hands, palms up. The blade bit into the leather of his gloves when the king handed it to him. It weighed more than he imagined. Both men's faces reflected on the two inches of polished steel - the faces of soldiers who had fought one too many battles; men who had given up a lot for their convictions and had now to sacrifice what remained.

The king landed a heavy hand on his captain's shoulder.

"I am sorry, Caid. For Morgan. And for Eileen."

The dreaded name yanked the man off his thoughts. He closed his hands on the sword, and bowed.

"I will honor my word, my king. No one but the rightful High King will find the sword, or fetch it again."

oOo

Derek backed against the opposite wall. He resisted the urge to bend his knees and sit. If he let himself down to the ground now, he was not sure he would be able to ever get up again. Sacha put one arm around his back as he bent forward to breathe, brushing his shoulder. He panted, "I… really… wish… you would… stop doing that."

She took off her hand immediately. Derek managed to crack a smile. His legs trembled under him but he held on.

"No, I meant… The visions…" he paused to straighten up, heaving out a breath "A warning would be… pleasant next time."

"What did you see?"

Air found its way into his lungs, blissfully.

"You know what. Caid took… the High King's sword. To hide it."

Her hand found his arm again, urgent this time, instead of comforting.

"Derek, let's backtrack to the crossing."

Worry modulated her voice like dissonance in a melody. Her fingers trailed above his elbow, hooking around it and refusing to free him. A few days ago, she would have snorted and make some sassy comment about stubbornness or idiocy, giving him the cold shoulder. Now, her body language simply caressed his ego, softly inviting him to reconsider his choice.

The emptiness in front of him scintillated, calling Derek's attention away from the tempting lady by his side.

"I want to know where that light comes from. You stay here."

Her grip on him hardened.

"Oh, no, this is out of question. Last time I let you go by yourself, the ceiling nearly fell on our heads. I'm coming with you."

Derek shrugged and stepped forward. The tunnel curved into an opening, not wider than ten feet squared. The gentle slope changed drastically in the middle of the chamber to rise in a spiral around a massive boulder, the flattened sides of which were reminiscent of a roughly cut cube. And in the center of the cube probed one foot of unpolished metal, ended by a cross: a sword, encased within the rock, forgotten under the dust of centuries.

"Derek, wait!"

He wasn't listening anymore. Sacha's image blurred into some vaporous form before brightness swallowed her. Light radiated from walls and the ground alike to concentrate in the blade, pulsing like a human heart, its call irresistible. His own was answering every beat, recognizing the ancient rhythm.

The golden hilt of the sword was large enough to fit a giant's hands, the pommel encrusted with topazes, diamonds and amethysts. The closer Derek came, the more the gemstones gleamed. The gold brightened. The double-edged blade cleared until it retrieved its mortal silvery glint. After God knew how many years lost in a cave, the metal looked still sharp, deadly.

Derek stretched his left hand to touch it. Sacha gasped.

"Derek, oh my God!"

He looked down, not fully understanding why she cried. The bandage around his hand was soaked with blood. Red drops were plopping on the rock, and that was where the beat came from. Derek tried to escape her attempt to grab him and reach the sword, but she circled his waist with both arms and put all her weight in one desperate pull.

'Narijt drole Forra. Akilten emen Forra arkanic Drakor kiomlot.'

The strange words bang in his head, the language foreign, and yet so familiar. One step was all it would take to close his fist around the hilt and pull. Derek shifted sideways, too strong for Sacha to stop but she refused to budge. His motion brought her down, her knees hitting the stone.

"Derek…"

Tears wet the emerald eyes pleading with him, delicate falling pearls which diluted the blood on the back of his hand. Suddenly, her face pressed against his palm; he received its contours. He brushed hair and tears away from it.

"You're crying…"

The caress nearly overwhelmed him when relief illuminated her smile.

Sacha pushed onto her feet and forced him to pivot so that his back was to the altar, surprised that he obeyed without a protest. Her arm secured around his shoulders, an anchor in his chaos. Away from the aggressive light, the pulsing in his head reduced to a headache, the boil in his veins more bearable by the minute.

Derek squeezed her hand.

"I'm okay. Let's get out of here."

oOo

Fillin tossed a strand of blond hair above her shoulder before she turned another page. The only book her father had allowed her to study contained nothing but stupid spells to favor a good rest, cure a cough or keep rodents away from the pantry.

She clasped her tongue impatiently. She needed something other than old wives' remedies for domestic problems! She wanted magic that was efficient against an enemy, a way to entrap the stupid girl and even take away her powers.

Fillin beamed to herself. Oh, yes, that would be so perfect... She was going to disrobe Elwyn's beloved sister of her magic all by herself, and if it worked properly, Elwyn himself would be next. She nearly clapped her hands in pleasure. Yes, it was an excellent idea.

Ambushing the seer could not be that difficult, she had perused spells able to exterminate vermin for hours in that stupid book. This page, thinking of it, displayed how to cast some invisible glue board; it was written that it worked like a spider web, really. Once the fly was caught, it couldn't escape until the board was obviated. Her lopsided grin matched the dancing flame in her bronze eyes. Who cared if one little dragonfly never flew again...?

No, the how and where were more of a challenge.

The blonde pushed onto her feet to glimpse the empty corridor. Her father was still shut down in the library, deeply involved into whatever magic he felt was more important than teaching his "impatient and immature" daughter. Fillin snorted. She flattered herself to be impervious to insults. She was eager to learn, not impatient. What her father called immaturity, she called inexperience. And she was a quick student. She had proven so many times.

She also had good hearing and an even better memory. Although the Great Wolfryth took care to close himself off to perform the Dark Arts, little did he know about how thin the panels were near the chimneys of adjacent rooms. Fillin chuckled. The spells to break into one's mind would sure be useful one day, but far less than the one she had heard several weeks ago, when his father had stolen the secret of this despicable place from the priest of those druids.

Three words would serve her needs. Three little words, spoke loud with a clear voice, looking at the seer directly in the eye. *"Pantswa nekem maorenia."*

Closing the door behind her, Fillin tiptoed to the stairs leading to the caves, book in hand. There was only one thing the pair would seek before confronting her father. If she set her trap near Elwyn's cell, she was sure to catch her prey.

Chapter 28

The sunset fringed the line of clouds with yellow and red copper, as the solar disk disappeared behind the horizon. On the left, the sea mirrored delicate pink and gold. On the right, the storm was nearly upon them, straining the sky with dim grey and heavy marks.

The duke looked for a gush of wind, the distinctive fresh smell that always came before the rain. The hush was unsettling; no thunder rolled, far away in the heart of the coming tempest. The wind had not risen yet. The banners pooled sadly, with the dark bear, Pemfro's protector, sleeping wrapped around the mast.

Geraint lowered his gaze to the now empty courtyard. The merchants had packed their goods, and even the last onlookers were deserting the place, quietly going home. A man, fully armed, caught his captain's short nod, and lifted his arm in return. The order was forwarded to another guard, until a tired squeal broke the silence.

A loud *bonk* bounced on the inner walls when the beam secured into place. The sentinel hurried through the courtyard, en route to the other posterns. Geraint turned away from his position on the crenels. For the first time in fifteen years, Haven would close its doors for the night.

He wished he could protect his children as easily as his city. For the thousandth time in three days, he wondered where they were, and if they had found a shelter for the night. He could only pray they were safe.

The mid-aged man resisted the urge to massage his temples, and shot one last glance to the quieting courtyard below him, readying for his first guard inspection in years. The small silhouette that appeared in front of him startled him.

"Lady Sonia, what you doing here?"

The young woman bowed her head gracefully, not at all bothered by his arch welcome.

"I was looking for you, Sir Geraint. I have a favour to ask."

The duke reciprocated the salute. He had heard the queen had met with her the previous afternoon, though Ylianor had been very discreet about the encounter. Was that so-called request anything related to their conversation?

"Please do ask, Lady Sonia."

She smiled sweetly as he offered his arm to escort her off the walls.

"I would like to send word to my mother, my lord, and wondered if I could borrow one of your doves."

"Of course. Garrett will-"

"I was hoping to send my message tonight, my lord."

He recognized the smile. Sacha mustered the same, when she wanted to charm her dear old father into agreeing to some fantastic indulgence she hadn't or couldn't dragoon out of her brother. Geraint raised an eyebrow to mask his amusement at the display.

"The bird cage is closed for the night."

Sonia answered with the faintest flutter of lashes, her intelligent brown eyes scrutinizing his face. He felt too old for these games.

"Lady Sonia, I am sorry, but you will have to wait for Garret to open the cage tomorrow."

Her hand dug into his forearm briefly, as he helped through the low passage leading the stairs.

"I'm afraid I have to insist, Sir Geraint."

The sweet grin was gone, as well as the flirty ways. The older man held the darker stare without blinking.

"Really. And why is that, pray tell?"

"I-" She choked on the first syllable and clasped her mouth shut instantly, finally breaking the eye contact.

"I need my mother's advice."

The words bumped against each other in her haste to have them out. "On private matters."

Sonia lifted her gaze back to his defiantly. Her discomfort hadn't lasted very long. Did Sonia's meeting with the queen regard these "private matters" as well? For all he knew, Sonia had barely communicated with her mother in the last year; thus why now?

What did she discuss with Ylianor that required some advice? It had to be related to Derek, in some way. Derek, whom everybody, Sonia included, was supposed to think was scouting the northern border.

The brunette's face revealed nothing except her obvious dissatisfaction at being denied, or even questioned. She would not disclose anything more to him than she had to the queen. Geraint made a mental note to inquire about their meeting. In the meantime, he presented his best paternal grin to the young woman at his arm.

"Do not trouble yourself. I am convinced the Lady Ylianor will answer any of your questions until you get word from your mother. Tomorrow."

The glance she shot him froze the air in the staircase. Geraint kept his smirk in place. The bottom of the steps offered the perfect pretext to excuse himself. He had spent enough time on a battlefield to know when a strategic retreat was best; or when additional information was required before starting a war.

oOo

The light knock on the door pulled Sebastian out his sleepy reverie. The half-drawn curtains made it hard to tell exactly what time it was, but a growl low in his stomach dinner time was close enough.

"Come in. Ah, Agnes..."

He received a small smile in return for his greeting, while the servant installed her tray on the nightstand near him before helping him up. The smell of food provoked another reprise from his stomach, making him blush slightly, as he perused the mashed potatoes and glazed ham. At least Jeffrey seemed to think he had had enough of chicken soup.

The young man doubted the physician's judgement with the first bit. His jaw cracked painfully when he took in the first forkful. Swallowing also cost him. He paused before taking another one, allowing the load that had fallen into his stomach to settle down.

Agnes busied herself with the jug, realigning his medicine unnecessarily, or ruffling a cushion on a seat near the chimney. He watched her doings for a few minutes, before deciding her nerves were more annoying than funny.

"Agnes, can you just... Just sit down, please."

Doe eyes widened on her face briefly before they fell to the floor. She curtsied and moved to a corner to sit on a stool to wait. Sebastian sighed and cut another piece of ham, smaller this time, hoping that coating it with mash would help it down. Eating without real company was dull, especially when chewing hurt this much.

Another visitor took his attention away from his plate.

"Good evening, Sebastian."

"Good evening, Uncle. You look tired."

Geraint laughed, and the grin washed away some of the worries weighting his features.

"Thank you. You don't look that fresh yourself. How's your dinner?"

Sebastian wrinkled his nose and pushed the rest of his food away.

"Please never tell Elwyn and Derek I said this, but chicken soup has its perks."

The mention of his two best friends dimmed the light atmosphere their bantering had brought about. Geraint took the tray away to the main table and put a small scroll on his nephew's lap. Sebastian didn't grab it immediately, watching his elder walk around the room instead. Finally, Geraint ceased his inspection and took the seat by the bed.

"It came in two days ago."

The young man picked up the missive; he recognized Derek's handwriting and went carefully through the enigmatic message.

Geraint stared at his nephew while he read. It was hard to say if the color on his cheeks came from bruises, or from eating properly. His shoulders were hunched, his back round against the pillows, and he read with the paper close to his chest to avoid lifting his arms up too much.

"So. Wolfryth."

The older man nodded.

"I fear so. Reports confirm his mercenaries are marching to the north too."

A small wrinkle marred Sebastian's forehead.

"It's more complicated than that, isn't it? They could have killed us all, or simply waited in the woods until we left. We would never have found them. Those men moved and fought like animals."

A shiver crumbled up his spine at the memory. Geraint waited for his nephew to go on.

"He used us as a bait, to get Derek. He hoped you sent your best men after us. You didn't, but the fool jumped in nonetheless. God, when will he learn?!"

Agitation took its toll and Sebastian fell back in his cushions, exhausted and furious at his friend for being so careless, and at himself for being weak. If only he had been conscious, he would have convinced his best friend not to go. He would have seen through his cousin's torturous schemes and stopped her beforehand. He would have... Sebastian turned his head toward his uncle.

"Do you think Wolfryth knows Derek is to enter Camelot's territory?"

"Maybe not yet. We can only hope."

"How long can we keep up the pretense?"

Geraint pushed onto his feet to go to the window and stared at the courtyard below.

"A day, two at most. I ordered the doors to be closed for the night."

"We need a diversion."

Sebastian pushed his head back into his pillow, closing his eyes for an instant.

"Recall your men from the north. And declare war on Wolfryth, on Derek's behalf."

A yelp and a crash echoed Geraint's own gasp. Both men had forgotten the maid, who fell on her knees to pick up the pieces of the tray she had silently gathered from the table. Geraint waved his hand and she hurried out.

"Are you serious?"

"Well, we want Wolfryth's attention away from Camelot's border."

"What will we do then? We won't stand a chance if he attacks us with magic."

Sebastian met his uncle's clear eyes with dark, serious ones.

"I know. But do we have a choice?"

Geraint shook his head.

"You are asking me to risk the life of hundreds of people to save only one."

"Not one man, Sir Geraint. All of us."

Ylianor signalled Sebastian not to move, but for once accepted Geraint's bow of deference with a short nod.

"I have some information I must share with you."

She settled very straight on the chair the duke had deserted.

"Several things were related to me yesterday afternoon."

Geraint furrowed his brows slightly, not daring interrupting the queen.

"I have still to decide which part is true and which part is pure superstition. However, I was told only Derek can stop this madman from bringing more damages upon the kingdom, and this I believe."

She turned to the duke with a tired expression on her graceful face.

"I won't ask for your assistance as my vassal. I am not your queen anymore. I am asking for a friend's help, as my husband did fifteen years ago."

Sebastian watched the battle on his uncle's face. He knew what answer he would have given, he already had, but he was young and inexperienced. He hadn't the weight of a duchy on his shoulders, or to balance lives against honour. Suddenly, he regretted his suggestion. Surely there was another way. They could continue to act as if Derek were among them, and... And believe in miracles.

"And a friend's help you will receive, Madam. I will reunite the council tomorrow."

"Thank you."

The duke bowed over the offered hand, and left.

Sebastian noticed for the first time the shaking on the lady's hands when she picked up the book he had abandoned earlier in the afternoon, too drowsy to read.

"*The Odyssey*... I must say Derek always preferred *The Iliad*. The fighting suited him better than the tale of waiting and patience."

Sebastian smiled as Ylianor caressed the cover gently.

"I was about to start with Book 21."

"Hmm, Penelope's last challenge to the lordly wooers. Do you want me to read for you?"

"Would you?"

Ylianor grinned at the boyish glint in the young man's stare and ruffled through the pages until she found the delicate lace of the bookmark.

"*And then Athena, the goddess with the bright eyes, inspired the daughter of Icarius, the wise Penelope, to present the wooers with the gray iron and the bow in the halls of Odysseus, weapons of her challenge and carriers of death.*"

Sebastian backed in the pillows to listen, eyelids half-closed. It seemed everything talked about bows and arrows lately. He played with a fold in the sheets.

"Thank you for staying, Lady Ylianor."

Ylianor offered a warm smile and read on, the book open on her lap.

Chapter 29

By the time they reached the crossing, Derek felt stronger on his legs; or at least he was steady enough to stagger into the main corridor and lurch over to the wall without Sacha's help. The young woman searched their bag for the shirt she had already torn apart, handing him a sugar cane in passing. He opened his mouth but the glare she shot him at the same time made him gulp back any form of protest about the food, or the tending.

Derek scarcely picked at his treat while she untied the ruined dressing from his left hand to replace it. She poured water on the wound to wash away the blood with another daring look and he was relieved to see the flesh was healing, if still raw.

"I don't know how it reopened. I didn't hurt my hand. I think."

He recalled testing the sharpness of the strange crystals on the rock face and bearing on the roughly cut altar for leverage, nothing major. Derek nibbled at the sweet more out of habit than anything else. He used to heal quicker than that. The sugar made him thirsty.

Sacha didn't answer, paying more attention than strictly necessary to put away the soiled fabric and arranging their goods. Derek took a swig, leaning back against the wall.

"Do you understand what happened?"

The trouble was gone' that crystalline cocoon around him so everything seemed to move slowly. It had passed, just like it had in the forest. Sacha shook her head, still avoiding his stare. Derek waited.

"What this place does to you, it scares me to death."

Not really the answer he would have liked to hear, especially when a good part of him squirmed in agreement. Her green eyes finally met his, blocking the wheels turning in his head.

"Derek... The sword is yours. It's your birthright. It calls for your blood and-"

The blue eyes on her widened then narrowed, almost silver in eagerness. She felt him jitter under her hand, muscles tensing to get up and go retrieve what was his. Sacha gripped his forearm harder.

"You must not take it. Derek, it's important. Please, this one time, listen to me. Don't go for that sword. The Source must remain sealed."

She hammered the last words, eyes blazing. She couldn't explain why, she just knew. She was ready to beg him if she had to. The strange words in a language she didn't speak were branded in her mind.

Narijt drole Forra. Akilten emen Forra arkanic Drakor kiomlot... The Source is revealed. The Source shall be unsealed by the Dragon's blood revealed. The sword was made for him; it was his, by all means. Yet, its time had not come yet, and if he took it... She had seen the world shrunken into blackness.

Derek swallowed. Her face was too serious. No smile brightened her pale eyes and damned him if he didn't understand why. Suddenly, he wanted everything to go back to normal, back to the way they were, before they embarked together on this mad journey and he began to be so aware of her; more than he already was, anyway.

"Now you sound like a true prophetess."

Her stare darkened drastically.

"Your wit is returning so I take it you are strong enough to walk?"

The ice in her voice sliced through the pleasure of teasing her. Derek groaned internally. He should have wished for normality minus the constant disdain. Her defiant stare accompanied him as he pushed away from the wall, testing his legs.

"So it seems-"

A long screech interrupted him. Derek flashed his sword at once. The noise flew past them, reverberating on the rock which glow flickered softly.

Derek didn't wait for the noise to cease and started down the corridor, gesturing to Sacha to follow. When she failed to obey, he grasped her arm harder, ushering her up. He walked briskly, stopping every few steps to crush against the wall, covering them from the potential enemy waiting ahead. The ground became rougher the further they went. Soon she had the feeling of stepping onto fragile needles, which broke under her boots. One particular crack made her wince; it reminded her of the sound of bones crumbling into dust, but she refused to look down at her feet.

The unnatural cry seemed to go on forever then it finally stopped. Derek pressed against the wall once more. She nestled against his back.

"What was that?"

"Shush."

For once, she obeyed, her arms wrapping around his waist. In the renewed silence, their hard breathing echoed indefinitely against the now glooming walls . Protecting her with one arm - or maybe preventing her from moving forward before he ordered her to do so - Derek peered at the empty space in front of him.

The corridor ended abruptly, the rock cut into a hard staircase. From the bottom, he could merely see a platform about two or three hundred steps above, then more steps. The walls on each side were flat, without a turn or a curve to hide and take a safe rest. A long climb, completely devoid of cover - the perfect trap. Instinct screamed inside Derek's head to backtrack and forget it all: Caer Lon, Elwyn; run back to the waterfall, dive and run some more. He breathed in deeply.

Sacha's murmur almost made him jump out of his skin.

"Are we going up?"

Derek swallowed his fear and nodded before he secured his grip around the hilt of his sword.

oOo

Elwyn eyed the blonde lurking outside of his cage, suspicious. She had been turning around in circles for God knew how long. Her concentrated look could only mean trouble. He snorted, ready to harangue her, when suddenly the stone started screaming.

The sound poured silver liquid in his bones, exquisitely cold until it caught fire and threatened to burn him into ashes.

"What are you do- AAaaarghh! Stop it, stop!"

Elwyn tumbled down to the floor like a rag doll, twisting while the magic Fillin had unleashed gnawed at his magical link with Earth, biting, chewing, trying to tear it apart with teeth not sharp enough for a clean cut. He screamed and screamed for what seemed an eternity, and then the agonizing ripping stopped.

Exhausted, he toiled to push up on one elbow, just long enough to see Fillin licking her lips with a smug on her face which reminded him of an animal ready to feast. Elwyn rolled on his back, and let darkness engulfed him.

oOo

Her heart was trying to punch its way out of her chest and the feeling was excruciating. Every breath she took added pressure to her stomach. The lack of oxygen made her dizzy. Or it was the terror of hearing that terrible howl again. Derek squeezed her hand lightly.

"We're nearly there, Sacha, just another flight of steps."

She had no idea what he meant. The stairs in front of her nose went on forever. She could barely breathe. Her lungs felt as if they had been severed and the cut splashed with salt. The light from the walls was nearly a souvenir. She couldn't make out the tunnel they came from, let alone the top of her current nightmare. Sacha sucked in air with difficulty and forced her legs to obey, putting one foot on the next uneven step and pushing up. Then another. And another. Pull, press, push. And again. Her knees threatened to break.

Her foot slipped on a particularly high step. Her back protested when she twisted to keep her balance, only ceasing its grouching when Derek put one arm around her to help her onto a surface which seemed wider than the others. She offered a smile though she feared it might look like a grimace. The hole inside her was still growing, wider by the minute; so painful. Then it disappeared.

Sacha leaned against the wall, breathing through her open mouth, uncaring how unladylike it might look.

"Water?" asked Derek.

To her satisfaction, he too sounded a little breathless. She took the jug, finding it uncomfortably light in her hand. She restrained herself to a small sip, barely enough when her throat was so parched...

"I think..." he breathed in deeply to settle his voice "I don't like stairs."

She chuckled and whined instantly as her abdomen squeezed painfully in the effort. Sacha swallowed her complaint, awfully conscious that Derek had put away the water without drinking when he was probably just as thirsty as she was. Keeping her head up sucked at her strength, dragging her toward the abyss.

"We'll have to make you exercise more when we get home..."

In the semi-darkness, she nearly missed the smirk flashing in his stare. Sacha pulled a face at him; the short pause had steadied her sufficiently that she could look up. She saw nothing but the shadows of uneven shapes cut into the dark rock.

"How long do you think we need to climb?"

"I counted 284 so far, but I think I missed a couple."

Sweet Lord, he had managed to keep tabs through the torture?

"... about a hundred feet, maybe more."

Sacha struggled to push off of the wall, unsure if he meant they had climbed that distance, or it was still to come.

"Elwyn will owe me for this, and I assure you he is going to pay every penny."

Derek hauled the bag higher up on his shoulder.

"Take a number."

They stared at each other for an instant before resuming their climb, silently sharing their thoughts. Both hoped Elwyn was all right and would be fit to go down the stairs after they found him. If they found him. Derek nodded with a lopsided grin, and gestured her to move first.

Her heart skipped a beat, strangely puffing with gratitude. In his own clumsy overprotective way, Derek had offered more than the initial help she asked for. Sacha stopped on the first step to turn. With the difference of height, their faces were nearly at the same level.

The hug took him by surprise, yet it ended before he could react.

"Thank you."

"My pleasu-"

Unwilling to hear what his ego had to say, Sacha silenced him with a kiss.

Surprised, he did not move until the soft pressure of her lips against his lightened. Then his free hand shot up to her hair to bring her closer, kissing her back passionately until her reserve melted. Sacha barely registered the sound of metal hitting the stone when he dropped his sword to press her against the wall as he abandoned her mouth to favour her neck and pressed devouring kisses just above her collar.

His tongue brushed on a particularly sensitive spot and her knees buckled. Derek steadied her somehow, pinning her harder to the stone with his lower body while his hands… Sacha refused to acknowledge what his hands were doing, except they were moving agonizingly slowly.

The danger they were in, the strange lights, the cavern, the sword, the magic which affected both of them, everything dissolved, pulsing in the back of her mind. She had never imagined that kissing him would turn into this ravaging fire that consumed her from within. She had pictured light brushes of her mouth, her inexperience blooming in hesitation and timidity, not such… hunger. The cold in her back contrasted with the heat blooming inside her, forcing some sense into her.

"Derek…"

She fought to push on his chest, when her fingers trembled to bring him closer.

"Derek… Derek, stop…"

This time he seemed to hear her plea and backed abruptly. She missed his body against hers instantly, her hips instinctively coming forward for more caresses. Her head fall against the wall, her cheeks burning, her ragged breathing matching his.

In the semi-darkness, Derek's dilated eyes burned with barely controlled emotions, his gaze fixed on her mouth, or maybe she was the one staring. Sacha forced her eyes away, embarrassed to feel so alive.

After a moment, the young man backed down another step and bent to grab his abandoned sword on the ground. Trouble perked under the mask of determination he was wearing again. He refused to look at her in the eye, so she took his arm.

"Derek I will not refuse you…"

She meant it. He was irritating and brave and bossy and honorable. She could not imagine a better man for her.

"You just did."

The impatient retort brought up a smile, instead of flaring her temper. She yearned to brush her lips on the small frown between his brows to smooth it, nearly did so.

"Because you have the worst timing ever."

Frustration bounced dangerously in the blue eyes now drilling into hers.

"You kissed me first."

Sacha laughed, determined not to let him have the last word.

"That you are better not to forget; my lord."

Derek shrugged and turned away, moving up the stairs again.

Chapter 30

The torch's flame flickered, bouncing on the gold lace sewn on Fillin's skirt. Elwyn crept away from the fence with his back to the wall, his gaze on his nemesis.

The noise of old paper being creased under bored fingers disturbed the silence of the dungeon. The blonde was seated on a stool in a corner, and fortunately didn't pay any attention to him. As far he was concerned, she could forget his very existence, and he would live perfectly happily for as long as her monster of a father would allow him to.

Elwyn pulled his knees to his chest, biting back a whimper when the position added pressure on his broken ribs. He preferred to keep his mouth shut. Whatever she did, it couldn't be a good thing for him, and it was better to make his presence as unnoticeable as possible.

The pain brought dozen of dark dots in front of his eyes; or were they fireflies dancing? He rubbed his eyes to chase the annoying glittering snow from them. The fireflies sparkled happily, brown and dark red. Each time he blinked, it seemed to be more of them. Elwyn pressed his fingers to his lids, hard. He didn't remember hitting his head in falling this time. Surely he had. In no way could insects fly to form square and diamond shapes. The small points in the air shone in straight lines, brighter at the nods, the same way cords linked together to form … a net.

Elwyn closed his eyes for good. Hallucinating nets of fireflies was a bit spooky, even for him. Sacha would tease him to no end. She always said he had too much imagination for his own good. Sacha…

oOo

The stone changed into the land surrounding the castle; in spring, it was covered with delicate patches of white and lilac she liked so much. She spent hours walking the land to bring back armfuls of heather grass, which she used to freshen her chambers and his.

Sure enough, she was whirling near the edge with her arms widely open to the wind, close to the abyss, so close... He called her name.

oOo

His hand tensed around the hilt of his sword helped him to think, Derek realized. Even if he could hear Sacha's light pants, and feel more than see her presence one step ahead of him, the cold contact eased the tingle urging him to grab her for more kisses. He surprised himself by running his tongue on his lower lip, teeth nipping at the flesh as if to bring her taste back into his mouth.

Surely he should say something. Not an apology, certainly not that; he didn't regret for a second kissing her back. She could not be so naive as to touch a man, embrace *him*, as she had and expect he would behave. Yet, he should really say something now.

He bit back a smile. Sacha and he kissed like they quarrelled: her passion against his willpower, until she allowed him to discover the tender, loving woman she also was. He wanted both. Derek tightened his grip on his weapon and heaved out a breath, half-rasp, half-jeer. Emotions had spiralled in her wonderful eyes; he wondered if her feelings mirrored his own. They would explore them happily later. For now, he had to focus on their mission.

"It's becoming darker the more we go up."

"Yes, I noticed."

Derek tempered his snap with a brush on her arm.

"Do you wish we use a candle?"

Her hair cascaded down her back as she shook her head, silk brushing his chest, distracting him.

"No, it's all right. At least the steps are smaller here."

Derek chastised himself internally. She noticed things to which he should have been paying attention. The steps were smaller, barely three inches high, if he had to guess. His boot bumped into the next.

"Sacha, the stairs are turning, I will take the lead, just step asid-"

She didn't give him enough time to finish the sentence before she disappeared in the spiral the staircase now formed. Derek rushed forward, taking the steps four at a time.

"Sacha!"

He caught a glimpse of her shadow when she entered another corridor. Derek lunged and grabbed her wrist before she escaped him again.

"Don't be foolish, we don't know what's ahead!"

"It's Elwyn, Derek. I hear him…"

She tried to free herself from the iron grip but Derek held tight.

"We'll find him, I promise."

The smile that blossomed on her lips was so adorable he couldn't do anything but answer it, releasing her forearm to link their fingers. Sacha used his distraction to untangle herself from his grasp and dashed off. Derek sprinted after her, cursing under his breath.

The corridor ended on another spiral staircase, except this one seemed made of cut stones bonded with mortar. In his haste, he put away the spider webs without wondering why the darkness had suddenly lifted so that he could actually see them. The screech of old metal in front of him made him move ever faster. It ate at him not to call after her at the top of his lungs. Was it another one of her visions? How could she outrun him after the exhausting climb? Idiotic, empty-headed little… the list of epithets unwound in his head.

Derek rushed through the fence he had heard shrieking open, the first of a long series of arches of stone and metal. Torches were suspended after metallic rings on the walls, lighting one after another the more they progressed up the passage. He didn't take time to notice when the last archway opened into a different room in which iron fences had replaced the stones on the sides.

"Derek no, stop!"

Her cry came too late. His next stride took him across something cold and sticky. His foot stayed glued to the ground whilst he wanted to move forward, the motion sending him rolling against the wall. His left wrist hit the stone violently and he yelped in pain.

"Derek!"

A chuckle answered Sacha's anguish, cold enough to freeze his blood.

"Oh, I would worry a bit more about yourself than him, if I were you. *Pantswa nekem maorenia!*"

A flash of silver whipped through space toward Sacha. She screamed, ducking her head instinctively with her face in her hands. Derek jerked to get free from the invisible net restraining him.

"Sacha!"

The holly wood comb in Sacha's hair lit up even before the silver lightning touched her. The bolt aiming at the dark-haired beauty quirked down, pooling around her like a halo. Sacha's eyes widened in terror, her mouth open in a mute cry. Derek pulled and tugged, desperate to reach her. The silver light darkened, then paled, taking the fantastic colors of a rainbow all at once. The halo hardened into a shell, waving like a soap bubble.

Their assailant gawped, holding one hand up in preparation to repeat the spell. Derek yanked once again, his fury climbing higher by the second. Behind her shield, Sacha seemed to shrink and quailed, slipping away from his reach. He was about to yell again, but a roar Derek recognized as Elwyn's stopped him.

"VANN JE HILSEN, SHER RELYOD!"

The silhouette in gold and blue hiccupped in a wet noise. Her malicious bronze eyes opened first in surprise and then into something Sacha would have sworn was fear, when the hand threatening her just a second before bumped into something solid.

The raven woman shivered uncontrollably as her own tears joined tips of water sprouting from the ground and the wall moss to surround her attacker. The woman's shape started to waver, losing its density in a whirlpool of fog and wind. Her pale hair spurted around her face and in an instant the only thing that was left of her was a puddle on the floor.

The net vanished. Derek jumped toward the young woman before him.

"You!"

The flames on the torches hissed angrily, spreading to lick the ceiling. Still protected by the iridescent bubble around her, Sacha saw a giant arm strike down. Derek crashed against the wall, knocked out. Within the second, his sword flew across the fence, straight to Elwyn. Her brother lifted his arms to protect himself.

"LEGI SKJOLD!"

The spell burst out of her mouth before she recognized the words. Droplets of metal rained on the floor with the noise of shattering glass when the sword exploded against a shield similar to hers. The large figure turned his golden stare on her instead of Elwyn.

"You won't defy me for long, young seer..."

Wolfryth snapped his teeth like the wild dog he looked like. The thin layer around her flinched and popped. Panicked, Sacha tried to move away but her back was already at the wall. Her throat squeezed painfully. She gasped for air, only meeting with agony. Darkness grew in front of her eyes. Her fingers clawed the space around her, unable to fight the shadows strangling her. Her head felt so light she dreamed about floating, exquisitely empty. Then all thoughts disappeared.

oOo

The young woman woke up in alarm, her breath laboured and her heart throbbing. Air hissed through her lips as she tried to calm down. Her throat cloyed disagreeably, hurting with every difficult heave.

Sacha wanted to push on her feet, and she realized she was lying on the floor. Standing asked too much of her, and she fell back on her backside with a little cry.

Her eyes adjusted to the dim light and she started noticing her surroundings. She crawled on her knees and hands, still unable to straighten up, and reached the facing wall and the body crouched against it.

Dried blood and dirt had formed a crust in the stubble on his jaw under her fingers. His left wrist was clutched to his chest at a bizarre angle. The bandage around it was ruined.

Sacha sat near the prisoner and touched his forehead gently. She felt pain, unable to tell if it was his or hers. Derek winced when she brushed the cut on his temple. His skin was cool under her fingers. Or maybe it was her who was too hot. She did not know. Sacha took her hand away, and nestled against him in the semi-darkness. Her head came to rest on his shoulder, as if it was too heavy for her alone to bear.

"I'm so sorry…"

Tears tingled in her eyes, too many to be contained, burning when they glided down her cheeks.

"You seem to say that a lot lately. Are you trying to make up for the last fifteen years?"

The quip was barely more than a whisper. Sacha straightened up and met serious blue eyes searching her face for any traces of injury. Finding none, Derek looked away and gave a pull to his bonds. A rattle answered his effort, but the chain did not budge.

"Now would be the perfect time for a trick or two, Sacha."

"I don't know any 'trick'. I…"

She bit her tongue before saying "I'm sorry" again. She slowly began to learn Derek used sarcasm like she used scowls and outburst of temper. He was baiting her so the despair of their situation did not crush down on her, or himself. Sacha leaned against his side again and he automatically brought his free arm around her. The contact comforted her.

"Where do you think Elwyn is?"

"Here!"

The voice came from the other side of the fence. Derek grunted when Sacha pushed on his shoulder to get up.

"Are you alright, Elwyn? How…?"

"I'm fine, I think. What about you?"

"Derek is wounded…"

"Am not."

She frowned at him and he glared back.

"I'm shackled to the wall, however, which is rather inconvenient."

The retort was strained with his usual arrogance. Sacha snorted but Elwyn laughed.

"Tell me about it. My former bedroom was far more pleasant, save for the company. So, what's the plan?"

The answer echoed into the semi-darkness.

"Awfully simple, magician. Pendragon brings me to the Source, or I kill you all."

Chapter 31

Wolfryth started on Elwyn.

Derek pulled Sacha to his chest, blinding her so she didn't see the tongues of fire darting at her twin brother. He couldn't conceal her from the screams though, and soon wished he too could hide from the screams. She jerked with every blow, every spell. Sometimes she whimpered even before Elwyn cried. Each burn, each whip, every mental torture Wolfryth inflicted to her brother, Sacha felt too. The horrible images the sorcerer drilled into her brother's mind - blood, death, monsters feasting on human flesh - she saw as well. She twisted and sobbed against Derek's chest, and the only thing he could do was looked at their suffering and bear it.

The display of cruelty would have been easier to understand if only the sorcerer had actually asked something. But the man was silent. Terrifying silent. The only noise the prince heard was the cracks of the torches and - his jaw clenched hard - bones.

An inhuman shriek tore the silence apart, and Elwyn's body went limp. The prince embraced the woman in his arms tighter, her face buried against his heart to muffle her cries of anguish. Her teary murmur took him by surprise.

"Take the comb, Derek, please… He must not find it."

His fingers brushed on the wood restraining her hair, the charm that had apparently protected her from the blonde's attack earlier, but would likely fail to spare her now.

"I'm next. Keep the comb with you. Please…"

"I won't let him touch you."

"Don't do anything; whatever he wants, he must not have it. He will kill us anyway."

The giant was already turning to the couple in the other cell. Derek nodded imperceptibly against her forehead, and the comb disappeared inside his clothing. Then he struggled to stand, shielding her from view. A roar of laugher welcomed the effort.

"You're just as ludicrous as your father… True to the knight's vow to protect the weak and the helpless… *Szarik*"

Sacha yelped in terror as she started slipping on the ground, pulled to her tormentor by some invisible cord. Derek lunged forward to seize her hand, but the bonds foiled his attempt. The shackles bit into his wrist. Derek almost hoped his wound would reopen, so the blood would oil his hand into freedom. He yanked twice at the handcuff, bringing up a laugh from Wolfryth.

The young woman was now kneeling at the giant's feet, prostrate. Her free hair flew over her shoulders to the ground, her arms loose by her sides. Derek growled in warning.

Wolfryth put two fingers under her chin to force her face up.

"What a pity to mar those angelic features." He cast a glance toward the chained prince. "Don't you think?"

"I forbid you to touch her!"

If he only had a weapon, a sword or even his dagger, he would throw it at the brute without hesitation. Derek fisted his hands, pulling desperately at his bonds. The sorcerer returned his attention to the woman at his feet, his fingers pressing hard into her cheeks.

"What do you say, seer? We are close already, after all those nights of sharing dreams."

Derek roared.

"Leave her alone! I'll kill you, I swear…"

"Snoeren!"

No sound came out when Derek bawled his frustration. He growled, the effort nearly tearing his throat apart and spat, "Let her go, now!"

Wolfryth twisted his head, the golden eyes a thin line of hatred. The sorcerer lifted one hand and the prince's shoulder cracked loudly. He gave a ferocious pull at his chains nonetheless, trying to reach for the immobile form of Sacha.

"Derek, don't."

Her order froze him into place instantly. Amazed, the young man saw Sacha slowly arise and brush off the sorcerer's hold with a backflip of her hand. Surely it was surprise that gave her the leverage. The top of her head didn't even reach the man's chin, and he was twice as large as she was.

When she spoke again, Derek barely recognized her voice in the deep cavernous tone.

"Your time is coming to an end, Wolfryth. You can't break Him; he is the Blood and the Source will obey to his command."

The giant took one step back, his scared face distorted with fury.

"The Source shall be mine."

"The Power obeys the Blood of the Dragon and only him."

"Enough!"

Wolfryth slapped her so hard Sacha fell on the floor again.

"Sacha!"

The weight in Derek's chest lifted partly when he saw her stir, stretching carefully her arm toward a still unconscious Elwyn. She reached her brother, first close enough to touch his arm then his chest, before she managed to push upright and take his head on her lap. Her fingers roamed over the ashen face, and Derek blinked in disbelief. Under the tender caress, Elwyn's bruises seemed to fade, the biggest marks shrinking to a copper flick before they vanished completely. He didn't know she had such magic within her. She probably didn't know either. Her eyes were dreamy, their focus very far from the body in her arms.

The prince rattled his chains to attract the sorcerer's attention back to him. If she needed time, he'd buy her some. But the wolf-man was already marching upon the woman who had defied him just a moment before, his top lip curled up to bare his teeth. Derek pulled the last card he had.

"I'll do it!"

He had no idea what the "source of power" was. His stomach heaved knowing Sacha wasn't really aware of her actions, too lost in magic to see the danger; he had to stop that man, and he only knew one way to do so: standing, with a sword in his hand.

"I'll take you to the Source."

Only then, he understood what it was. Sacha had asked him not to take the sword out of its sheath of stone. She had asked him to refuse, whatever happened. The sword was his, she said, his birthright. Whatever the sword really was, she had pleaded him not to reveal it, but it was the only way. He just couldn't stand seeing her and Elwyn tortured without at least fighting for them. God forgive him. He just couldn't.

"You leave them alone, and I'll unlock it for you."

Wolfryth was going to kill them all. But he could have at least one chance to bring down the beast. One chance was all it took.

oOo

The guard bowed before Sonia, apologizing for disturbing her evening.

"This letter just came in for you, my lady. It is sealed with red wax."

The mark of urgent messages. Above the crimson lace, the wax bore her mother's seal.

"Thank you."

The man bowed again, leaving her alone once more. The brunette pecked at the fire anxiously while she broke the seal.

My daughter,
The world has changed already. You know what to do.

She folded the piece before throwing it in the fire. Her mother always answered questions with riddles; such was the Guardians' way. What was worse was that she understood exactly what her mother meant. Some days, she wished that habit had not rubbed off on her so much. Sonia dismissed the thought. Too much was at stake for regrets or wistful wishes.

The brunette returned to the door to lock it before she opened one of her chests and took out the books it contained. When she reached the bottom, she pressed a small scratch in the wood. A panel slipped aside, revealing a piece of old tapestry rolled to form a case about three feet long.

Sonia slowly ran her index on the intricate gold and red stitches forming runes she didn't recognize. The symbols seemed incredibly fragile compared to the tired leather bond tied at one end.

After a few minutes, she stored the tapestry back in its hiding place and replaced her chest under the bed.

Her mother had the power to read all Elements, the first high-priestess with such gift in generations, and she, the elder of the Children, was the Carrier, as it always had been among the Faerlings since Caid had entrusted the Scabbard to their guardianship. Yes, she knew what to do.

oOo

He refused to associate the twitch in his fingers or the beating inside his body with impatience. Only fools would rush in without a second glance, and he was not a fool. The scar on his face reminded him of the cost of moving close to a Pendragon unprepared.

Wolfryth sneered disdainfully, eyeing the shadows in front of him. He had no more leverage on that one than on his father. The feelings the young one sustained for his friends gave him strength, more than his old man had fifteen years ago when fighting for his life. He would break the younger anyhow, just like he had his father.

The sorcerer reported his attention on the silhouettes jumping from step to step in front of him. The seer was helping her brother, one arm circling his waist. Her connection with Elemental Air and Fire was strong; nearly as strong as his. But the daze in her eyes while she healed her brother proved she hadn't mastered all their possibilities.

Such a pity, to waste useful resources when there were so few truly gifted. He pulled the wolf skin higher on his massive shoulders. Her threat was nothing. In a few moments, he would bath in the Ultimate Power Source, seizing up its energy to become a god among men. Thinking about a legacy was useless for one about to taste eternity.

oOo

Geraint turned from the armour on display to look at the seven men standing around the large table. Four of them were soldiers, friends and allies in charge of his fiefs. The other three were merchants, notables whom the inhabitants of Haven had chosen to represent them at the duke's council. They all shared the grey temples of age and rounding bellies. None were fit to go to war. He felt like a farmer about to throw his sheep into the lion's den.

A light knock on the door announced the last member of this particular council. Geraint escorted Ylianor toward an additional chair at the end of the table, grateful for the former queen's presence by his side.

"My friends, please take a seat."

Grifelt, one of the merchant with whom Geraint enjoyed a game of dice once in a while and the senior of his counsellors said: "You don't look like the proud father who is about to announce us the one news that could bring the delightful company of the Lady Ylianor at this table."

Ylianor bowed her head and smiled at the subtle welcome. Geraint cleared his throat, and began before he regretted his decision.

"Unfortunately, Master Grifelt, such an announcement is yet to come. No, I summoned you here tonight for less pleasant reasons."

The smiles born from the image of the handfasting of the fierce-tempered Lady of Haven and Prince Derek gave way to more serious faces.

"As you all know, the past weeks have brought worrying news. The northern and eastern lands are plundered. I dispatched a company in the east and it was attacked within our frontiers. Some information I received only yesterday confirmed that Wolfryth is the one threatening us."

Concern and wariness replaced seriousness on the seven faces turned to him.

"We cannot tolerate it any longer. I will not tolerate it."

The men looked at each other and back at Geraint, fear already perceptible, whispering against the heavy silence. Grifelt spoke first."What have you decided, Sir Duke?"

The seasoned soldier braced himself against his own words, sadness filling his voice. "I was one of King William's closest

friends, and his ally. Yet I failed to go to his help when I had to."
Ylianor placed one hand on his forearm, comforting. Geraint
nodded and stood. "I won't fail the House of the Dragon a second
time. On behalf of Prince Derek, who owns my vassalage, I am
declaring war on the usurper Wolfryth."

Geraint sat back down and waited for hell to break loose.

Chapter 32

The rattle of iron-heeled boots on the stone made Elwyn jolt with every thump. Sacha tightened her grip on him, feeling his jitters. Elwyn shivered and realized she was the one who was frightened. All their lives, they had understood each other with half-finished sentences, but now it seemed even that was dispensable, as he peeked into his twin's mind. Her feelings were a mix of fear and pain, which he understood, and a rainbow of emotions that amazed him: pride and warmth, trust, doubt. He wished he could reassure her, but terror was so deeply encrusted in his own bones he kept his mouth shut, focusing on the stairs.

Things before the stairs were still confused; painful and cold and pitch black. He had felt Sacha's magic curling around his soul, so tender and comforting that light replaced darkness inside him. Then Wolfryth had forced them to go down the stairs.

Elwyn glanced at the man on his left. Derek moved with his back straight, shoulders proudly squared, one hand fisted along his right side, the other hooked in his shirt. His clenched jaw spoke volumes about his state of mind. Derek's plan, if he had one, had the smell of a death wish.

'We need to help him, Elwyn.'

He jumped. Sacha squeezed his waist lightly to quiet him. Her mind brushed his again.

'Derek thinks he can kill Wolfryth, but he cannot; not alone; not yet.'

The caress was delicious. Soft and sweet, it had the delicate scent of roses his sister adored. The voice in his head giggled before the warmth iced and a hint of juniper spiced the roses to stir him up.

'It's important, Elwyn. Listen.'

Elwyn let himself relax in the arms of his sister and listened.

oOo

The storm lasted for five days and six nights. It fashioned the earth with an unthinkable hail of ice and stone. Where stones struck, fires blazed until all was left were bare grounds and lands ready for a new beginning. Save for a few lunatics who had left their refuge to venture into the chaos, the people were safe.

The cataclysm had built new alliances at the same time it changed the landscape forever. Where there had been plains, mountains overhung. Faults appeared where there had been hills. Where there had been Britons, Celts and Jutes, now stood the People. Even the invaders were now off the Land.

Romans offered their taste for planning and order to beat the chaos. The People brought their crafts and their knowledge of the land for food and goods. Winter succeeded the fall. Most survived, thanks to the communion of talents.

When spring left its place to summer, a new leader arose; a Roman who promised to serve all. To prove his word, he walked inside the hole the sky had carved into the highest mountain and brought back its heart.

Accepting the pact, the best craftsmen between both nations bound to create the symbol of the new order. The blacksmiths forged a blade of tempered steel out of the Celestial Stone. They gave it a length of three feet: one for the People, the first nation; one foot was given for the Romans, new to the country, and the last one represented their unity, survivors of the gods' hatred. Jewellers encrusted the hilt with precious gemstones: diamonds for strength and purity; topazes for courage and temperance; and amethysts for wisdom and humility. Their forging took almost ten moons to complete and spring came again before they finished. They called their masterpiece Caladbolg, or "hard cleft" - in Latin, Excalibur, the weapon of the Great.

The new leader was a warrior and he recognized the power of the sword. He also knew the value of compromise and asked to be reborn following the Rites, before he agreed to bear it. He cleaned in the sacred waters, observed a fast and chased the Divine Stag on the blessed night of Bealtaine. A man of principles, the leader declared the maiden he bedded that night would stay by his side as his legitimate wife.

Therefore, the guides of the People blessed her dowry, accepting the Roman as their true King. The scabbard she embroidered as a present for her handfasting became the protector of spilled blood. As long as the truthful king would wear the scabbard, he would be protected from mortal wounds in recognition for the new king word of honour.

The man known as Acturus swore to protect all and reign wisely and received the last name of KinDraco.

oOo

At first, energy circled around him, cautious like a cat watching a mouse. Then Derek felt it fizzling on his skin, fiddling with his nerves as a playful woman. The brush trailed up his tailbone to the base of his skull, diving under his scalp so every hair on his head bristled. It moved around his shoulders, tenderly, and then glided down his arms, tempting him to accept its embrace. His heart pumped madly in his chest, making it hard remembering where he was and why.

Derek clutched Sacha's comb to find an anchor in the rioting desires inside him. The energy flew away, going back to its previous lookout. The holly wood was pulsing heat and ice against his palm, maybe as a warning of what threatened to submerge him. The prince forced his grasp on the little object to relax, and slightly turned his head to his right to check on the twins.

Elwyn walked with his eyes half-closed, as if he was concentrating on something. Derek hoped he wasn't elaborating one of those mad schemes of which he was so fond. Wolfryth would kill them all within a second if he tried anything.

The sorcerer was built like an oak; thick legs, large arms and even larger shoulders. Even his head was massive. Derek had fought knights as big before. But knights were honorable. This man was a brute and an assassin. Their only chance was for him to gather the sword and strike as fast as possible afterward. He prayed that whatever Sacha had said about him not being ready for the sword was wrong.

They were nearly at the bottom of the stairs now. Sacha's torch bent forward to splash light on the flat ground below. She forced her arm to press up, the other still wrapped around Elwyn, more to steady herself than for him. Her legs wobbled under her. Her arms and her chest burned; yet exhaustion was drowned in the buzz in her head.

In the beginning, it had been easy to channel the voices toward Elwyn, so he heard the words Caer Lon poured endlessly into her soul. But the closer they came to the core of the mountain, where the Source lay, the faster the voices spun in her head, terrifyingly loud. Sacha trembled as they whispered about promises and trust. Her heart flipped when hisses about death and betrayal taunted her. The cries of terrible battles hurled in her ears, so vivid that she couldn't discern past, present and future anymore.

From the corner of her eyes, she saw blackness leaping around Derek. Her warning got stuck in her throat. The Throne was his by birthright. Power sang in his blood. The sword was his, it would obey to his command. Was it time for the High Kings to rise again? Fire flared on his frame, growing quickly to fight the night. Gold tainted with blood. So many images, so alike, so different… Her head throbbed, heart coming up her throat once more, and she tightened her grip on Elwyn.

Derek stopped.
"It's here. The tunnel in the middle."
"Get in."
The young man pointed at Elwyn and Sacha.
"Release them."
Wolfryth growled.
"Get in."
"Them first."
"Don't test my patience, son of the Dragon."

Silver and gold flashed in the heart of the tunnel. Derek's stare immediately glued to the sword in the stone, called forward by forces beyond his will. The blade had the purity of crystal. The hilt mirrored the magical light radiating from the walls closed on them. Oblivious of his friends and the massive silhouette of Wolfryth behind him, Derek approached the altar and climbed the short steps to kneel before the sword. Runes were pressed in the steel. They marked the double edge blade, encrusted into the metal. Their meaning escaped him, but deep down, he recognized them, their meaning was just within his grasp...

"Take it out now."

Greed thickened Wolfryth's voice. The prince stared at his friends, momentarily free from the fascination the sword held on him. Sacha hugged her twin brother so hard her knuckles had turned white. Her raven hair hid most of her exquisite face. Elwyn didn't seem to mind the deadly grip, his attention entirely absorbed by the sword in front of him. His eyes were wide with awe.

Derek put one hand around the hilt, then the other, flexing his fingers against the grip. The magic that prowled around him purred, sharpening its claws on the back of his mind. Fangs sank into his neck. He resisted the urge to shout his lineage: he was Derek Pendragon, son of William, son of Richard, son of Brenhin... His ancestors sprawled to life, names becoming faces, dozens, hundreds of them, men and women who had honoured their vows and reigned over the Kingdoms, united in peace.

The blood of the Dragon simmered in his veins, his senses becoming more acute to the world around him. The stone was an amalgam of dust bound by energy, as flexible as human flesh. Water ran through it, and so did air. He could see the missing two feet of steel encased in the mesh of crystals, ready to be fetched again.

Tightening his grasp, Derek pulled on the hilt.

Slowly, easily, the blade came out of its case of stone. Straightening up, Derek played with the sword. It was perfectly adapted to his hand. He tested its weight, surprised to be able to handle the deadly weapon with only one hand.

"Give it to me."

Derek stepped back from the sorcerer, eyeing his enemy carefully. Suddenly, the steel seemed a little clearer. Light reflected on the blade.

"Let my friends go."

He pointed the sword to Wolfryth's throat.

"Now."

The sorcerer grimaced. His wrist hinged forward almost absently.

"Brann erar."

Derek jumped sideways. A tongue of fire whipped toward the place he had been. The now empty stone hissed like an animal in pain. Wolfryth snarled.

"Hand me the Source, Pendragon. Its power is mine."

"Never!"

Derek held the sword above his head and lunged forward. The blade ripped on some invisible shield the sorcerer created around him. Wolfryth swept the air in front of him. A brutal gush of wind slapped the young prince violently, so that he crashed against the still smoking altar. Derek grunted in pain, but pushed up on his knees to riposte.

"I'll crush you like I crushed your father. *Angrep*!"

An arc of lighting erupted from nowhere and aimed at Derek. The prince parried the attack with the sword, feeble protection against the deadly bolt. The blast shoved him backward into the stone. The metal was already too hot in his unprotected hands. The steel paled to a blinding white. Excalibur seemed to absorb the energy that tried to kill him, but pumped his strength at the same time, as if it used it to resist the attack.

Behind the brilliance of the sword, he barely saw the furious face of his opponent. He gripped the hilt harder, refusing to let go. If he gave up, everything would be lost forever. His vision blurred.

'Svic af kiom e kiom af svic.'

Sacha's scream echoed in the small room, covering the impossible shriek of lighting against steel. Elwyn turned his stare away from the desperate fight to her. Light crowed her slender frame. Her entire being seemed to undulate like a banner in the wind. He grabbed the hand he had released for a few seconds, and felt energy invade his whole being. All a sudden, the earth under his feet became alive, and he breathed the water in the ground and in the air.

The voice cleared into a melodious tone he understood.

'Svic af kiom e kiom af svic.' 'Heart is blood and blood is heart.'

Derek fell on one knee then the other hit the ground. The brightness was so intense Elwyn couldn't watch at the sword any longer.

'SVIC AF KIOM E KIOM AF SVIC.'

The spell exploded in his head.

Elwyn dove forward, one arm still clutched around Sacha. He grasped Derek's ankle at the same moment Wolfryth realized his intention. Balls of fire lurched at the trio. Light and darkness clashed. The world spun faster and air got stuck into of his lungs. He had trouble breathing. Reality narrowed to a pulse, small and frantic. Wolfryth's yells of rage died on the wind. Every sound disappeared, reduced to that beating heart. And then the beating stopped.

Chapter 33

Sacha lost her grip on Elwyn and sprang up, panicked. Air scorched its way back to her lungs. She gasped and blinked. Behind her lashes, the shadows shaped into faces she knew, the dry silhouette of Master Bor, the blacksmith, and the plump Master Pelles. How…

"Derek, oh, thank God…"

Ylianor knelt before her son. Geraint, who was hugging Elwyn, dragged her in the same tight embrace.

Home. They were home.

Still a spectator whilst the world swirled in a painful ballet of sounds and images, Sacha noticed relief fighting suspicion on the counselors' faces. She turned her head to see Derek struggling to push onto his feet, his mother's arm secured around his waist. His face was twisted in pain. His hand still clutched the hilt of an enormous sword. It didn't look so big a moment ago when he…

The memory escaped her. She had trouble gathering her thoughts; they came and went too quickly in her head. Sacha tried to shake her father's hands off her shoulders without success. She had the strength of a newborn kitten. Anything more than a whisper asked too much of her.

"What happened?"

"I'm not sure and I don't care…"

Elwyn's answer came through the fog invading her brain. Someone else talked; the words meaningless to her.

"Sir Geraint, surely this changes your decision…"

"This council is adjourned until tomorrow morning."

She recognized the voice of Master Grifelt in the dismissal and then left herself to drift off.

oOo

When she regained consciousness, Sacha was lying on her bed. She didn't remember bathing or changing clothes, but she knew she had. The fresh fabric of her shift was a blessing on her skin. She ran a cautious hand in her hair, indulging in the soft contact. It felt so good to be clean again.

Home.

The grey light coming through the half-drawn curtains made it impossible to know if it was morning or afternoon. Sacha sighed and turned her back to the window before the gloom of that low sky chased away the well-being from her rest completely.

Her mind juggled with the last day's events, unable to fit them into a coherent puzzle. Like fragments of a lingering dream, every image stayed distinct only until she tried to connect it with another. Derek yielding to Wolfryth, the sword, the ancient magic filling her, and Elwyn screaming in her head. None of these memories seemed real yet each one had her heart pounding harder.

Sacha pushed away the coverlet, unable to stay still any longer. She slipped on a dress the color of the dark clouds hanging above Haven and exited her room.

The few people she came across in the corridors saluted her briefly before they went to their occupations in a furtive haste. Gloom seemed to have taken over the entire castle. Upright, her body remembered it hadn't eaten properly for days, and her stomach demanded that she find her way to the kitchens. Even there, the usually joyous atmosphere was tampered with hushes and thoughtful glances. The slowness that reigned around the cooking fires made her guess noon was a memory, for meals always sent the place in frenzy. A kitchen boy smiled shyly at her before a cook scooted him out to bring water with threats of pots to scrub if he didn't hurry.

Sacha was to sit down at the long table when a maid she didn't recognize asked:

"Will you join Master Sebastian for tea, my lady?"

She remarked the large tray covered with steaming cups and buttered scones, ready to be taken away, and nodded hastily. Her cheeks burned in shame. How could she have forgotten? Sacha hurried up the stairs leading to the wing where Sebastian, Elwyn and Derek had their quarters, refusing to listen to the protest of her sore muscles, now fully awake.

The door was open, so she neglected knocking and instead peeked inside. The two silhouettes by the bed stopped her from flying in the arms of the dark-haired man seated in the bed. Composing herself, Sacha approached quietly, avoiding both Elwyn and Derek's stares when she bent over her cousin to kiss his forehead.

"I'm glad you're awake."

Sebastian returned her bright smile, squeezing her hand gently.

"And I'm glad you're all back here in one piece." He nodded over her shoulder. "Put that on the table, thank you."

The maid put the tea tray down and bowed quickly before she closed the door behind her. Elwyn approached the food with a famished look on his face. Sacha's stomach shrunk in envy when he picked up a scone and shoved it almost entirely in his mouth. Sebastian laughed.

"Elwyn, why don't you serve the tea?"

Freed from her hostess' duty, Sacha released her cousin's hand to install herself at his feet on the bed with her legs under her, arranging her skirt so it pooled around her. She didn't care how unladylike it might look. It was just the four of them now, like when they were younger. Derek had seen her in far worst states in the last days, anyway.

The prince had taken his favorite position by the window, checking on the courtyard below, so she could only see half his face. He, too, had rested and looked much more presentable. Interest warmed the pit of her stomach as she noticed he hadn't shaved. Sacha glanced away quickly.

Sebastian let his stare ventured from one to another. Sacha suspected he looked for something to say. Surely, confined in bed as he was, with the sole visits of Jeffrey who looked gruffer than ever and servants who hurried out of the room after opening the curtains or helping him to a cat-wash, the news of their climatic apparition the night before had yet to reach him. She said: "We arrived yesterday."

Sebastian's short nod had Sacha swallowing. She failed to understand why suddenly chitchat was so hard between them and the feeling she was the cause of the pregnant silence thickened in a lump, blocking her throat. Derek turned away from his vigil.

"You already know of the council Geraint had summoned."

The statement of the prince seemed to conclude a conversation they had begun before she arrived. Elwyn continued to busy himself with the teapot and plates, his nose down. Sacha detached her eyes from the jewels scintillating on the golden hilt at Derek's waist to look first at her brother, then her cousin.

"You all seem to know something I don't. What's the matter?"

Elwyn answered first.

"We are at war, Sacha. Father declared Wolfryth a usurper and called on his vassal's duties to Camelot's Crown to revolt against him."

Her brother seemed on the verge of adding something but he shut up, looking at Derek intently before he returned to the plate in his hand. Color drained from her cheeks. They were safe now. They could resume their lives without risking more. War would bring death and desperation upon the people. Why...? Her stare collided with Derek's unreadable one.

"Derek, hundreds will die!"

He could die. And Elwyn. And Sebastian.

"I know."

Sacha opened her mouth to argue further. His hand rose from the sword it was absently caressing to silence her.

"I won't let that happen."

Something in the angle of his jaw transformed the thanks on her tongue into a chip of ice, which she forced herself to swallow. It chilled her to the bone. His eyes returned to the window, his hand finding his weapon once more, his back stiff to block her probing. She knew that stance by heart and she hated it. Sacha gathered her skirt to stand, determined to have the entire story out of him, one way or another. Sebastian interfered.

"Elwyn, do you have any intention to share, or should we call for more scones?"

The little joke fell flat. The young man wasn't eating anymore, torn between his loyalty to his friend and his twin sister. He had the same puppy look every time they bickered, but somehow the growing silence made it even worse for him than the icy barbs they used to throw at each other. Sacha took the cup her brother was holding and brought it to her cousin. Sebastian asked, "So where were you all this time?"

Elwyn washed down the last crumbles of sweet bread with a mouthful of tea.

"Wolfryth discovered the city of Caer Lon, and he brought me there after we were attacked."

Sebastian bowed his head.

"So no one else survived."

"I fear so."

Derek approached the table in turn. Sacha tried to catch his eyes, in vain. Keeping her hand from trembling when she handed him a cup demanded an effort of her. She wanted to believe his elusiveness irritated her; that she was just annoyed; not anxious.

"How Derek and Sacha got there, I have no idea. Wolfryth tortured us to force Derek to bring him to the sword trapped in stone, and…"

Sebastian turned his head to the prince. Derek fetched the blade out of its stealth slowly and presented it for all to see. The tarnish was completely gone, as if he had spent hours polishing the metal and sharpening its edges. Sebastian held one hand to touch the sword and Derek instinctively withdrew his hand, before he noticed and displayed it fully so his friend could admire the weapon.

Finally, Sebastian abandoned his inspection.

"It's a fine piece of work. But how did you escape?"

Derek sheathed Excalibur.

"I guess it was more Elwyn's and Sacha's doing."

Elwyn beamed.

"I did magic I never dreamed about before!"

Sacha broke from her reserve to scowl.

"I am not sure it's a good thing Elwyn."

"But Sacha-'"

"She's right."

Derek's intervention turned three pair of eyes to him, all of them amazed by his statement, though for different reasons. Sebastian cocked an brow. Elwyn wondered when Derek had started to take her side in an argument. Sacha suspected she would regret his change of attitude as soon as he explained himself.

"If Caer Lon increased your powers, what do you think it did to Wolfryth's?"

oOo

She returned to her room with a disagreeable throb in the back of her mind. Derek's question had hung above their heads for the rest of their tea, despite Sebastian and Elwyn's obvious intents to deflect the conversation on lighter topics.

After hours of trying to figure out what it was they were not telling, she was tired and edgy. She wanted nothing more than to relax in a bath and crawl in her bed after a light supper. Unfortunately, when Agnes finally showed up, her maid announced her father requested her presence in the courtroom.

The usual cheer escorting the invitation was absent from the servant's voice. Generally Agnes loved pampering her beautiful mistress, probably more than Sacha herself. Her lack of enthusiasm was definitely a surprise. But not as much as seeing the maid at all. Sacha didn't doubt for an instant she had had to answer about her disappearance, and she was even more amazed she had not been given her notice. The girl looked at her feet more than her lady's hair while arranging the long curls in a braid.

"Which dress will you wear, my lady?"

Sacha tore her thoughts off the penitence her father would unmistakeably announce either tonight or tomorrow morning for her elopement. Though Elwyn's return was a blessing, she was certainly to be punished. As for Derek…

"The velvet one, thank you."

It was a deep purple velvet dress with front laces and golden band on the sleeves and the bodice. The neckline was low for a simple, familial dinner, but the fabric was soft and warm, and exactly what she needed to comfort her.

The light knock on her door arrived just when she was putting her evening cloak on her shoulders.

"Come in."

She had not expected to see the person who stepped the threshold.

"Good evening, Sacha."

"Sonia."

The two women detailed each other, the elaborate embroideries on the countess's dress eclipsing the simpler adornments of Sacha's. The raven-hair beauty regretted her choice of attire. She blushed, more in annoyance than in embarrassment. The mixture of emotions was a familiar bother in front of her rival. Sonia's dark eyes sparkled in mischief.

"Your father was kind enough to invite me to dinner. Shall we go together?"

Sacha tried not to choke in surprise. Sonia and she were hardly friends. They grated on each other nerves like metal on stone, to say the least. Why on earth did the countess show up at her door to escort her to dinner? And why her father had invited her? She pushed away the idea Sonia's presence at dinner had anything to do with the boys' silent messages of the afternoon. Derek had been definitely ill-at-ease. What if…

"Sacha?"

Sonia's light reminder forced her to bow her head in agreement.

They walked down the corridor in silence for a few minutes. All the while Sacha tried to figure out what to say, if anything.

As if she could read her thoughts, Sonia paused at the doors of the courtroom.

"Thank you for saving him."

The last pronoun achieved to awaken every jealous fiber in the enchantress's heart.

Chapter 34

The last minute announcement had sent the castle into a chaos of harried servants and nervous nobles. The former ran for food, water and fresh flowers, while the latter wondered if they would put on the same clothes they wore for the Yule ball or pressure their seamstresses for that new garment they had requested for May Day. The result bloomed in a rainbow of strange looking plates and garments either too hot or too thin for the weather.

Ylianor watched Sacha part from Sonia as soon as the two women entered the room. She wished she knew why the countess had decided to seek Sacha's companionship for coming in. Undoubtedly, it had to do with Sonia's personal interests, though she couldn't fathom which one.

"The mark is no more, Majesty. She's free."

Sonia's whisper startled Ylianor off her thoughts. By the time she turned around, the brunette had disappeared into the crowd once more. The momentary relief on her face faded when her stare seeking the elusive Faerling fell on the tall frame of her son.

For the first time since he came of age, Derek was wearing a circle of gold in his hair, and the red cloak on his shoulders was rimmed with ermine. The symbols of royalty suited him. They claimed beforehand what he was about to announce to the whole Court.

A small white hand came around her elbow and Ylianor quickly composed herself to face Sacha. She smiled at the young woman, while her gaze wandered toward her son again. He was talking with Elwyn and Thomas, the newly appointed second-in-command of Geraint.

"I thought we were to have a simple family reunion."

The queen turned to her friend, vaguely surprised to see worry tangled with doubts in the green eyes fixed on her. If only she knew…

"Well, I suppose your father is as glad as I am to have you back in one piece."

They fell silent for a while. The occasional laugh simmered, out of place, as if the party was thrown for remembrance more than joy. Sacha scanned the room in turn until her gaze stopped on the blonde head crowned with gold. Ylianor heard her gasp and braced herself for a question that never came. Sacha whispered.

"I hate it. I can feel something's wrong, but I don't know what-"

Geraint clapped his hands twice sharply and she fell silent, her fingers gripping Ylianor's. The queen looked away when Derek marched to the center of the room. She wished she could close her heart as easily she closed her eyes.

"My friends…"

He sound so much like his father Ylianor couldn't help a small smile.

"Sir Geraint made a courageous decision, but I cannot accept it. I refuse to lead you into a war which is only mine."

Sacha's death grip on her hand stopped being painful as Ylianor returned the grasp.

"I will confront the usurper myself, as it is my right, and my duty. I'm leaving tomorrow."

Geraint bowed.

"The duchy of Pemfro will wait for your victorious return, Prince Derek."

In the silence that followed, Ylianor saw a small boy running into her embrace, showing her the new wood sword his father had offered. She dried the tears that flowed when he broke his arm falling from his horse. She chastised the young man parading with his friends after his knighting, and hugged the teenager who demonstrated his affections with small gestures, rather than speaking them aloud. Yesterday he was just a child, fisting his hands while standing proudly by her side while Geraint welcomed them in Haven, and this morning a man had knelt before her to say he could not let anyone die in his place. Her hand left Sacha's to press on her mouth. She prayed her anguish didn't escape. A sob trembled, though the nearly inaudible cry was not hers.

"Ylianor-"

"He has to…"

The mother's voice broke midway in her sentence. Ylianor forced her lungs to accept air before she went on.

"Derek can't back out from this any more than his father could. Don't ask him to. I didn't."

Ylianor slowly took her arm from Sacha's lock and walked to her son, her head and shoulders proudly straight. The young man welcomed her with a smile, before he continued his exchange with the knights regrouped in front of him.

Sacha stepped away from the crowd. She had to get out, before her heart exploded or she made a fool of herself. She looked for an excuse to flee and found none. It seemed every eye went from Derek to her and back. Every sigh pitied her. Her head pounded. Her face burned. She couldn't take it any longer. She needed…

A cup crashed on the floor somewhere, the world shattered and she realized no one was looking. No one gossiped about her lost prince. The people around her buzzed about his desperate fight like they would have talked about the next tournament. She wanted to scream.

Sacha gathered her skirts, readying to run out of the room. Derek caught her arm, forbidding her to leave him behind without a word. Sacha tried to free herself, but she couldn't shake him off without making a scene. He was far too strong, his fingers circling her wrist in an iron grip. She met his stare, and stopped fighting.

"I need some air. Please…"

With a nod, he escorted her outside, and they turned a corner to find the next corridor deserted. In the dim light of the torches, his blue eyes paralyzed her. Derek didn't hesitate to pull her into his arms and cover her mouth with his. Breathing became a strange notion. Her knees weakened, and she had to grab him for balance when heat tensed her spine as their tongues brushed.

When he lightened his kiss, allowing her to take in air again and one or two coherent thoughts to reach her head, Sacha noticed he had pushed her against the wall again, hiding her from the view of wandering eyes; or forbidding her to escape, as if she had wanted to go anywhere away from him… Her breath caught as he pressed tiny kisses into her neck and her eyes fluttered closed. One caress lower on her throat made her pulse jumped to even higher rates.

"Derek… Derek not here… At least take me to your chambers…"

He ceased his ministrations, grinning.

"I thought you'd never ask…"

She wanted to chastise him but he captured her lips once more, then scooped her up bridal-style to walk down to his apartment. They were only feet away from a room full of people, her father, his mother, Elwyn… She couldn't care less.

He managed to open and close his door without putting her down or ceasing kissing her; such a mystery she would ponder on later; much, much later. Derek eased her gently on the bed, pushing away to untie her evening cloak and remove it from her shoulders. The intimate gesture made her shivered slightly. His movements were very gentle, almost reverent when he caressed the length of her neck, his mouth following the brush of his fingertips. Sacha leaned into him when her bones melted under his kisses.

Derek growled when her curves pressed against him, a low possessive sound. The contact of hard muscles under her hands was unusual and amazing. She felt him shake under her hands as he restrained his desire to hurry things up. Sacha tensed instinctively. She had been told it hurt the first time, and it scared her; a least a little. Rumors said Derek was… She didn't even know how to name the attentiveness he avowedly showed his partners. She was inexperienced, while he…

Sensing her hesitation, Derek stopped nuzzling her jaw and plunged his gorgeous blue eyes into hers. Seeing alarm there, he kissed her lips again, more gently this time, and pulled her into his arms, resisting the urge to help her down into the pillows. Sacha nestled against his chest, burying her face in the crook of his shoulder.

"We don't have to rush things if you are not ready."

He had no idea how he would keep that promise. Every part of him was ready to break with the softest sigh. Every nerve screamed for her, claimed to touch, to taste, to possess… Waiting was driving him insane, but he would die before pressuring her in any way.

His heart bounced under her hand. Sacha murmured, "I don't want to wait," hoping her voice sounded steadier than she truly felt. She reached for the laces of her corsage, loosening them so the fabric pooled around her. Derek inhaled sharply. Sacha covered herself with both arms shyly, alarmed by the hunger on his face. Instead of reaching for her, he took his shirt off then offered his hand, inviting her to the security of his arms again.

He was beautiful. Sacha wanted to look at him some more, but touching him was irresistible, so she took refuge against his bare chest, enthralled to feel his skin against hers. When his hand moved from her back to her side, brushing the soft swell of her breast, Sacha felt her blood sing in her veins. Curious, she started an exploration of her own. She ran her fingers from his shoulder to his collarbone and down his ribcage. His groan surprised and troubled her as she investigated the flat planes of his stomach, curling the short hair around her fingers.

Derek pushed her into the pillows as his mouth found the curve of her neck. She closed her eyes to enjoy the unknown heat growing inside her, welcoming his weight on her with a sigh. His hardness pressed against her thigh, remaining barriers gone somehow. Sacha lost her breath slightly, unsettled by the urge to have him even closer.

Her eyes opened wide when he pushed inside her and she closed them back quickly, biting back a whimper of pain, trembling in the effort not to get away from the white-hot blade tearing her apart. She hid her face on his throat for comfort, her fingers clinging into his shoulders.

Derek felt her wet lashes flutter against his neck and tightened his embrace, fighting his desire to move with all his will. She was incredibly sweet, and so hot he feared he could not resist. Being inside her was more delicious than he had ever imagined and he had to…

He cupped her face to look at her, worried to read hurt on her adorable features. Her cheeks were flushed and her brows slightly frowned in concentration, as she tried to adjust to the male invasion. He stretched to caress her hair, and her eyes shot open. Her green stare, both radiant and clouded, fascinated him. Her luscious lips parted and he stole her breath in a soul-binding kiss.

Passion engulfed him completely when her hands slid along his arms to fasten in his back. Derek arched, instinctively begging for more caresses, and the movement allowed more of him inside her. Sacha gasped and closed her eyes tightly shut again. Then he felt it, the soft pressure of her stomach against his, just a brush of tantalizing soft skin, and again. Her nails bit into his back, his name bubbling in her throat.

Derek abandoned her face to secure his hands around her waist, careful not to crush her under him when he set a slow pace that sent waves of pleasure through every part of them. Her hips followed his moves, timidly welcoming his thrusts. Unable to wait any longer, he accelerated his moves devouring her mouth to possess her thoroughly, body and soul. Suddenly she bucked into him with a little cry of surprise. His grip matched hers in ferocity as Derek pinned her back down on the bed, muffling her name in her neck, a curse or a prayer, she couldn't tell.

Lightheaded, Sacha listened to his heart calm down against her breast, its strong beat bouncing against her skin. The erratic pulse seemed the only thing real around her. She itched to stretch but couldn't find the strength to move and break from the comfortable cocoon of pleasure closed around her. She kept her arms around his chest, refusing to free him just yet.

After a while, Derek rolled off her on his back and brought her with him. She felt sated, thrilled and embarrassed. It hurt too, but the satisfaction was greater, so the burning sensation low in her stomach was more a discomfort than a scorch. Derek pulled her up to look at her. The blue stare caressed her face silently, lovingly, before he simply kissed her forehead and allowed her to cuddle against him again.

Now the passion was fading, tiredness dazzled her and she wanted to fall asleep in his arms, in that special nest they had created together. As if reading her mind, Derek pushed some curls from her face.

"Will you stay?"

The question startled her, shattering her bubble of peace to force her back into reality. Sacha straightened up slowly, using the sheet to cover herself.

"I cannot... If someone finds me here..."

Derek frowned and opened his mouth to protest, but she silenced him with one finger before she stood gracefully to dress. The fire and the candles made her skin glow softly. She had never been more beautiful to him than now. Her dress flew over her, hiding her body from his sight. Derek pushed away the coverts.

Surprised, Sacha looked back at him.

"What are you doing?"

He arranged his shirt and breeches, fishing for his boots from under the bed.

"I won't let you venture around the castle by yourself at this hour."

His tone was hard, almost impatient. Derek fastened his belt around his waist and sheathed his sword, then handed her cloak. Suddenly she felt helpless. The pressure in her stomach chilled her to the bone. He sounded aloof, his voice completely devoid of teasing or warmth, pushing her away. Now she had given him... She shivered and closed her cloak tighter around her. Derek held his hand:

"It will not surprise anyone to see me walk the corridor at dawn... If you... If you allow me to your chambers."

By chambers, he meant bed. He wanted to spend the night with her. She could not stay with him, so he asked her permission to stay with her... Her heart skipped several beats happily. Sacha flushed and smiled, and blushed some more. She took his hand, letting their fingers entwine. Derek brushed a kiss over her knuckles, his cobalt blue eyes never wandering away from hers. His tenderness erased the growing awkwardness between them.

They walked side by side in the dark corridors, Derek some feet away from her. The distance would protect her from gossip, in case they came across guards or, anyone who would realize they had slipped away from the banquet together. She wished he were closer. Once at her door, he took her hand again, contemplating her delicate fingers, so small in his hand. He looked enthralled by the sight and Sacha smirked.

"Do you need an official invitation to come in?"

He grinned and the emotions spiralling in her stare found their match in his. Their relationship would never change. They would always challenge each other, until one of them yielded, never the same twice in a row. She liked that. He liked it too. They were opponents, accomplices, friends, lovers; equals in every way.

Derek brushed another kiss in her palm and she closed her eyes, the soft caress too much to take already. Sacha fumbled with the knob behind her back and soon she was in his arms again. Cloak, shirt, dress fell around them as desire took over.

This time, she knew what to expect when he pressed against her, and she wanted him to make her his again. But Derek had other plans, caressing her hair, her throat, covering her body with kisses, worshiping her lips, her chest, her stomach with mouth and hands, stealing every nerve in her body until she nearly lost her mind. When their bodies finally fused, she could only murmur his name and how much she loved him.

Chapter 35

The soft light of dawn played with her lashes, stirring her gently out of slumber. Derek slept on his back with one arm wrapped possessively around her, the other across his forehead to block the brightness. His face was tensed, and his hand fisted the pillow like a shield ready to be used. She stretched to brush a kiss on his frown, her hair cascading on his chest. His breathing eased as both caresses apparently relaxed him.

Sacha nestled back against his side, the glee of waking up near him for the first time tainted with worry. She could lose him today; this fight was do-or-die, and what could he do against magic so powerful? She wished she could give him her strength, her faith, whatever he needed to pull through.

"I love you…"

Her whisper grazed his biceps, rising goose bumps on his skin. Intrigued, she blew the words on his throat, rousing more quivers. Her lips followed the same path, curious to discover more than he had allowed her so far, the ridges and plates of his neck and more mysteries down his breast. The brush of her mouth over his navel brought up a strangled sound, dark and almost primeval.

Sacha looked up to find him staring under half-close lids. The deep blue of his eyes captivated her so she forgot about exploring and cuddled under the arm protecting her, embarrassed by her boldness. Derek lifted her head to him to kiss her gently on the lips before he lay back with her in his arms.

"Did you mean it?"

His heart pumped hard under her cheek.

"I want to go with you."

He preferred to keep their last moments together light and carefree. Derek grinned into her hair, teasing so she abandoned the topic.

"Sometimes you can't have what you want."

"Oh, really?"

Sacha pushed up for another kiss. His hand slipped under her to help her knees on either side of him. Derek let her control the kiss, but the caress under her thigh arose other desires she still didn't completely understand, except they both bested her and made her feel powerful. Releasing his mouth, she let him guide her hips down, trembling slightly when he entered her but only because the urge to have him inside her was too strong to repress.

Derek arched as she moved slowly, unable to look away from her, fascinated by the flush on her skin, her breathing erratic already. Her gaze never released his, emerald against sapphire, the gemstones fighting for control as she resisted his guidance, just for a second, torturing him, simply because she could, but never for long, because she needed him as much as he did her.

When she grasped his arms for support, his hands circled her hips to rest between her shoulders, first gentle brushes, then greedy when Derek couldn't wait any longer to feel her all around him, sure his heart was going to explode when she followed him over the edge.

Their pulses beat in perfect match, as Sacha watched golden light flowed over their entwined bodies from the windows. It was joyous and peaceful, the promises of new beginnings. Derek kissed her lips lightly, still wrapped in her arms, serious again.

"I have to go."

"Not yet."

She refused to release him, stretching on his chest like a cat. Derek caressed the silk ebony pooling around them so he could twine his fingers with the loose ribbon still tangled in her curls. Sacha snatched the purple lace from him, tying it around his wrist. He smiled, finally pushing onto his feet to dress.

"It's late. I'll take the services stairs, so no one will-"

"I don't care."

Derek brushed a finger on her petulant mouth.

"I do. And I bet your father does, too, at least until I come back."

Her eyes shimmered, the half-mouthed proposal a brutal reminder of why she had wanted to share his bed in the first place.

"Derek-"

This time a kiss replaced his hand.

"No. I will come back, Sacha."

Her hand moved across her midsection and he followed the caress with his eyes, dying to take her back into his arms and forget the world.

"You'd better."

Derek grinned.

"You really can't resist bossing me around, can you…?"

She rolled her eyes, her pout swinging from annoyance to laugher. Seriousness won. Derek sat on the edge of the bed, touching her face lightly to grasp a few more seconds of bliss.

"Will I see you in the courtyard later?"

Sacha didn't want her last image of him to be one of a soldier clasped in cold steel instead of one of the man he was now, with mussed hair and bribes of unruly emotions dancing in his eyes. Two different men. Two faces of the same heart.

"Yes, of course."

oOo

Elwyn finished tying Derek's breast and back plates, a ritual the friends had shared for years. Elwyn helped Derek with his armor and Sebastian helped Elwyn with his before joining the spectators while his elders entered the arena. This time, no tournament would take place. Derek would fight alone, to the death.

Sebastian watched as Elwyn secured one last leather strap and landed one hand on his friend's shoulder.

"Done."

The prince nodded curtly. The armor weighted a ton on his shoulders. Ever since he had quitted Sacha's arms, a chill he couldn't shake off clutched his insides, the cold grip hardening by the minute. Derek blew air through his nose, trying to retrieve some of the confidence he had left with her.

A maid knocked and entered the room, a white handkerchief in hand. She delivered her message in haste, visibly taken aback by the three men frowning at her.

"My Lady Sonia of Gosharling sends her favor as a proof of luck and she would be delighted to express her best wishes herself."

Elwyn grinned, ignorant of Sebastian's imperceptible frown. Derek shook his head.

"Please thank your mistress for her wishes. She is welcome to join the company in the courtyard in a few minutes."

The maid choked at his refusal, but she bowed and exited the room. Elwyn turned to Derek, his eyes like saucers. Sebastian inclined his head to mask his smile.

"Derek, are you out of your mind? Mighty Sonia refused half the court!"

"I know."

Derek fidgeted with the hilt at his waist. The contact comforted him, somehow. Elwyn continued to stare. Derek knew he had to say something, but could not find the words just yet. His light blush attracted Sebastian's attention from the door back to him. Derek ran one hand through his hair.

"Hell, forget it."

Elwyn's gaze suddenly turned a piercing blue. He grabbed Derek's forearm in a surprisingly strong grip, pushing his sleeve up to reveal the purple ribbon Sacha had tied around his wrist at dawn.

"What's that?"

Derek's stare fell on the display and his blush intensified. Elwyn paled.

"Those are my sister's colors. Why? When? What did you do?"

Derek's crimson face answered for him. The hold turned into a tight grasp. Derek pulled away, hands up in a peace offering.

"We both wanted it, Elwyn, and I fully intend to-"

"Whatever!"

He stormed out of the room. Derek sat at the table behind him, defeated, and Sebastian chuckled.

"This is not funny, Sebastian."

"Come on. You just told your best friend you unmaidened his twin sister. You're lucky he did not jinx you."

"God. Do you have to make it sound so gross?"

Sebastian laughed harder.

"Right. You did so much better. It is not so much of a surprise after all. You and Sacha played cat and mouse long enough. Don't worry; he'll get over it. I would worry more about Sacha if she learns about Sonia's offer."

"I don't care about Sonia."

"Good."

Derek glanced at his friend, but let it go and walked to the window to look down. A horse was ready for him. A lad was leading two more for some early riders. A few people had gathered in the courtyard already. Time was flying too quickly. He wished he had a few more moments. A few minutes to tease Sebastian about Sonia, a couple more to talk to Elwyn. Hours to spend with his mother. Days to bicker with Sacha and nights to make up for it. He wished he had not to leave. The chill in his stomach reached the size of an ice pack.

Derek turned away from the window.

"Don't forget that you promised to knight me."

The young prince nodded and grasped his friend's forearm in the traditional knight's grip.

"I'll see you soon."

He had to believe it.

oOo

When he stepped in the courtyard, funnily enough he wasn't the center of attention of the little group crowded on the steps. The shouting match involved one imperious feminine voice Derek knew too well and two deeper ones he also recognized.

"I am going."

"So am I." added Elwyn.

Geraint shook his head.

"This is complete madness. You both stay here."

Elwyn and Sacha tweeted in unison.

"Derek needs our help."

Giving in meant not facing Wolfryth alone; not dying alone if he failed. Agreement dripped warm over the knot in the pit of his stomach, loosening it for a second before pride rebelled, hooking its claws deep in his chest. He didn't need anyone's help. He had Excalibur to fight magic and his rights to strengthen him. Failure was not an option. He had prepared for this fight all his adult life. His crown, his battle. No one else's. He stepped forward.

"No."

"I don't remember asking for your permission."

Derek's ears grew scarlet. Did she have to be that difficult? Couldn't she let him go with the memory of the endearing woman she was earlier in his arms? He glared. She scowled back. Derek towered over her, uncaring for Elwyn's snarl and Geraint' frown.

"I said no."

Blazing eyes threw jade stings at him. Derek smirked, kindling more anger. Her fingers curled, promising a hit she restrained at the last minute. He wondered how she would react if he grabbed her waist to kiss her into submission in front of the entire court.

Derek broke the stare contest, shaken by the need to try anway.

"I don't have time for this."

He waved at the servant to bring the horses back to the stables. Turning tail, the prince caught an amused expression on his mother, quickly erased.

"Prince Derek."

He noticed a small hiss in his back, and bowed his head in greetings with a smile that roused another grumble, the words too low to catch.

"Lady Sonia."

"A sword is not enough to defeat Evil, even this one."

Derek lost his smile. What now?

"Caladbolg was forged to bring balance to the world of men."

Instinctively, Derek put one hand on the sword at his side. Sonia approached further.

"It will serve the Blood as long as the Blood serves all. Yet iron without velvet is useless for the arm which fetches it."

She was holding some old piece of fabric or a tapestry of some sort. His hand jerked on the hilt, flexing with impatience.

"My people watched over Excalibur's Scabbard for centuries, waiting for the new High King to fulfill the prophecies, and deliver us from our vows."

Last week, he could have laughed his head off at the excessive drama. Before he could even realize it, he had pulled Excalibur from its stealth for all to see. The blade gleamed in the pale morning light. Energy flowed down his arm and swelled in his heart. The silver runes carved in the steel branded their meaning in his mind.

"One face to conquer and one face to protect. I will."

Derek dropped the useless sheath on the ground and buckled the Scabbard at his waist. The sword hummed under his palm. He felt different and the same; stronger; complete. Sonia bowed deeply.

"Good luck."

Chapter 36

The next hours disappeared in the clap of iron shoes on the road. Derek let his mind empty with the ride, making one with his mount so doubts and regrets kept quiet.

He had considered stopping in Lann Stefan when he reached it barely an hour before dusk, then decided against it to finally stop in the clearing Gaul had indicated a few days before. Mistress Marion would ask too many questions if he appeared at her door fully clasped in armour, and without Sacha.

The named lady had probably started listing unpleasant ways to make him pay for leaving her behind the moment his horse disappeared from view, if not earlier. Derek didn't doubt her list counted more than a hundred ideas by now, from sharpening her dagger on his rib-bones to disdainful cold glares. He played with a stick to shake the embers. If he pulled through, he'd even bless public humiliation.

The fire sparkled, the noise sending his heart into a frenzy. The night was quiet around him, not an owl squeaking, not a leaf moving. The forest was completely silent. Too silent?

Derek fidgeted to find a more comfortable position against the boulder, his frustration growing. He needed to rest. A tired man made a sloppy fighter. He had to rest but the more he tried to relax, the more his mind brought up random images, which either made him smile or disturbed him: his mother, bent over her little cauldron preparing a new remedy that would smell heavenly and taste foul, Elwyn, crouched against the wall in the dungeon, Sacha, surrendered in his arms while she slept, Geraint's hand squeezing his shoulder after the council the previous morning, Wolfryth's mask of rage when they escaped.

The young man changed position again to play with the tokens at his wrist. Sacha's comb was twisted with her ribbon to keep it in place against his skin. He wasn't sure why he had taken it. An impulse. Superstition. The holly wood was soft under his fingers, not warm but not really cold either. The magic he could feel around wasn't a treat. Yet. Derek closed his hand around the comb, and finally decided to push onto his feet. Since sleep eluded him, he might just as well get into the High City.

He tracked crushed leaves and combed grass, footprints, every tangible sign they had left walking the very same path three days ago, but his efforts were useless. The trail scintillated softly, its irregularity familiar in the moonlight. The same low energy reeled under his boots, welcoming him back or daring him to approach.

The weapon at his waist became heavier. Derek paused to gather his bearings, his breath short. Had the climb been so strenuous the last time? The lump in his throat didn't feel like exhaustion.

Branches above his head sprang to life. His blood boiled through the block of ice his forearm had become under the comb's impulse. Derek gritted his teeth preventing a yowl of pain. The wind swirling around him seemed to scorch him alive. The roll was more of a pulse now, similar to primeval battle drums. His heart throbbed to mimic their rhythm. Eyes were watching in the dark.

Yellow flared, and the trees changed into columns of stone, the canopy into a ceiling with thick beams. Tiles replaced leaves at his feet. Derek fetched Excalibur, pushing its point forward.

"Do you think your toy impresses me?"

A clap of fingers, and dozens of torches fired on the walls to chase the shadows away. The young man kept his eyes on his adversary, immobile.

"Hand me the sword."

"Never."

Derek lunged forward, meeting only air.

"You're laughable. *Szarik*."

Derek felt his boots slide on the floor while an invisible hand pulled him forward, crushing his chest until breathing became an impossible luxury. Cold racked the top of his neck. He tilted his blade up to ease the non-existent grip in desperation for air. The stifling grip disappeared instantly. Wolfryth's hiss reminded him of a wounded animal. Derek sneered but kept his mouth shut, circling his adversary with his sword pointing forward, the blade parallel to the ground and the pommel up his shoulder. His eyes trained on the sorcerer. The giant in front of him wore only a wolf skin for protection. One quick thrust and he could…

The torches on the walls roared in warning.

"Brann angrep."

Flames exploded all around Derek, dashing, fencing, trying to rip his chest and back apart. Excalibur swirled widely, cutting the angry tongues. Sweat glided along the young man's spine. As soon as he destroyed one, two or more whips sparkled to life and attacked him. His shoulders burned as never before. Raising the sword again and again became difficult, then next to impossible. Fog came out of his mouth when he panted, the sharpened teeth of frost biting in his heart. He felt so cold…

Suddenly the brands retreated to solidify into their master's hands. Derek stumbled back, gulping air, his head heavy. His armor slowed his movements, making him easier prey. The comb now bit into his flesh to undermine his strength. How stupid he had been to take it with him. Derek fought with his gauntlet to get rid of it and access the purple lace around his wrist. His fingers were numb with cold, forbidding him to tear away Sacha's tight knot.

Wolfryth smirked. The sword in his hand was completely formed now, twice as large as Excalibur and several inches longer. With only one gauntlet on, the weight of the weapon felt wrong and Derek shook his other hand bare for a better grip.

Excalibur buzzed in his naked hands, the enchanted sword nearly singing its impatience to fight. Derek grabbed it more tightly, resuming his stance just in time to parry Wolfryth's next blow. The clash echoed in the room, bouncing on the ancient walls until it was joined by another and another. Tendrils of a blizzard circled his temples, the cold emanating from the comb no longer contained on his body.

Derek almost welcomed the heat from the fire sword of the sorcerer when it approached his forehead. He blocked the cut with the hilt and riposted, aiming for the massive neck. Wolfryth broke his step, fire blade pointing up. His passing back was too slow, and Derek lunged in the opening. The attack at the sorcerer let his upper body unguarded one second too long and fire bit into his pauldron. But he found his mark.

Pain shot through Wolfryth instantly, right before the eager sword vanished in a greyish puff of smoke and he bawled in rage and hurt.

"Legi skjold. Legi skjold!"

The acrid cloud its weapon had been convulsed, failing to obey his command.

Half blinded with sweat and pain, Derek jabbed forward. The vibration of steel piercing flesh shook the bones of his arms up to his neck. Wolfish eyes assaulted him, too close, and he pressed harder. Hands as large as hams tried to circle his throat. The prince tilted Excalibur up and pulled. The greedy claws went limb. The fire in the wild stare died, and the enormous man collapsed on the ground.

Derek tore out his sword from the lifeless body, gasping. In a daze, he pulled away the wolf skin to grab the hair clasped in the leather bond, exposing his enemy's neck, and slashed. Pandemonium erupted in the empty room. He jumped back, tottering to keep his balance, while black and green flames engulfed the beheaded corpse to consume it. Finally the only thing left of the sorcerer was the wolf skin at Derek's feet.

His legs wobbled. The young man controlled his trembling just long enough to wipe the blade of Excalibur finding only brown ashes staining the steel rather than blood. He fell on his knees, shattered, as dawn brought three majestic thrones back to life, coated with gold and crimson, bringing...

Epilogue

The crowd murmured as the young man walked along the red carpet, his walking stick clanging in rhythm above the whispers. The sun poured from the enormous windows washed over the coats of arms on the massive shields hanged on the opposite wall. A golden dragon spewed out flames on a crimson bed on the one closer to the thrones. Next to it, on the second, a large yellow cross cut through azure. The last one, which had been hanged during the night, invited a beautiful black swan to sing, its wings wide open on silver.

Finally, Sebastian reached the two-step stage, where three people were waiting for him. Ylianor bowed her head and he returned her salute before offering a quick smile to Sacha, ethereal in her blue dress, a fine crown circling her head. Derek stepped forward and the knight-to-be forgot about the oversized thrones in front of him.

"Sebastian, son of Connor of Kernow, why are you before me this day?"

Despite the solemn question, Derek's grin warmed his voice.

"I, Sebastian, last son of Connor, am kneeling in front of my king to swear an oath."

"Then speak loud, so those present hear you and report your words to others."

Sebastian closed his eyes, and spoke up.

"I will honour my suzerain and bravely defend anyone who needs my arm. My mouth will speak only the truth I know and I won't fear the truths I don't. Such is my oath, shall it please God and the High King."

Excalibur gleamed in the sunlight.

A gasp escaped the crowd when the large blade fell hard on Sebastian's left shoulder. The young man winced when it ripped on his chainmail toward the swan embroidered on his collar, before it rose again. Bending his head in acceptance, the young man caught a glimpse of a pale hand clasped on blue skirts right before a moan froze Derek's gesture in mid-air.

oOo

A feminine hand smoothed some of the tension in his back so unclenching his hands became easier. His best friend-advisor-new knight-self-appointed-godfather had picked up the baby, expertly putting one hand under its fragile head. The feelings rioting in the pit of the father's stomach felt like jealousy, protectiveness and panic merged together.

"He is not going to break, Derek. Sebastian is doing just fine."

He reacted instantly.

"You should not be up."

Sacha gave a little smile, one she offered more and more often now, which made him wonder if marriage and motherhood had increased her powers so that she read him like an open book. Did she know about the day before? Did she know about the pacing? Or his yelling at each servant who entered and exited the room without telling him anything? Or how agony smashed his bones to dust every time she bawled her pain through the door?

He pushed the memories away and forced air into his lungs, as Sebastian cradled his baby ward. Next to him, Elwyn bent over his nephew and beamed.

"He frowns exactly like you do, Sacha."

She pulled a face at her brother whilst securing her son in her arms again. Her face illuminated when the tiny fingers curled around hers. The funny feeling inside Derek's chest shifted to balance between amazement and pride. Sacha settled their son in the ornamented cradle, the dark wood glowing in the late afternoon light.

"Sacha doesn't frown."

Surprised that her husband defended her, she looked up. "She pouts."

Sebastian and Elwyn laughed. The sea-green eyes narrowed on the tall blond man in front of the bed.

"At least, I'm neither stubborn nor impatient."

"I am not."

"Really? Then who broke into my chambers fully armed and smelling like dirty stables to drag me to my father in the middle of the night?"

The memory was happy, but he just could not let her have the last word.

"And who decided to cut our betrothal down to two months?"

"You got me with child!"

Elwyn growled and covered the baby's ears with both hands. Sebastian shook his head.

"And *you* told me about it in the middle of the crowning ceremony!"

The rising voices finally disturbed the infant who whined, the cry growing alarmingly quickly. Sacha was near him in an instant, soothing his discomfort with small caresses and light words. The baby squeaked and calmed down. Sebastian rocked the crib gently.

"He is more reasonable than the two of you."

She blushed. Derek wrapped his arms around her, kissing her temper away. Sebastian overlooked Elwyn's protest to ask: "Have you finally decided on a name?"

The royal couple stared at each other, ruffled feathers forgotten. Sacha gave that small smile again and nodded. The new High King cleared his throat: "Arthur."

The end is only the beginning
November 2011

Also by Claude Dancourt

Second Chances

oOo

Claude Dancourt lives in Montreal, and wherever her job as an engineer takes her. She is fascinated by books and museums. To discover more about RETURN TO CAER LON, Claude Dancourt's work or simply drop a word, visit her website: www.claudedancourt.webs.com

www.ingramcontent.com/pod-product-compliance
Lightning Source LLC
Chambersburg PA
CBHW021951170626
46808CB00001B/109